This book is a work of fiction. Names, characters, institutions, organizations, places, events, and incidents either are the product of the author's imagination or are used fictitiously. Any resemblance to actual persons, living or dead, events, or locales is entirely coincidental.

Written and edited by Farhana Uddin

https://linktr.ee/farhanabooks

Human-generated content. All the words and ideas within this novel were created solely from the author's own writing skills and wild imagination. There was no use of any AI-generators in the making of this novel.

ISBN: 979-8-9892524-6-6

FARHANA UDDIN

For those who hunger
for a destiny far greater
than a little life.

Contents

Chapter 1:
What am I missing here?

"Enemies are like lovers. They're nothing but strains on our energy, always testing us in some way, forcing us to make all manner of uncomfortable decisions. They exist merely to teach us hard lessons... Lessons about who we are, what we want, what we're willing to fight for, what we're willing to die for... what we're willing to kill for... But don't you worry... You're still young. You have yet to meet all the people who shall love and hate you in equal measure."

J.R. can't remember who told him this. It sounded like something his father Lucien or his elder sister Lex might have said on those rare days when he'd catch them being honest, heartbroken, and human.

But don't you worry, son ... He could picture Lucien monologuing it to him, his tone charming and condescending.

But don't you worry, Little Wing ... He could also imagine Lex delivering such lines, her face soft and icy.

Still, he can't remember which one of them said it.

That was J.R.'s trouble. He couldn't remember a lot of things. Names, passwords, flossing, sunscreen, underwear, to name a few. Nevertheless, he was great at remembering people. Maybe their names escaped him. Maybe the conversations they had shared eluded him. But he never forgot a face... not until the new Grey King came along.

J.R. doesn't remember his first meeting with the Grey King. He doesn't understand why the man hates him so. Sure, they came from rival kingdoms, but that was merely business. The Grey King's hatred felt more personal than political. Then again, politics were personal.

Judging by the man's cruel smirk and the way he had swept his eyes past J.R. like a drive-by shooting, it was obvious his rival knew everything he didn't. J.R. couldn't comprehend it. Was he missing something? He felt like he was missing something.

With gaping holes in his memories, J.R. was at a disadvantage. The Grey King was gliding through the darkness, while J.R. was wandering in a fog where everything felt elusive, unreal, and warped.

J.R. blamed himself. He had taken the man's hand, believing it was an offer of friendship. When in actuality, it was nothing more than a trap.

What J.R. doesn't know is that it wasn't his fault. It wasn't a bout of forgetfulness or foolishness on his part that gave his enemy the upper hand. This was Divine intervention at work. Whomever was out there governing the cosmos had purposefully stepped in to mess with his mind. They did a bit of editing – snatched out a few crucial scenes which took place many years ago under a starry night sky in the middle of a dark desert – and left behind empty spaces where memories ought to be.

But the first thing they made him forget were all the little lies that brought him to the wasteland.

Chapter 2:
The little Prince is a big liar, isn't he?

He had to get rid of this woman.

He didn't harbour any ill will toward her, but getting rid of her was the only way to save her. She was all wrong for the job.

One look at her and he knew she was completely unfit to marry into his family.

Prince Lucien Justus Rex Valenta II – *J.R.* was what he'd go by in the future, but for now his family called him *Junior* – was born and bred in a Kingdom of Gold where the higher standards prevailed. That's how he knew when someone wasn't up to snuff.

He hailed from a family of formidable figures. You had to be equally fascinating and frightening to live, thrive, and survive amongst his kin. The House of Valenta was like a well-heeled wilderness. Lush and beautiful on the surface, but there were always vultures circling above, waiting for you to die.

The woman on the bench didn't seem particularly spellbinding or scary. She looked shy and sweet. She wouldn't last three seconds with his family. It would be like tossing a kitten into a colony of hungry eagles. His sister alone would tear this lady apart with those talons she called hands and have her for an appetizer.

Junior needed to rescue the woman from all the grief that would inevitably come from being a daughter-in-law for the Valenta family.

Yes, he would save her by getting rid of her. He was a Prince, and protecting pathetic, pretty girls was in his job description. At least, that's what a lot of books with bosoms on the front cover had implied.

"So, you're one of Mike's new girlfriends, huh?" Junior leapt up from behind the backrest of the bench, his cherubic face and tiny arms hovering over it much like a baby panda on a tree branch.

"Oh, err…" Putting a hand to her chest, the woman startled. She whirled her head around and scattered back a little on her perch. She had been expecting her host. She hadn't anticipated her host's seven-year-old little brother.

"Well," the little Prince demanded impatiently, "Are you, or aren't you?" He already knew the answer, but he needed to egg her on deliberately.

Finally finding her voice, she replied softly, "Actually, I haven't had the pleasure of meeting His Majesty Phantom King Michael in person yet. This is my first time here." At Junior's blasé stare, she added, "I have an appointment with his sister… with your sister."

"Ohhhhhhhh," Junior nodded, feigning innocence, "So you're one of *those* girls."

There was a huge discrepancy between Michael's regular roster of girlfriends that casually came and went as they pleased – *"Mikey's bad decisions"* as Lex called them – and the slew of prim and proper young ladies that she had been entertaining for the past week.

Entertaining, was what Lex had said. *Interviewing*, was what she meant.

It was why they were here in the United Phantom Realm, instead of back home in the Gold Kingdom. The sole purpose of Lex's visit was to find their eldest brother Michael a consort.

"Someone respectable, reasonable, and routine so that she may be a trustworthy and amenable addition to our little family," Lex had told him on the jet ride over. Her smile revealed far too much teeth to be genuine.

"Someone simple, stumpy, and stupid so that Mike never loves her more than he loves you," Junior had mimicked, arms crossed sourly as he gazed out the window.

Junior was ordered to tag along and accompany his sister, if only to give his Father a much-needed respite from his youngest son.

The Prince didn't enjoy travelling back and forth between the Golden and the Phantom realms. But there was no way around it.

You see, most royal families lived together under one Kingdom, but that didn't apply to the Valentas. Their current family tree went like this:

- Parents: Lucien I (Father) and Lana (Mother, *temporarily* deceased)
- Eldest son: Michael
- Second son: Gabriel
- First daughter, third child: Alexandra (Lex)
- Third son, fourth child: Lucien II (Junior)

The family hierarchy sounded simple enough – if they were living in another world where kingships were acquired through hereditary succession. But they weren't.

Things worked differently on this Earth. Being a Prince or a Princess didn't necessarily mean you would inherit the throne. Here, Kings were Divinely chosen by mystical entities called Totems. Each Totem carried a supernatural energy that appeared in a specific colour to the mortal eye. There were seven Totems presently: Gold, Red, Blue, Indigo, Black, White, and Silver.

Mind you, there were a few more Totems, which were currently absent. Most notably, the Green and Grey Totems had been missing in action for quite some time. The previous Green King had mysteriously died nearly a century ago. The last Grey King had died seven years ago, shortly after attacking Lana and leaving her in a comatose state (a temporary death, if you will). There was a lot less mystery around the Grey King's death: Michael had avenged his Mother by punching a hole straight through the man's face, effectively killing him. Neither the Green nor the Grey Totems had chosen any successors since.

Whenever a Totem chose a King, they installed their Divine energy inside their mortal host. If a King died or went into a coma, a Totem would select another soul, thereby shifting their energies into another body. Sometimes, they'd choose a new King immediately after the death of a former one. Or, on other occasions, they'd take their sweet time with the selection process, and there would be a gap of several years, centuries even, from one King to another – hence the currently kingless state of the Green- and Grey- realms.

There was much the public didn't know about these mysterious Totems, but two things were evident: their energies wielded inconceivable powers, and they chose their Kings freely, without much regard to gender, class, age, or background.

An *extremely long* time ago, the Golden Totem had picked Lucien.

A reasonably long time ago, the Black and White Totems had picked Lana.

And, more recently, after Lana had gone comatose, the Black, White, and Silver Totems had picked Michael.

Hand-picked by mankind's spiritual superiors, Lucien, Lana and Michael had become absolute monarchs of separate nations. Having multiple Kings in the family meant the Valentas were united by heredity and divided by divinity.

At present, the two realms functioned as followed:

- The Golden Empire consisted of the Gold Kingdom and a large handful of exoplanets – "*the colonies*" – within their galactic postal code. The entire dominion was owned by Lucien, but these days, he was pushing most of the managerial duties over to Lex. He had all the power, but she had to do all the work. Basically, the hierarchy was: Gold King Lucien I > Golden Princess-Regent Lex > Golden Prince Lucien II.

- The United Phantom Realm consisted of three Kingdoms (Black, White, and Silver), all of which were owned and governed by Michael and overseen by Gabriel. With Lana gone, the current hierarchy was: Phantom King Michael > Phantom Prince Gabriel > Phantom Queen (*to be determined, currently hiring*).

12

Junior belonged to the Golden Royal Family, but he came to the Phantom Realm every now and then to visit his brothers.

"How old are you, anyway?" Junior asked the current Phantom Queen-candidate.

Physically, the woman looked like a run-of-the-mill 18-year-old human female, but Junior knew she was a valensman. She had to be. Humans who were valensmen rarely ever mixed and married with the *other* class of humans – the primigens as they were labelled.

"I'm in my Second Century of life," the young woman said politely in a well-rounded Earth Standard Sole dialect.

"Oh, just like my sister." Junior averted his gaze toward the waterfall in front of them. "You like this display?"

"Yes, it's stunning."

"It's as fake as Lexie's smile," he snorted. "The water's not even real."

They were outside in Michael's black granite-tiled courtyard, which was located neatly between a triangle of skyscrapers. *Talon Towers*, was what Michael had named the place. Smack dab in the middle of the area was a massive metallic wall of a thousand lights, all of which were artistically arranged to look like a three-headed eagle.

Now that the sun had gone down, the structure did as it was told and released mist and rain out of all its lights. Junior watched the water splash to the ground, glazing over the tiles. The entire aesthetic was very much reminiscent of a cold, gloomy night in a city haunted by ghosts and infested with sad souls.

Lex had the structure commissioned last year for Michael's birthday. She had described it as the perfect embodiment of the Phantom King: *inscrutable, untouchable, and unstoppable.*

Junior disagreed. It wasn't any of those things. The lavish waterfall was entirely artificial. It was merely enchanted – or *charged*, as the Kings liked to call it – with Michael's Black, White, and Silver energies to *look* real. But it was all fake. Nothing more than an illusion. All this steam and spray came from nowhere and was going nowhere… much like this woman.

The Prince swept his eyes across her form in scrutiny. The lights glinted intensely behind all the false-water, giving him a better glance at her profile. He wondered if she was really human or human-passing. For all he knew, she could've hailed from one of the colonial planets.

"Where you from, anyway?"

The woman smiled kindly at him. "Aww, I think you meant to say, 'where *are* you from?'"

Junior knitted his brows together. "Do you know who I am?"

"Of course," she cooed sweetly. "You're quite the famous little lad. Everyone knows who you are."

"Well, I have no idea who you are. And I bet no one else does either. No one important, at least." Junior smiled meanly. "So, answer my question. Where ARE you from?"

The woman tightened her smile. "Well, I…"

"Are you from the Golden colonies?" Furrowing his little brows, he said with a searching squint, "Wait, you're not from the Red Kingdom, are you?"

"Err, no… I was born and raised in the White Kingdom, back when the Phantom Realm was first established."

"So, you're from here, then?" Junior clicked his tongue. "That's not good. My Father-King won't approve of that."

"The Gold King doesn't want a daughter-in-law from the Phantom Realm? Why ever not?"

"Father says the women here can't be trusted 'cause they're all wild and wicked."

This time, her smile slid right off her face. "I assure you I don't fall into either category."

"That's not good," he repeated with another click of his tongue, "Wild and wicked is exactly my Brother-King's type."

The woman's face visibly fumbled upon hearing that. "Oh, oh… is it, really? I …I … suppose I could be wild too…er…"

"Oh yeah? How?"

"Well, I – I – I've been known to let my hair down every now and then."

The idiom went right over Junior's head. "Pfffttt, that won't help. Mike doesn't care about hair! I've seen him shack up with girls who look like they've got birds hidden away inside their manes."

The woman gave him a curious look. "Well then, what does His Majesty King Michael prefer in a consort?"

"He likes girls with big bosoms. All his girlfriends have them. They have bosoms so big, I bet they can't even see their feet when they look down… But you don't seem to have that problem." Dropping his round dark eyes to her chest, he said, "You don't look like you have any bosom at all. That means Mike will never love you."

Making firm eye-contact with her, he continued, "Come to think of it, you don't look very smart either. That means my Father will stomp all over you like a bunch of grapes, and Lexie – don't get me started on Lexie – she'll have an easy time turning you into one of her trained b—"

"Junior!" He heard Lex shriek from behind. "What in Heaven's name are you saying?!"

Jumping off the bench, he spun around and gazed up at his sister. Her face was youthful, beautiful, immaculate, and outraged. The first three adjectives were her default. The fourth one – the outrage – only surfaced whenever Junior was around.

"Hey Lexie. You were taking too long finding Mike a trophy wife. I thought I'd help you out by *thinning the herd* a bit."

"You're not helping anyone by making such ill-mannered remarks," she said sternly. "Apologize to Lady Lettice at once!"

"Pfffffttttt," Junior snickered over at the woman, "Your parents named you after *lettuce*? Seriously?"

"Junior," Lex said forebodingly.

The little Prince whirled back to his big sister. "What? I was doing everyone a favour. This one's all wrong for him," he jutted a thumb back at Lady Lettice, "Besides, I liked the last girl you had better. Lady Uggzilla."

"Lady Ursula," corrected Lex.

"Yeah, her. She was better. She curtsied at me and told me I was the cutest thing ever. And then, she hugged me and gave me a chocolate caramel egg—"

"Oh... er... I brought something as well." Lady Lettice twiddled with her clutch. "I – I have a packet of tolu gum?"

Ignoring her, Junior went on, "And when the other girl held me, I could tell right away she had ample bosom! This girl has zero bosom, Lexie! Look! Her chest is shaped just like yours."

"That is enough!" fumed Lex as she grabbed her little brother's right arm.

Before Lex could drag him away, Junior quickly turned back to Lettice and jumped to snatch the packet of gum she'd been holding out.

"Come along, Junior." Lex stormed off with Junior in tow.

They went inside the south building of Talon Towers, past the foyer and down a long corridor lined with doors leading to bare rooms. Junior never understood why Michael had so many empty rooms in his primary royal residence. Maybe he needed a ton of space to fill up all his bad decisions?

It wasn't until they reached a private office that Lex came to a halt, parking Junior on a curved, off-white chaise.

"How many times have I told you to stop sneaking off on your own?" Lex reprimanded. "Everyone," and by *everyone*, she was namely referring to his security detail and his nanny, "Absolutely everyone has been a complete wreck searching for you this past hour." Releasing an exasperated huff, she said, "Ugh, I knew I should have had you microchipped last year."

It nettled her nerves whenever Junior pulled one of his disappearing acts. It was a mystery to her, but somehow, he'd learned how to dodge all the cameras and evade every guard.

When he wasn't lurking like a shadow, he was making a spectacle of himself, cartwheeling half-naked down hallways and vaulting himself into walls. He was either too silent to catch or too loud to ignore. It was always one extreme or another. Sometimes, the only way to keep him properly contained was to have the entire residence under lockdown.

"It's not my fault they can't keep up with me," said the little Prince tartly. "And I wasn't *sneaking off*."

Junior detested the accusation. *Sneaking off*, she'd said in that fault-finding tone of hers, as if the little Prince had been up to something sinister. He wouldn't have to slip away from everyone if they would just tell him where his Mother was being held. Rumour had it, Lana's comatose form was hidden somewhere inside Talon Towers.

He had never seen his Mother in person before. Or, at least, he couldn't remember seeing her face to face. Seven years ago, when Junior was an infant, Lana had been severely injured while battling the previous Grey King. What happened to her afterwards was, to this day, a source of great public debate. If you asked strangers on the streets, they'd tell you Lana was either in a coma, a coffin, or another celestial body. The general consensus was that she was *"temporarily deceased,"* meaning she

17

was alive, but unconscious and insensate. However, there was still a portion of the population who swore she was as dead as a mackerel in a fishmonger's basket and the Valentas were covering it up. Then, there were the conspiracy theorists who surmised that Lana had faked her own death and fled the planet.

Regardless of what anyone thought, it didn't change the fact that Junior held no memories of his Mother.

That was all he wanted. A single moment with his Mother. To touch her face. To hold her hand. To hear her heartbeat. To make sure she wasn't completely dead. But Lana's exact whereabouts were known only to his siblings, and they were purposely leaving him out of the loop.

"I was having a chat with Lady Lettuce is all," Junior said. "No need to make a fuss! ... Want some gum?" He offered, pulling at the wrapper.

"Oh, give me that!" chided Lex, confiscating the packet and stuffing it into her left pocket. Her dress didn't have any pockets two seconds ago. It did now. She had previously charged all her garments with Golden energy so that anything she wore would align with her emotions and needs. Her clothes knew better than to disappoint her. The same, however, could not be said for her little brother.

"Lady Lettuce seems nice enough. But she's weak... I bet she's the kinda girl who'd cry out a bunch of rivers if I shaved her eyebrows off in her sleep," Junior said disapprovingly. "I can tell she's not gonna be combustible with our family."

"You mean *compatible*."

"That's what I said – combat-able," shrugged Junior. "Father's never gonna approve of her anyway, and I told her as much."

"Why would you say that?"

"Cause it's true. He says all the ladies of the Phantom realm are wild, wicked heathens."

That brought a little smirk to Lex's face. "He ought to know. He married one of them."

"He did? So, wait, you're saying our Mother was—"

His family rarely spoke of Lana. Predictably, Junior had many questions. What did his Mother like to do? What did she hate to do? What did she love most in the world? Who did she love most in the world? Who did she hate the most? Who was her favourite child? Why did she pick a total square like his Father? Why did he pick a heretic like her? Where is she now? Where are you keeping her? *Tell me everything! Tell me anything!*

"—Mother was wild and wicked?!" Junior was starving for information about Lana. He was prepared to beg for whatever breadcrumbs Lex was willing to offer when it came to their Mother. "Was she really, Lexie?"

"Among many other things, yes." Fondness struck Lex's features for a moment, but it quickly melted away. "But never mind that," she said coldly, now back to business. "Junior, we must discuss your behaviour, which I hope you realize was entirely inappropriate. No respectable gentlemen, let alone a Prince, should speak so poorly of a woman in such a manner. Especially not to her face."

"I didn't say anything about her face. I was talkin' about her bosom."

"You are never to speak about anyone's bosom ever again. Do you understand?" admonished Lex. "You are a Golden Prince and as such you're expected to maintain a level of decorum, dignity, and elegance at all times."

"I know, I know." Junior released a puff of air, blowing his bangs away from his temple. "Can I have some gum?"

"Forget the gum, Junior. Do you really believe you exhibited Princely behaviour in front of my guest?"

"Yes, I did," said Junior defiantly. "A Prince's job is to save dumb young ladies from peril, right?"

"No, that's not—"

"Yes, it is. All the books say so. And that's what I was doin'."

Lex raised a brow, curious as to what *books* his nannies had been reading to him as of late. "You mean to tell me you were saving that young woman by making crass remarks about her body and her intelligence?"

"I was saving her life!" Junior insisted. "She's not Mike's type at all. I bet he'll throw her away, right out of his office window," he pointed toward the ceiling as a way of indicating to the 33rd floor where the Phantom King's private study was lodged, "The same way he does with guards he doesn't like… and advisors he doesn't like … and everyone else he doesn't like."

"Mikey doesn't do that," she lied easily.

"Yes, he does. I saw him do it yesterday. And the last time we came to visit. And the time before that, I saw him grab this one guy by the neck and snap—"

"OK, I get it." Lex released an exasperated sigh. She needed to remind Michael to refrain from disposing of people in such a cruel and cavalier way, especially with Junior creeping around the vicinity.

When Lucien executed people in the Gold Kingdom, he did so with discretion and formality. Unlike their Father, Michael had no class when it came to capital punishments. The Phantom King snapped necks and carried on with his day.

"Regardless, Mikey would never behave so savagely to his own consort," she maintained.

"Even if he doesn't like her?"

"That hardly matters," said Lex evenly.

"I don't get it." Junior shook his head. "Why does he wanna marry someone he doesn't like?"

"It's not up to him."

"It's not?"

"No," she said resolutely, "Mikey doesn't get a say in this."

"He doesn't get a say in who's gonna be his wife?" Junior was confused. He knew Lex played a huge part in the decision-making process of all familial matters, including spousal selection for her siblings. But he had assumed Michael would get to express his opinions and cast his vote in this specific issue, seeing as it was *his nuptials*. Apparently, Junior had assumed wrong.

"Certainly not," said Lex austerely. "Mikey, bless his cold little heart, can be relied upon to win wars and eradicate enemies. But an important, life-altering decision like the future Phantom Queen – our future sister, no less – can not be left in his hands."

"That's even worse," snorted Junior. "If it's not up to him, then that means it's all up to you, Lexie, and I know *you*."

"Junior—"

"I don't want another sister! I already have to deal with you!" he said, speaking over her. "And you don't want a sister either—"

"That's not t—"

"You want a patsy you can boss around like you do everybody else. You'll tear Lady Lettuce into a side salad and then you'll probably toss her aside like a …a … umm… like a … like a side salad! I was doing her a favour, shooing her away before she could get hurt."

Then, at Lex's unstirred countenance, he yelled, "I was just being honest with her! She needed to know what she was getting into."

"Honesty is not always classy, Little Wing," Lex sighed and brought a hand up to massage her temple. "And it's high time you learned to distinguish the difference between being direct and being discourteous."

Junior slumped back on the settee. "Am I gonna be grounded for this?" he asked miserably.

"Yes… the second we're back on Golden soil." With a low murmur, she put in, "We can use the time to plant a chip in your arm."

Junior groaned, smashing his face into one of the throw pillows. He didn't think it was fair. Lex and Lucien were always giving him "*timeouts*" for one reason or another. They claimed it was because he ran his mouth off too much, saying all the wrong things. Saying things a "*proper Prince*" should never say. But he didn't mean to. He was simply being honest when he told people things like:

- "You know, Count Mavis, you're super nice… It's too bad you're also super old. I think you might die any day now. I promise to look sad at your funeral."
- "Which one are you again? Diana or Sara? … Oh right, now I remember. Diana's the pretty sister."
- "I like you, Lady Bristlefront. I realllly like you. I like you a lot more than Lord Bristlefront's last two wives. You're the best one yet. And if he ever trades you in for another wife, I'll tell her you were my favourite of all the Lady Bristlefronts. Even if the new wife is prettier than you. I'll still say you were my favourite."
- "I'm confused, Baron Whitestilt. Can men really get pregnant or are you just fat?"
- "My sister doesn't really love you. She's just using you to make her ex-boyfriend jealous."
- (After learning about taxidermy.) "Father, I love you so much. When you die, I'm gonna have you stuffed and keep you with me forever."
- "I really like how your butt jiggles when you walk, Viscountess Nightjar."
- "What kind of music do you love the most, Tarquin? … I see … Well then, Tarrrr-quinnnnn, let's listen to

the exact opposite of that … Because I *hate* you, Tarrr-quinnnn. I HATE YOU AND EVERYTHING YOU LOVE!!!"

Junior's list of verbal offences went on, really. And every single time, he'd get an earful from his Father-King and his Sister-Princess-Regent.

"*You little hell-griffin! Not even a decade old and already a menace to society!*" His Father-King would wail and scold whenever his youngest son did or said something he found untoward, unfavorable, and uncouth. "*Your consistently egregious behaviour has besmirched our family's good name. By way of explanation, I've had to tell people that you have a hormone imbalance. But this must stop, Junior! I can't go on for the remainder of my centuries telling everyone that one of my sons has a hormone imbalance!!!*"

For his part, Junior didn't understand what he was doing wrong. He was being himself. He was being honest. Isn't that what adults were always telling him to do? *Be yourself. Tell the truth.*

"Junior, are you listening to me?"

"Bits and pieces," he mumbled morosely.

"I want you to go and apologize to Lady Lettuc—" Lex stopped herself and amended, "Lady Lettice."

"But I'm not sorry."

"Clearly," said Lex coolly. That was her little brother for you: guilty but unremorseful. "Even so, you're going to take Princely action and issue a full and unequivocal apology for the offensive and shameless comments you directed toward her person."

"Sooo… I have to tell her I'm sorry she doesn't have any bosom?"

"*Junior*," she said, this time in a tone that felt akin to a bullet being fired in a straight line.

"OK, OK. I'll say *sorry*." The Prince sighed and pulled himself up and off the chaise.

Adults were so confusing. They demanded honesty and candor, but they desired lies and deceit.

Fine! Junior internally snapped. If that's what everyone wanted ... If that's what it took to be a proper Prince, then he'd do it. He'd become the best liar in the world.

A few days later, Junior and Lex returned to the Gold Kingdom. They were back home in their family's primary residence, the Chrysos Citadel. That's what their Father-King had dubbed his castle, but everyone else called it the Gilded Cage.

Nothing had changed in the Cage. Nothing ever changed in the Cage. But something was different with Junior.

Within a week, his family had stopped being exasperated with the Prince's cruel honesty and began to feel alarmed by the streak of blatant lies coming out of the boy.

He lied about brushing his teeth at night. He lied about his guards being "*sneaky smoochers.*" He denied raiding the kitchens for sweets, even when the security footage revealed otherwise. At school, he told his instructors his Father-King would lock them up in their castle dungeons if they assigned homework ever again.

At that point, when the little lies turned into petty threats, Lucien knew it was his fatherly duty to intervene. The Gold King decided to summon his son to the east-wing library so they could have an honest discussion about lying.

"Lying won't do you any favours, son. But the truth – the truth shall always save you. Remember what Jesus said to the Jews," Gold King Lucien smiled down at his youngest child.

His Father's face was beautiful. His lounge suit was impeccable. And his tone was as condescending as ever as he held up the Bible (*King Lucien's Version*) with one hand and said, "*'You will know the truth, and the truth will set you free.'*"

Junior nearly rolled his eyes. His pious, God-loving, God-fearing, overly Catholic, Father-King was always harping on about Jesus, as if he knew the guy personally. Always going on about the Bible, too. As if he wrote it himself – which he hadn't. He had merely translated it from the original Aramaic, Greek, and Hebrew into the Earth Standard Sole Language (ESSL) everyone used today.

"Pppffffffft," scoffed Junior. Having just returned from a Griffin-Cub Scouts meeting, the little Prince was still dressed in his mustard-coloured uniform shirt, shorts, and neckerchief. "And they bought that snake-oil pitch? No wonder they were stuck in the desert for so long."

Lucien's grin plummeted into a grimace. "How dare you speak such sacrilege, you wretched boy! I don't know what I find more vexing – that I have a son who can utter without stutter such profanities or that I have one who forgets how the Jews wandered in the wilderness long *before* Jesus incarnated into the physical world."

Before Junior could get another word out, Lucien held up his free hand, commanding silence. "You leave me no choice but to issue you a timeout," he said, as though sending his son to another opulent room within the palace was the equivalent of exiling him to purgatory.

"How long this time?" Junior scowled up at him.

Lucien lifted one of his elitist eyebrows as he handed his son the Bible.

Junior reluctantly took the tome from his Father's grasp. The cover was laser-engraved with a detailed tree design. Did it represent the good tree that humans were allowed to eat from? Or the bad one they should've resisted but couldn't and didn't? He had no way of knowing.

"Until you've read everything from Genesis to Leviticus. And completed a 10-page handwritten report on all your learnings. No help from others. No *double spacing*-it either."

"But what about my dinner?"

"I shall have it sent to you when the time arises."

"But I'm hungry now!"

"I shall personally prepare some nutritious snacks to sustain your energy."

The little Prince made another face. His Father was a man who ate for health instead of happiness. Junior knew from experience that those *nutritious snacks* would look like vomit and taste even worse.

With his nose raised high in the air and one long arm pointing dramatically towards the door, Lucien ordered, "Now march yourself over to the nearest prayer chamber posthaste!"

Junior stormed off in a sulk. He didn't care how much his Father-King preached about the power of the truth. He already knew the truth was a trap, and only a good lie could get you out of it.

A thunderbolt of a thought suddenly struck him.

Maybe that was the problem. His lies weren't good enough. *Not yet*.

It took him awhile, but Junior had done it. He had finally learned how to lie the *right* way. Mind you, his first few years of deception hadn't led to much success. But it was through trial and error that he realized being a liar wasn't a bad thing. Not always.

Lying was a necessity. Especially when dealing with adults like his Father who got fussy and worked up over all the wrong things. "Sure, that *looks* like my handwriting, Father, but I really didn't pen that note to my teacher. Honest," Junior (age 7) had told Lucien after being confronted with an egregiously forged letter stating, '*please excuse prince junior from doing his homework forever. it's too hard and i'm too old and stupid to help him. signed, his father.*'

Lying was a way to restore balance to this unjust world. Especially when dealing with jerks who needed to be taught a lesson. "I didn't hit him," insisted Junior (age 9) after being accused of punching one of his classmates, Tarquin Wadsworth-Herringbone IV. He hated Tarquin, but he didn't want to strike him. He only did it because Tarquin had been bullying his friend Taurus Reed III. "Honest, I didn't hit him! Tarquin's mug always looks like that. It's not my fault God manufactured it that way."

Lying was a survival tactic. Especially when dealing with assassins. "You know, if you're gonna plot a kidnapping, you need to work smarter, not harder. Anyone can find me in this warehouse you've got here. What you ought to do is take me to that nameless isle by the Silver Sea. No one ever goes there." Junior (age 10) had suggested to his kidnappers. What he purposefully omitted was that particular isle, which housed an ancient penitentiary, was protected by Lucien's handmade thunderbolts. Anyone who stepped foot inside or outside that island without the Gold King's permission ended up deep-fried and dead within seconds. Junior would've been safe though. His Father's bolts knew better than to hurt him.

Junior never got to find out whether his abductors would've gone ahead with his recommendation. Not a moment later, his Sister-Princess-Regent and his Father-King had blazed in through the roof, ferocious streaks of gold lightning following their silent commands. It was the first time the Prince had witnessed them electrocute people with their powers. Afterwards, Lex had stroked his hair back and gently lied to him, "Oh, we didn't electrocute them, Little Wing... We *neutralized* them is all."

Above all else, Junior understood that lying was an act of kindness. Especially when dealing with ... well, everyone.

- "Why, Count Kestrell, are you really in your Fifth Millennia of life? To look at you, I'd say you were only in your Fifth Century."

- "Ah, Mr. Reed, it's *lovely* to see you again. Absolutely *looovvve-ly*."

- "Oh, Viscountess Nightjar, I probably shouldn't be around you. The mere sight of your face could send any man into cardiac arrest." (It wasn't her face he was he looking at.)

- "Aww, Lady Plover, why would anyone ever ask for your hand, when they could beg for your heart instead?"

- "Of course I don't hate you, Tarrr-quinnnn ... What ever gave you that idea?"

- "Errrr, Meryl, I see you got another perm ... another perfect perm that perfectly compliments your –your – your head."

Those were a few of the many polite lies he had told at age 11.

By the age of 12, he had learned how to lie with confidence and charm. He had become the *proper Prince* everyone wanted him to be. He had transformed into a beautiful liar. It did wonders for his brand appeal. Most people seemed pleased by his change in attitude and demeanour. The only exceptions were his family and friends. They were immune to most of the Prince's lies. His family, especially, could see right through him, much like they were doing now:

"Oh, Father, of course I remembered today is your birthday. I didn't forget. Honest. How could I?" said Junior.

"My birthday is a month from now," frowned Lucien.

"I know that." Junior's mind reached for a quick save. "It's just... I consider everyday a celebration of you, my Father-King."

"I'm sure," Lucien clipped dryly. "Anyhow, I was thinking of venturing to the Neutral Realm this year where I shall resume my Great Spiritual Quest to find Heaven on Earth." Gesturing carelessly to Lex and Junior, he added, "With you kids in tow, of course."

"Soooo ... you wanna go to the desert?" said Junior, unimpressed.

"You'll love it, son. It's a place to be revered and respected. A place to purify our mortal bodies and cleanse our immortal souls. There'll be no distractions there, none of these creature comforts you'll find here," the Gold King said, waving a hand around his private quarters as if to indicate to the entirety of the Gilded Cage.

"But – But I rather like these creature comforts," whined Junior.

Talon Towers felt more like a corporate office than a King's castle, with its minimal interior designs and sharp edifices. By contrast, the Gilded Cage was a traditional citadel, only better.

Lucien's massive palace was perched atop a tidal island. It had every luxury one could ever ask for. There were nearly 2,000 rooms. Apart from the numerous bedrooms, bathrooms, state rooms, dining halls, and servants quarters, the Cage also had a two cinemas, five indoor swimming pools, stables, a petting zoo, three tennis courts, five recreation rooms, five prayer chambers, fifteen libraries, ten art rooms, five private gyms, an intricate maze garden, an infirmary, a surgery room, and half a wing for their in-house designers, stylists and jewellers.

The Gold King's primary palace was a slice of Heaven, as far as Junior was concerned. The Neutral Realm … was a desert. Nothing but hot sand beneath their feet and a blistering sun above their heads.

Ignoring his son, Lucien went on in a dramatic tone, "—It'll be the three of us. At night, we'll sleep under stars that shine like diamonds on black velvet. And by day, we'll navigate through the silence of barren land where we shall fulfill our family's destiny by reconnecting the entirety of mankind to God." Swinging his eyes between his children, he continued, "Of course, it's a family vacation. We all get a say in it, and I shan't go if you kids are opposed."

Junior scrunched up his face. He didn't want to go to the desert. Apart from the lack of desire, there was also a record scratch in his thoughts, abruptly halting his mental facilities. A quick, disruptive beat in his internal narration. A second later, it was as though the record had been replaced with a quiet voice telling him, *'Avoid the wasteland where there is fear in the sand. The magic there will leave you in enemy hands.'*

"Junior?" his Father prodded.

Snapping back into his usual inner programing, Junior blinked up at Lucien. "Er—look, Father, I know you find these family trips very binding—"

"*Bonding,*" corrected Lex.

"Yeah, that's what I said… it's – well, I – I don't think—"

Lex elbowed Junior's side. "That sounds wonderful. Doesn't it, Junior?" His sister gave him a pointed look.

Junior really didn't want to go, especially after hearing that cryptic little ditty in his head. But it was for Lucien's birthday. It seemed wrong not to oblige him, especially since his Father always gave Junior whatever he wanted and more whenever his own birthday came along.

He shook off the voice in his head, warning him to stay away. The omen had been absurd. Fear in the sand? Enemy hands? Ridiculous. Absolutely ridiculous. The Neutral Realm was the most peaceful place on Earth. The most harm it could do was give its visitors a sunburn.

Nodding over at Lucien, Junior proceeded with the answer his Father wanted to hear.

"Yes, of course, Father." Putting on a bright smile, he lied perfectly. "Let's go to the desert. It'll be fun."

Someday in the future, J.R. would look back on this moment and cackle miserably at the butterfly effect it had created. It was amazing how one simple lie could unleash such unimaginable ripple effects across the entire world.

Chapter 3:
Is this necessary?
Can't we just buy him a girlfriend?

"Junior... Junior ... Junior!"

"What?" Junior snapped at Lex. He didn't bother looking her way, but his tone of voice and the annoyed frown crossing his preadolescent features made it very clear he didn't appreciate his sister's pesky interruptions.

"Didn't you hear me calling your name?" said Lex.

"Not the first hundred times, I didn't."

"Don't get smart with me, Little Wing," she said sternly. "Are you even paying attention to our Father-King?"

"Are *you*?" Junior threw back at his sister.

They both shifted their heads eastward to face their Father, Gold King Lucien, who was also known under his many other sobriquets: Emperor of the Golden realm, the First Chosen King, the First and Only King of the Golden Empire to date, the Eternal Monarch, etc. etc.

Not that anyone could ever forget who he was, thought Junior. His Father was the most famous King this side of the universe. Lucien's reputation preceded him and even if it didn't, there was always some Knight or another – the Volucris, as all the Gold King's soldiers were called – to stand around and recite all his titles whenever he entered a room.

Lucien was currently on the other side of their "*tent*." He was towering over a foldable table full of ancient maps. By his side were three historians he had brought along for their trip to the Neutral Realm. Two of the men were valensmen and the other one was a primigen.

They were all dressed in similar attire – white linen shirts and beige trousers, athletic boots, and safari jackets – but the trio of men looked so tiny and plain standing next to a being as tall and divinely handsome as Lucien. Junior suspected those men didn't care much about appearances. Otherwise, they wouldn't have chosen to waste their lives tucked away in dusty archival libraries, reading about dead people and events that simply didn't matter anymore.

If Junior really thought about it, he supposed he could understand why the two valensmen-historians pursued this type of knowledge for a living. They were both young – only in their Fifth Century of life – and had several millennia to spare. The primigen-historian, however, was the odd duck. He was already 45 years old and probably only had another 45 years left in him (if he was lucky).

For a moment, Junior reasoned the man must have been a complete idiot for wasting the remains of his short lifespan in such a futile profession.

Not a second later, he felt a little remorseful for thinking so poorly of the man.

"We must always be empathetic to our primigenious counterparts, Junior," Lex had once told him, "They are every bit as human as we are, but they are not like us … They die young even when they're old."

In ancient times, people had mistaken valensmen for demigods and vampires. It took them awhile to realize it was simply a difference in human biology. Primigens (homo sapiens) and valensmen (homo vis) were both part of the human race, but valensmen physically aged at a far less drastic rate due to specific mutations in their epigenome. Those mutations essentially slow down a valensman's natural aging process by the time they reached age 17. That was why his Father-King still had all the looks and vitality of a 30-year-old man, even though he was in his Third Millennia of life. Same went for his Sister-Princess-Regent, who looked like a teenager despite being in her Second Century. She wouldn't even get her first facial wrinkle until another six or seven centuries time.

Junior frowned at the men. Valensmen or primigen, he didn't care. He found all three of them equally annoying. They had taken up the better part of their Father's attention from the moment they had arrived on Neutral soil. *So much for it being just the three of us*, Junior thought bitterly.

Each historian was desperate to catch the Gold King's ear. They were garrulous as they went on and on about a couple of missing rivers.

"Your Majesty, I assure you the Book of Gensis clearly states that *one* single river went through the Garden of Eden," said one of the historians.

"I already know that," scoffed Lucien. Many centuries ago, the Gold King had translated biblical texts from the original languages of Greek, Hebrew, and Aramaic into the Earth Standard Sole Language they had today. It had resulted in the widespread publication of the Bible (*King Lucien's Version*).

"—Yes, but when it exited, it parted into *four* rivers: Pishon, Gihon, Tigris, and Euphrates," piped in another historian.

"It's like watching a snake chasing its own tail with you lot," Lucien rolled his eyes. "Enough with all this circumlocution," he demanded, loudly tapping one long finger against a spot on the map. "Tell me frankly – and I shall know if you're lying – are you positive *this* is where the riverhead used to be located or not?"

All the historians exchanged uneasy glances. None of them wanted to state the obvious, which was that the main river supposedly leading up to Eden no longer existed. Two of those rivers had most likely been wiped out over six millennia ago due to mass flooding and the other two endured a detrimental fate in the year 1027 AD – on the very day Lucien had been Divinely chosen.

It was common knowledge by now that all the Kings of Earth were selected by beings of Divine energy called Totems. Every Totem appeared in a different colour and a different shape whenever it chose a King to lead. Lucien was allegedly the first to be chosen, back in 1027 AD when he'd witnessed an entity of pure golden light shaped like a griffin.

The symbiosis of the Golden Totem's power and Lucien's body had caused the most intense global earthquake the world had ever seen. Chunks of land had been separated while others had melded together. In one massive energetic sweep, all the ancient domains – the Roman Empire, France, Kashmir, Japan, Liao, to name a few – were literally torn apart. In its place came the emergence of new realms run by Chosen Kings.

The Golden Bang was what they called that event in modern times.

In the process of such a seismic shift, some bodies of water had been introduced to large amounts of sediments whereas others completely changed their original course.

In the back of Junior's mind, he could still remember his second big brother Gabriel, explaining the Golden Bang and the history of Chosen Kings to him. "*All beings are made of energy, Junior,*" Gabriel had said, "*But Chosen Kings have the ability to carry an additional source of Divine energy that appears in different colours to the mortal eye. When this energy synergizes with a King's body, they can use it for supernatural means… Some say there's no limit to what a King can manifest with this energy. Take Father as an example. As the Gold King, he can easily conjure up thunder, electricity, shields, and…well, gold.*"

The historians kept looking at one another. None of them wanted to say outright that they couldn't pinpoint the exact location of said rivers because their King had inadvertently changed the structure and fate of their planet forever.

"*See*, you're not listening to them, either," muttered Junior, from their table on the opposite side of the tent.

Not that the Golden Royal Family were by any means in a traditional sort of tent. Right beneath them was 2,000 square feet of carpet made from the finest wool, silk, and cotton materials. Above and all around them was a massive, glowing, golden dome that Lucien had made with his Kingly energy. It was one of the Gold King's Shields. It was completely impenetrable.

Lucien had a knack for making sturdy Shields in any size and shape, and they always ranged in various shades of gold. Sometimes he created these barriers in such a transparent creamy tint that no one even noticed there was a Shield present – not until they smacked themselves face first into one. No force or elements could get through a Golden Shield created by the King himself, not unless Lucien allowed it.

"I'm listening," insisted Lex, and at Junior's disbelieving look, she added, "Well…bits and pieces…" Staring over his shoulder, she asked, "What are you doing?"

"Colouring some of these monster pictures Father brought along," he said, keeping his attention on one of the drawings sprawled across the table.

Colouring wasn't an ideal pastime for a boy a few months shy of his 13th birthday, but what else was there to do? His best friends had come with their respective noble families, but they were situated miles away in another area of the desert. Junior wouldn't get to see them until later tonight at Lucien's party.

Lucien had said this would be a family vacation, and yet he'd seen fit to invite a team of historians, a handful of his household staff (domestic servants, private assistants, chefs, and the like), and nearly half the members of the Golden Royal Court (*the Osprey*, as they were known) to tag along.

"Oh, you jealous boy. You and your sister always want your Father-King all to yourselves!" Lucien had beamed earlier this morning, throwing his arms around Junior and Lex, effectively caging them in.

Junior had wrinkled his nose in annoyance. He hated it whenever Lucien referred to himself in the third person.

"Errr... yeahhhh, that's it," lied Junior, squirming in his Father's octopus-tight embrace.

"How lucky am I to have children who constantly covet my attention?" Lucien continued to gush. "Well, you young creatures needn't despair. We'll have plenty of quality time to ourselves. Our courtiers shan't interfere with us. They're only here for the party... think of them as a necessity for display purposes, if you will. Today is a day where I celebrate my existence after all, and you know what I always say, there's no point—"

"There's no point in existing if there's no one around to see it," Junior and Lex had finished off dully. "We know, Father, we know."

They did know their Father-King, all too well. Lucien's life's mission had been to conquer the world. His life's pleasure, however, was to show off everything he'd conquered.

Junior's eyes trailed leftward. Members of the Osprey weren't the only ones here for *display purposes*. Junior's Secutor, Jeremiah, was here with him as well, sitting beside a woman – Lex's Secutor – on a bench by the south side of the tent.

Secutor. It meant official companion.

Jeremiah was his age, and he was paid to be Junior's consort whenever and wherever the Prince travelled. *Some companion he is*, Junior thought with an internal snort as he watched the boy gaze indolently at the ground in silence.

The Prince knew very little personal information about his Secutor. But based on a conversation Junior had overheard between his nanny and one of his bodyguards, Jeremiah was an orphan who allegedly came from "*the kind of neighbourhood where the 'for rent' signs looked like ransom notes.*"

Junior didn't understand why Jeremiah was being so weird these days. The two of them used to have fun playing together when they were younger. But in recent years, Jeremiah had become so cold and closed off towards the Prince. Junior sometimes wondered if he had offended the boy somehow. Had he done something wrong? His friend, Peter Porkina (a.k.a Porki) told Junior he had a foul habit of doing all the wrong things without even realizing it.

"*You're an idiot, my Prince,*" Porki often said, but the words were usually laced with a smidge of fondness.

With his attention momentarily focused on Jeremiah, Junior didn't take notice of Lex's outraged expression.

"Junior!" She whisper-yelled, tugging the coloured pencil out of his grasp. "That's not a colouring book! You realize those are ancient sketches of angels... Ugh, I told Father we should have brought along copies instead of the originals."

"These are angels?" said Junior, perplexed. "They look like beasts... this one's got five faces and four of them are animal-heads ... and this one is nothing but a row of blood-shot eyes with a bunch of feathers around it."

"I think that's a seraphim," observed Lex. "Well, at least you only coloured in one of the drawings and it appears to be of a low-grade principality," she said, a little relieved. Lucien would've thrown a fit had Junior ruined images of entities higher up in the angelic hierarchy.

"*Prince*apality?" Junior held up the picture of the angelic warrior, who was now crimson from head to toe. It wasn't done. He still hadn't finished colouring in the flaming sword the angel had in its grasp. "So, this one was a Prince of Heaven?"

"No. Based on theological studies, only archangels like Gabriel, Michael, and Raphael were considered Princes of Heaven."

None of those angels were in the pile of depictions lying about the table.

"Then … Father named Gabe and Mike after heavenly Princes?" he asked, referring to their older brothers, Gabriel and Michael.

At Lex's nod, Junior said, "What about *me*, Lexie? Who was I named after?"

Lex tilted her head to the side and stared down at him. "Who do you think, *Lucien* II?"

"Oh, right," mumbled Junior, feeling a little dumb for asking the question.

Junior's eyes briefly flickered over to his namesake before lowering back down to the drawing in his hand. "So why were they called Principalities if they weren't Princes?"

"I'm not sure. I think they were meant to be protectors, guardians of men and nations."

"Why not just call them Guardians then?"

"I don't know," she shrugged, "I wasn't around when angels allegedly conversed with mortals."

"I bet Mike and Gabe would know. Guess you're not as ancient as them, huh?"

"Certainly not!" Lex placed a hand to her chest, affronted. "I'm only in my Second Century of life as you well know … and Mikey and Gabby are far from ancient. Why, neither of them have even surpassed their First Millennia yet and – wait a minute, aren't you supposed to be completing your homework? I distinctly remember you having a family history report due the second we return home."

"I finished that ages ago." He thrusted a sheet of paper toward her face. "Here."

Lex poured through its contents:

- Father: Lucien Valenta
    - Born 23 October of yesteryear (*God knows when*) → Divinely Chosen → 1st Gold King → Semi-retired
- Mother: Lana Valenta
    - Born 31 October of yesteryear (*I dunno when. She's as ancient as my Father*) → Gold Queen → RESIGNED → Divinely Chosen → 1st Phantom King → Semi-dead
- Eldest brother: Michael Valenta
    - Born 31 April 1035 → 1st Golden Prince to King Lucien → FIRED & EXILED → 1st Phantom Prince to King Lana → Divinely Chosen → 2nd Phantom King
- Second elder brother: Gabriel Valenta
    - Born 3 June 1111 → 2nd Golden Prince to King Lucien → FIRED & EXILED → 2nd Phantom Prince to King Lana → 1st Phantom Prince to King Michael
- Elder sister: Alexandra "Lex" Valenta
    - Born 21 November 1828 → 1st Golden Princess to King Lucien → Golden Princess-Regent

"*This* is your idea of a report? It's nothing but a few dates and professional labels."

"In the end, isn't that what we all are, sis? Dates and labels," he said with a superficial display of thoughtfulness on his face.

"You'll have to redo it." Lex shook her head. "This is much too short, Junior."

"Best to keep it short and sweet, I rather think," said Junior. "Focus only on the key deets... Not for my sake. It's to save my instructors all that time and energy."

"How solicitous of you," said Lex flatly, plunging the paper back down to his chest. "I'd like to see a revised draft by tomorrow. And stop telling people Father fired Mikey and Gabby. You know that isn't true!"

"He may as well have fired them," he muttered under his breath.

"And why didn't you write down Father- and Mother's birth years?"

"Pffft," snorted Junior, "Did they even have numbers and calendars back then? I'm surprised Father even knows his own birthdate."

"Our parents are not as prehistoric as you think," Lex chided, but Junior could tell she was biting her cheek to keep from smiling.

"Pfffttt, please," guffawed Junior, "I bet when Father was born, people spent their nights sitting around the fire, wondering how it got there."

"Shhh," she hushed him, "Look alive, Father's coming this way. Quick, hide that Prince you just coloured."

"He's not a Prince, he's a Principality," said Junior as the two siblings tried to tidy up all the papers on the table, their hands fumbling awkwardly in haste.

"Are you kids ready to have some fun with your Father-King?" Lucien came toward them with a wide grin.

Junior tried very hard to keep from rolling his eyes. He and his Father had very different conceptions of fun.

"Father," Lex started hesitantly, "Are you sure about this expedition?"

"Have a little faith, my dear," said Lucien, smile still intact. "We're in the Neutral Realm, the holiest and most mystical place on Earth. This is the land where our Savior was born, where He defeated the Devil, where His disciples were chosen, where miracles were made long before the time of Chosen Kings. This is where ..."

Lex's thoughts began to drift as Lucien went into a tangent.

The Neutral Realm, also called the Neutral Desert, was a barren region that didn't belong to any King and maintained no citizens, only visitors set to make a pilgrimage. The theory was that this desert was the modern-day area that once consisted of some of the most sacred places known to man – places like Nazareth, Bethlehem, and Capernaum. Because of this, it was marked as a place of peace, untouched by the ownership of a King, unsullied by the madness of men.

The land was currently governed by the Convocation of Kings, a global organization whose members included nearly every chosen King on the planet.

"Did you come up with that name, Father?" Junior had asked Lucien once. "You know the abbreviation spells COK, don't you?"

Current members of the Convocation included the Gold King, the Red King, the Blue King, and the Indigo King.

While the Neutral Realm didn't have an official ruler, members of the Convocation had still installed a few laws to *"maintain peace"* within the land. The two biggest rules were: no bloodshed of mankind and no use of a King's Gift. The only people who were allowed to use Divine energy in this part of the world were the owners of said energy – the Kings themselves.

All that said, Lex didn't entirely agree with Lucien's sentiments regarding the Neutral Desert.

Was it the holiest place on Earth? Debatable. The Golden Bang had literally muddled up the world, to the point where it looked completely different on a map. After the Bang, the First Five Chosen Kings (Gold, Red, Blue, Green, and Grey) had gone off invading and conquering as they pleased. Thus, creating a brave new world with new-fangled Kingdoms.

And as for the Neutral Realm's mysticism… Lex couldn't deny there was something enchanting about the desert under the moonlight. But by day, everything felt like a sun-kissed deathtrap.

Right now, Lex didn't fancy putting a single toe outside. Inside, they were protected from the harsh sun and dry weather, thanks to the Shield and the portable air-conditioners they had brought along. Not to mention the oxygen tanks, which were a necessity since nothing could get past one of Lucien's Shields, not even air.

What made it worse was that Lex couldn't even use the Golden Gift to protect herself from the extreme heat and dryness awaiting them outside. *Ugh*, she internally groaned. What was the point in having a King's Gift if you couldn't use it whenever and wherever you pleased? It was like caging a bird with perfectly healthy wings, forbidding it to fly.

With a sideways glance at Junior, she wondered if her brother fully understood the concept of the King's Gift. If he didn't already have a solid grasp on how it all worked, she would have to explain it to him soon.

You see, when a King is chosen and given proprietorship over Divine energy, they're free to share a fraction of said energy – or *powers*, if you will – with whomever they pleased, including their family members, Knights, etc. This is referred to as the King's Gift.

43

It went like this: Totem (Divine energy) → Chooses a King → Divine energy merges with the Chosen King → Chosen King shares said energy with whomever they please (the Gift) → Receivers of the King's Gift pull from the energy stored within their monarch.

For most people, a King's Gift often came with various restrictions in place. For example, law enforcement could only use their Gift for defense and combative purposes. In Lex's case, however, Lucien had granted her unrestricted and unlimited access to his Golden energy. This meant she could do whatever she pleased with her Divinely-charged superpowers… provided she was anywhere except on Neutral soil.

"…Now, I know what you're thinking, Lexie – my previous trip to find Moses' burial site was an exercise in futility, but that shouldn't hinder us from our path to God," Lucien prattled on, "We're all here on a journey and that journey includes partaking in at least one successful spiritual quest."

"Is there a difference between a journey and a quest?" Junior wondered offhandedly.

He regretted asking not a moment later.

"Is there a difference? Is there a difference?" Lucien tossed his head back and laughed like a drain. "Of course there's a difference, you silly boy! The desert is the journey. It's a literal and psychological excursion of isolation and introspection. For the desert is a lonely place, but so is the human mind. All this burning chaos and emptiness is a reflection of our subconscious. The macrocosm in the microcosm. Here, we are all Moses in the wilderness, wandering and waiting for the Lord. The quest, however, is the mission – the purpose of our journey. What we're here for, which is the pursuit of paradise, of enlightenment, of God."

Lex waited a few beats to ensure he was done talking. She took a moment to inspect Junior, who looked like he had fallen asleep with his eyes open during Lucien's entire spiel.

Turning back to Lucien, Lex said in a listless tone, "*Right*. About this quest for the Terrestrial Paradise. From what I recall of the story of Genesis, there was a particular reason mankind was cast out... Wouldn't Eden be guarded by militant angels ready to smite us without mercy or at the very least be shielded from our mortal eyes?"

"Nonsense. As a Chosen King, I have the spirit and energy of God running through my veins," said Lucien imperiously. It was his way of saying, *I'm untouchable because I'm God's favourite.* "They wouldn't dare smite me or the fruit of my loins. We're Divinely protected beings, Lexie. You must rejoice in it!" Then, he added airily, "The archivists and knights tagging along, however, are fair-game for death and dismemberment. But they know what they're getting into. I had them all sign liability waivers ahead of time ... And if there's a shield in the way, then that's perfectly fine. Afterall, who knows better about Shields than your Father-King?"

Mistaking his children's glazed expressions as understanding, Lucien nodded happily. "There you are then... off we go, children." He strode past them, bopping Lex on the nose and ruffling Junior's hair along the way.

Junior and Lex turned to watch Lucien as he strutted out the dome-shaped Shield like a ghost passing through a wall. The archival team followed him in a similar manner, but with far less finesse. Lucien had given them temporary access to pass through his Shields for the remainder of their time here. Anyone who tried to do so without the King's authorization, however, would have broken every bone in their body in the process.

Outside, in the desert, were a handful of sport utility vehicles and Volucris Knights waiting to accompany them on their quest.

Still looking at the spot where Lucien had been standing, Junior said, "I hate it when he calls us the *fruit of his loins*."

"I'm not too fond of it either," agreed Lex as she smoothed out Junior's hair. "But it can't be helped," she sighed. Looking over her shoulder, she said to their Secutors, "You two go on ahead. We'll be along shortly."

"Do we really have to go, Lexie?" whined Junior.

Lex hoped Lucien wasn't hearing this. Their Father had created the dome around them with a soundproofing mechanism, but she knew he could easily eavesdrop through it if he so wished. Thanks to his powers, Lucien could hear through vast distances – but only if he really wanted to. Lucien usually turned a willing ear to what he wanted to hear and disregarded everything else.

"It's his birthday," Lex held out her palm, indicating for him to take it. "We must indulge him for today."

"Can't we indulge him by buying him a pet … or a girlfriend?" said Junior, reluctantly getting up from his seat.

As he clasped Lex's hand, he felt the metallic coolness of her golden cygnet ring against his palm. The ring had a circle divided into three neat sections like a pie chart. Each sector depicted a different bird. A black eagle for Michael, a silver raven for Gabriel, and a gold swan for Lex. It was a ring exclusive to the Valenta siblings. Lex promised Junior that his symbol would be added to it someday; but first they needed to figure out what Junior's avian honorific would be.

"You can't buy someone a girlfriend."

"Pfffttt, yes you can," said Junior. "Mike does it all the time over in the Phantom Realm."

"I don't like that type of talk, Junior," said Lex primly. "It's not appropriate for a Prince of the Golden standard to be saying such things."

"Well, I don't hear you offering up any show-stopping gift ideas," retorted the Prince. "If you had, then maybe we wouldn't have had to come here lookin' for Jesus."

"We're not here to – oh forget it." She didn't care to explain the quest to her little brother. Again.

Lex also thought Junior may have had a fair point. She didn't have any stellar birthday gift ideas in mind for their Father-King. Nothing that could possibly distract him from undergoing a *spiritual quest* across the desert.

Lucien not only had the looks and fame of an A-list movie star, but he also had god-tier level of superpowers, which allowed him to do many things, including making his own gold, which in turn made him richer than God. To say that Lucien was a difficult man to shop for was an understatement. He had more than everything and wanted for nothing... Except... except maybe bringing his wife back from the dead. Not that their Mother, Lana, was *dead*-dead. She was more in a coma of sorts. Still, resurrecting her was beyond Lex's abilities.

"Buck up, Little Wing," she said. "Who knows? Maybe we'll find paradise after all, in which case, you may very well come across a principality ready to slice us all apart with a flaming sword."

"Cool!" said Junior as the brother-sister pair effortlessly stepped through the Shield and out into the extreme heat of the desert.

Chapter 4:
Being mummified doesn't make them any less dead, does it?

Like most quests, spiritual or otherwise, it didn't entirely go to plan.

It had been a long commute back and forth across the Neutral desert and by the time the Valentas had returned to their tent, boiling daylight had converted into a chilly evening.

Members of their staff had already retreated to their resting areas. Their individual camps were properly Shielded like the one the Valentas were occupying, but they were much smaller and compact. Some of their employees were impressed with the way Lucien had whipped up all the tents with a quick curl of his left palm. The more seasoned workers were unfazed. A few makeshift shelters were hardly awe-inspiring to them – for they'd been around long enough to witness their King accomplish far more magnificent feats with his powers.

Besides, it never took Lucien long to manifest anything he desired. Usually, he only needed less than a second to picture it in his mind's eye before willing it to materialize.

The three Golden royals were now alone in their large camp. They would be heading off to Lucien's birthday celebrations in an hour. They needed to change clothes, but instead of getting ready and glamming up for the party, they were sitting around sulking.

"At least Junior enjoyed himself," Lex told Lucien.

"Of course, he had a blast," huffed Lucien. "The boy got a kick out of meeting those satanic nuns."

"They were pagan priestesses, Father," Lex chided. "And they were holding a prayer ritual."

Lex and Lucien were sitting across one another with a long smoked white oak table between them. Lying atop the table was a map Lucien had been examining earlier: the one that allegedly ascertained all the ancient rivers flowing from Eden.

It came as no surprise – to everyone except Lucien – when the Golden Family had failed to find the eternal Paradise lost to man. They had, however, come across a hidden tomb full of mummified cats and women dressed in ceremonial robes and metallic feline masks.

Lex suspected they were worshiping a goddess once revered by Ancient Egyptians – long before the Golden Bang, that is. She found it rather fascinating since she wasn't aware there were still people who paid tribute to the Ancient Egyptian gods.

Then again, maybe she shouldn't have been too surprised. Many pagan religions had seen an upswing in their following ever since her Mother, Former-Phantom King Lana, had been Divinely selected to lead. Lana was a classical pagan and follower of the Ancient Greco-Roman gods. Her time as a King had brought forth a renaissance of sorts for the "*old ways and the old gods.*"

"You call what they were doing prayer?" Lucien scoffed. "It looked more like a demonic summoning, with all those obscene noises they were making—"

"Those were sacred chants, Father," said Lex.

"—the way they kept rubbing oil on each other—"

"They were dabbing perfumes as a form of anointment."

"—not to mention all those dead cats—"

"They were mummified."

"Being mummified doesn't make them any less dead, does it?" Lucien said haughtily.

"Isn't mummification such a fascinating spiritual practice, Father? I've read that before a corpse was interred, all the internal organs had to be removed and mummified separately from the body. Everything except the heart, of course, because the heart was considered the throne of a person's soul and needed to be protected at all costs. Mind you, they didn't give an owl's hoot about the brain. Why, you'll never believe how they got the brain out of the nose during embalming. Supposedly, they used a pair of vicious-looking metal hooks to break the nose bone and scramble the brain to mush—"

"*Thank you*, Alexandra," Lucien said with disgust. "But we can do without the detailed history lesson."

Releasing another reproachful scoff, he continued, "Honestly. *That's* what they call spiritual? You'd think those broads were possessed with the way they were flailing and floundering about like… like oily, salty strumpets in a broth—

" He paused mid-sentence, remembering he was in the presence of his preadolescent son, whose young ears were far too delicate to be exposed to such coarse language. "In a house of ill-repute," he whispered hotly to Lex.

Perched nearby beside a small table, Junior snorted at Lucien's selection of words. *House of ill-repute*, the Prince scoffed to himself, *Father's so pretentious. Why can't he just say whorehouse like everyone else?*

"Oh, stop it, Father. Those women were doing no such thing," said Lex defensively. "They were only dancing is all. It's part of their ritual."

"A ritual for demonic possession, no doubt," sneered Lucien. "And to think, all this false idolatry was taking place on holy soil. The flagrant impiousness of it all!"

Lex could only sigh at her Father's prejudice toward pagans. Such biases were a contributing factor to the deterioration of her parent's marriage. "They were performing a prayer for protection and good health."

"They aren't likely to find either one of those things from whatever demon they were beckoning," muttered Lucien.

"I assure you Father, there were no devils and demons involved. It was all perfectly harmless."

At least, Lex was relatively certain it was harmless. She wasn't entirely sure what they were chanting and which goddess they were worshipping. Lex had only been able to make out a few words of their speech thanks to an elective class she had once taken in secondary school, *Lost Languages: The Ways We Spoke Before the Earth Standard Sole.*

Like most ancient languages, Egyptian was not familiar to the masses. The final stage of the Egyptian language was written in Greek letters, and it was still the ceremonial language of the Coptic Orthodox Church. But apart from Coptic clergymen and a few surviving pagan sects, Egyptian was practically a dead language, one that hadn't been widely used since the Golden Bang.

Despite the language barrier, Lex was confident those priestesses hadn't been up to anything sinister. But, if a demon was what they were after, then she figured they got their wish, seeing as how Junior had showed up. The Prince had unceremoniously cartwheeled himself over to the middle of their ritual and joined their collective dance.

"If good health is what they seek, then perhaps they should stop hitting the sauce," said Lucien censoriously.

"They're not praying for their well-being in this lifetime, but rather what comes after it," she said, "Their dances weren't so much a celebration of life as it was a plea for an exalted afterlife."

"Spare me," snorted Lucien as he leant back on his chair, throwing one long arm over it.

"You know the history of it better than I do, Father. Don't pretend otherwise," said Lex knowingly. "I've read the Ancient Egyptians were obsessed with the afterlife. Most of their prayers were dedicated to it. They believed life was merely a transitory phase that one needed to endure before reaching everlasting joy."

Glancing over at her brother, Lex found that Junior was sitting at his usual bench on the other side of the tent. This time, instead of colouring angels, he was trying to make sketches of the women he had seen. Junior truly enjoyed meeting those priestesses, but there was one thing that still bothered him.

"How come those women weren't bare-breasted, Lexie?" he hollered at his sister.

Lex's left eye twitched. She had lost track of how many times he had asked this question.

"In *Global Geographic* Magazine, pagan girls are always topless," the Prince continued.

"I don't know, Junior. Maybe they only whip them out for photoshoots," said Lex sarcastically.

Lex was growing irritated at Junior's constant commentary about the women they had seen and their fully clothed bosoms. It was all he had talked about on the ride back. Well, that, and some odd-shaped cloud he had spotted in the sky.

"What?!" Junior's eyes bugged out. "Why didn't you tell me before? Had I known, I would've brought along our in-house film crew," he said, referring to the production team that Lucien had on staff for the sole purpose of shooting Golden Royal Family exclusives.

The Prince's frustration faded as an idea shot into his head. "Say, maybe if we go back tomorrow with my camera, they'd be willing to writhe around and flash their bre—"

"That's enough, Junior!" snapped Lex, finally losing her cool. "I swear I've heard nothing but *breasts* from you for the last three hours."

"Your sister makes a fair point, son," agreed Lucien. "It's most uncouth for a young prince to say a word like *breasts* as often as you have today."

"Sorry Father, I hadn't realized I was exceeding my quota of breasts per day," said Junior dryly.

"Do you even grasp how insulting and misogynistic you're being?" Lex crossed her arms. "Expecting those women to remove their facial masks and lift up their dress robes for your viewing pleasure."

"They can keep their masks on if they want," said Junior bluntly.

"Junior!" Lex shouted, appalled. "They are priestesses who have devoted their lives to a higher calling. One which does not involve entertaining the lecherous advances of a pervy little prince like you."

"They didn't seem to mind having me around today!" Junior refuted, puffing his chest up a bit. "If anything, they seemed to thoroughly enjoy being on the receiving end of my attention. And why wouldn't they? Father says all Valenta men have that heart-stopping quality that makes everyone enchanted with us upon first sight. Isn't that right, Father?"

"Hmm?" Lucien was only half-listening to his children at this point. "Oh, I was mostly referring to myself when I said that. But I suppose my natural-born charisma could extend to the fruit of my loins as well."

"Nevertheless," said Lex, "Those women—"

"They weren't all women," Junior cut in.

Lex blinked. "What?"

"They weren't all women," repeated Junior. "There was a boy there too. I spotted him lurking in the corner."

"That's impossible," Lex shook her head. "There were hieroglyphs of muliebrity etched across that entire tomb. If I interpreted those symbols correctly, then membership to that community is exclusive to women."

"Then your interpretation was wrong," shrugged Junior, "Either that or they made a special exception for that boy."

"How do you know it was a boy? They were all wearing the same masks and garments."

"Hmm… well, he didn't look tall enough to be an adult man," reasoned Junior. "And he was far too flat-chested to be a woman. Even girls my age aren't *that* itty bitty titty."

"Such flawless deductions," Lex rolled her eyes. "You do realize people come in all shapes and sizes regardless of age and gender."

"I'm telling you he was a boy!" Junior slammed a hand to the table. "He had no breasts!"

"Everyone has breasts! … Or rather, we all have breast tissue when we're born. But people assigned male at birth generally don't grow more breast tissue than—Oh, this is ridiculous!" Lex threw her hands in the air. "Why are we even discussing this?" Pointing a finger at her little brother, she ordered, "Junior, I don't want to hear any more talk of breasts."

Lucien began in a mollifying tone, "Now, now, children—"

As if sensing Lucien was about to say something that would, no doubt, spike her aggravation, Lex turned to him and bit out, "And Father – Not. Another. Word. About. Your. Loins."

Junior scowled and went back to his sketches. He was internally kicking himself for forgetting his gear bag when they left for their quest. While on Neutral soil, they were prohibited from using devices charged and fueled with the King's energy, but they were allowed to have ordinary non-supernatural gadgets with them. Junior had remembered to pack his camera. Unfortunately, he had neglected to take it with him upon leaving the tent.

Not only had he missed out on taking pictures with those pagan priestesses, he also didn't get to capture that incredible silver flare he had seen soaring through the sky as the sun went down. He'd eyed it from the car window on the ride back. He had tried to bring everyone's attention to it, but no one believed him because it had disappeared by the time they had followed his gaze. Lex had insisted it must've been a dissipating cloud. Junior didn't know what it was, but he knew it wasn't a cloud. It was a fast, shiny ball of silver – or was it grey? – and it moved like a comet.

After taking a moment to calm herself, Lex got up and went to Lucien's side. She placed a hand on his arm. "I'm sorry this trip wasn't what you expected, Father," she said softly.

Lucien patted her dainty hand and smiled kindly at her. "Oh, but I'm not disappointed, my dear. Truly. 'Tis nothing but a minor setback. The quest carries on! We shall return another year and try again."

"Super," said Lex in a subdued voice. "… Well, we best get ready for your party then."

"There's no rush. We have plenty of time. Besides, one can't expect one's King to arrive early to his own birthday party," chortled Lucien as he loudly clasped his hands together. "Now, I have an important decision to make: What speech should I use tonight? Shall I go with my famous "*Glory Drenched in Gold*" address or the "*These are the Hours of Our Eternity*" declamation? Mind you, the latter hasn't gotten the recognition it deserves in recent centuries, but it was a huge hit when I first orated it back in 1506."

Lex and Junior exchanged a look.

"Wellll…" said Lex slowly. "All your speeches are winners. You can't go wrong either way."

Lucien looked between his two youngest children. He didn't understand why they seemed so unenthused, and then it hit him. "Silly me, what am I saying? You two youngbloods weren't around when I wrote my *Hours of Our Eternity* speech."

Junior and Lex nodded quickly in unison.

It wasn't that their Father's speeches were tedious. On the contrary, Lucien was a great orator and speechwriter, and unlike many other Kings, he actually wrote everything himself. But that was half the problem: Lucien was the longest-reigning King in history, which meant he had written and spoken *a lot* of speeches. It was impossible for anyone – besides Lucien himself – to remember every single address he had ever given. The other part of the problem was that Lucien was never short on words and could, most likely, rant on for all the hours of eternity.

"Yeah, that's it, Father," Junior piped in. "We never heard it 'cause we're not old like Mike and Gabe."

"We couldn't possibly judge which speech fares better," Lex nodded in agreement.

"I see … In that case, I shall recite both speeches to you kids now, and then we can deep dive into a thorough comparative analysis," said Lucien, his large white teeth on full display as he grinned widely. "Problem solved!"

Lex and Junior sighed in unison and in despair.

Chapter 5:
Am I the last beautiful man on Earth or what?

The Golden Family were running late. The last ones to the party.

"Father, they're all waiting for us," said Lex. "You told everyone to come early."

"My darling, you ought to know by now that when I say *everyone*, I'm never including myself … Besides, the hero always enters last," Lucien said as he winked down at his children, sparkles and splatters of Golden energy leaping off the corners of his eyes as he did so.

Junior and Lex agreed with that last statement. That's why they didn't really mind being late. What irritated them was the *reason* for their tardiness: their Father-King had spent the better part of two hours trying to figure out which speech to use, only to come to the realization that both the speeches he had in mind were more fitting for a victory parade than a birthday party. At which point, he had decided to change course and rehearse a few of the verses he'd written for his latest series of epic poems. And then, after another hour pouring through lines and lines of iambic pentameter, the Gold King had simply declared he'd "*wing it*" and come up with something on the fly.

This was followed by another thirty minutes of Lucien deciding what to wear. Plus, another ten minutes of him awaiting appreciation for his appearance and expecting praise for his existence.

"Well, how do I look?" Lucien held out his arms as he beamed at his children.

"You look great, Father," Lex said in a mild tone. "Can we please leave now?"

"Great?" Lucien's smile shifted into a sneer. "*Great*?"

Both Lex and Junior found it remarkable how Lucien could take an ordinary word and turn it into something insulting simply by uttering it with such contempt and derision.

"Is that it?" pressed their Father-King. "Is that all you've got for me?"

"Er... you look really great?" supplied Junior.

"Surely, you kids can appreciate the fact that there are people across this galaxy who literally stagger back in admiration upon first sight of your Father-King," said Lucien primly.

"Stumbling back in irritation, more like," Junior muttered quietly under his breath before saying to his Father, "Does it really matter how you look?"

Lucien gawked at his son as though he'd asked the dumbest question in the universe. "Of course it matters! Everyday is a day of judgement for our kin and Kingdom. And I'm not alluding to judgement from others – though that still applies to a certain degree, mind you – I'm referring to holy judgement from God! One can only judge a Kingdom by its men," he said pointedly. "And the way men behave is directly influenced by the conduct of their monarchs."

Sensing Lucien was about to descend into a lengthy tangent, Lex attempted to trim down his monologuing. "Well said, Father. Shall we head out now?"

"—We're not like *other* Kingdoms, son," Lucien preached on. "As Golden monarchs, we are duty-bound to uphold perfection in all aspects of life, even appearance. Our subjects expect it of us, but more importantly, God expects it of us. I've always said it's our responsibility to ensure the welfare and protection of every Golden citizen in our realm. And that remains true, but it's also our responsibility to inspire them every day and in every way with our elegance, beauty and grace. We must always look our best, be our best, and show to the entire breadth of the cosmos that we are epitome of Golden manhood. For we not only represent the Gold Kingdom. We *are* the Golden Empire, where the higher standards prevail!" He finished proudly.

Smiling down at his son, he said, "Do you understand now, my boy?"

"Uhhhh…. yeahhhh," lied Junior.

"Good," nodded Lucien. Spreading his arms out once more, he said, "Now, I shall ask again: How do I look?"

Lex and Junior stared at him mutely.

Lucien dropped his arms at their continued silence. "Oh, never mind," he said peevishly. "I swear, it's at times like these, I miss your Mother. She always knew exactly what to say."

"Which would be what exactly?" Lex inquired with a raised brow.

"That I look like the most beautiful man on Earth," he tossed his head back haughtily, "That I am the human embodiment of perfection. An ethereal entity encased in ephemeral flesh."

"Mother never said any of that," said Lex.

"She did. She said it all the time." At his daughter's disbelieving look, he went on, "Shouted it to the Heavens, more like! Practically shattered glass with her flagrant declarations of love toward me. It was, quite frankly, rather mortifying at times, to be on the receiving end of her amatory attentions."

"Oh Father. Come off it!" Lex shook her head, scoffing out a laugh. She wasn't buying Lucien's latest verbal nonsense. She and Lana had a complicated and somewhat strained relationship, but she knew her Mother well enough.

Did Lana believe Lucien was the most beautiful man on Earth? Probably. There was a long list of people who agreed with that sentiment and Lex wouldn't discount Lana from that list.

Would Lana have ever admitted it out loud to an ego-inflated man like Lucien, who had never been humbled a single day in his 2,000+ years of existence? Not a chance.

"Alright," Lucien conceded reluctantly, "Perhaps she didn't say it all the time—"

"She *never* said it."

"She certainly thought it. Constantly."

"I can accept that much *may* be true," Lex went up to Lucien, grabbing his hand. Her smile faltered and took a fast turn from amused to melancholic as she admitted, "I miss her too, Father."

Junior kept silent, carefully observing the father-daughter pair as they exchanged looks of remorse. It was a rare occasion to see either of them, especially Lucien, talk about Lana. For the briefest of moments, it felt like the Family Spell, the enchantment hanging over the Valentas, had been lifted.

It wasn't a real spell, of course. Real spells involved old-world sorcery complete with incantations, rituals and spiritual invocations. *The Family Spell* was a nickname Junior made up in reference to the delusions his Father-King had tried to cast on himself and by extension, Lex and Junior. Lucien genuinely wanted to believe it was only the three of them. The three members of the Golden Royal Family, the Golden Trio. He usually refrained from mentioning the other three *former* Golden Royals, the ones who had moved to the United Phantom Realm (UPR) over a century ago.

Junior's family had a very long, complicated history, one that he found profoundly difficult to express in words. Not that he really needed to expand and explain. He figured that out a couple of years ago.

"My Father and Mother are both Kings, you know," Junior, age 8, had once said to his friend Porki while they were building snowmen by the wintry bluffs surrounding the Gilded Cage. "Well, my Mother used to be a King, she's not anymore... I mean, she started off by my Father's side as the Gold Queen, but then she was Chosen by the Black and White Totems and became a King. Most Kings only get picked by one Totem, but my Mother got her powers from two."

"Uh huh," said Porki, rolling up a large ball of snow.

"My Father even gave her some land so she could have her own realm," Junior had prattled on, "My big brothers chose to go with her and that's why he fired them as Golden Princes. So now, I'm the only Golden Prince in this Kingdom."

"Uh huh," repeated Porki, still focused on the production of his snowman.

"I was supposed to go live with my Mother too... but a little while after I was born, she got hurt in a fight with the Grey King. And then she died — But she's not dead-dead, she's ... she's sleeping..."

"Like she's in a coma."

"Yeah, exactly like that!" That about covered the trajectory of his Mother's life, more or less. She went from Orphaned → Married → Golden Queenhood → Procreated (3X: Michael, Gabriel, and Lex) → Phantom Kinghood → Procreated (1X: Junior) → Attacked → "Died"

"After she di—after she got hurt, her Totems chose my brother, Michael. He got his powers from the Black and White Totems, but also the Silver Totem. I don't know why three Totems chose him."

"He must be special," remarked Porki off-handedly.

"He's really not!" Junior fumed. *"... Anyhow, a little while after that, my Father made Lexie the Golden Regent... I mean, he still has all the power, but my sister has to do all the work. That's all it is."*

Porki stopped shaping his top snowball to fix his attention on the Prince. "Yeah, I already know all of this."

"You do?"

"Of course, my Prince. Everyone in our galactic postal-code knows. Your family's more famous than God."

"Oh... right."

"Junior! Junior! Are you listening to me?" Lucien snapped his fingers in front of his son. "If it's one thing I can't stand more than another is people not listening to me."

The Prince blinked away the memory as he returned to reality. It appeared that whatever *moment* the King and Regent were having was now long gone. There was no more talk of his Mother; the Family Spell was back in place.

Lex and Lucien were gazing down at him, awaiting a response. Had they asked him a question? He had tuned out entirely.

"Errr... yeah I was listening," he lied again. "But I was thinking that...that...maybe I should go change into something else," he pulled at his collar, "So that I can look like the embodiment of Golden manhood ... just like my Father-King."

Chapter 6:
Tripping the light fantastic?

The sky was now a dark lavender canvas freckled with tiny white stars. It was well past sundown when the Valentas arrived at Lucien's birthday party, which was being held in another area twenty or so miles away from their homebase-campsite.

The Golden Family's in-house decorating committee had ensured a massive circle within a circle was laid over the sand. The inner circle had an ivory vinyl surface with Lucien's coat of arms – a growling golden griffin with a massive wingspan – painted on it; it was designed to be the dancing area and where the King would address his subjects. The outer circle was made of 70,000 limestone tiles, each one containing fossilized remains that reportedly dated back to the Jurassic period.

"What was it like for you, Father?" Junior had inquired when he first caught a glimpse of the fossils.

"What was what like?"

"Riding a dinosaur back in the day?" The Prince said innocently, ignorantly. Judging by the twitch in Lucien's jaw, Junior figured it had been the wrong thing to say.

Lex tried not to laugh as she informed Junior that their Father-King was still a young valensman, only in his Third Millennia of life. Contrary to Junior's assumptions, Lucien wasn't well over 30 million years old, which was around the time dinosaurs became extinct.

Lucien had also lent a helping hand with the decorating this time. Back home in the Gold Kingdom, Lucien only needed to charge generators with his powers to install Shields across their castle grounds. He claimed that charging an item, such as a generator, to create a Shield took up a lot less energy than "*creating it from scratch.*"

Charging, was what the Kings called it.

Whenever a King *charged* an item with their energy, it meant they used their supernatural powers to install a specific set of instructions, explaining exactly what they wanted said item to do. There were millions of generators situated across the Gilded Cage; the majority of them were instructed to put up impenetrable defenses against intruders, unauthorized weapons, poisons and toxins.

But the Valentas weren't in their Home-Kingdom right now. They were in the Neutral Realm, which meant they were on diplomatic territory co-managed by the Convocation.

Many years ago, the member-Kings of the Convocation came to a lengthy agreement regarding the Neutral Desert. To sum it up, there were a few key rules:

- No violence against people from all walks of life.
- No use of the King's Gift by anyone, be they Princes, Princesses, or Knights.
- No use of technology charged with Divine energy.
- Only Kings hold the right to use their Divine energies on Neutral soil.

So, what did all this mean for Lucien's birthday party? Since none of Lucien's Knights, nor Lex for that matter, could legally use their Gifts here, the onus was left on Lucien to create another makeshift tent.

Another dome-shaped Golden Shield hung over the entire perimeter of his party and buried itself deep into the sand. Lucien had created the Shield and would keep it up all throughout the night relying on nothing but his own will. *From scratch*, as he called it.

Unlike their personal tent, Lucien had made this Shield semi-transparent so that his guests could see the stars above them through a light filter of gold. In essence, it felt like they were viewing the world from within a citrine crystal. Apart from the pretty aesthetics, the Shield was set in place to protect the King's guests from the cold night air, dust storms, and any other potential threats.

Not that there were any manmade threats out here. The Neutral Realm was considered the most peaceful place on Earth. Still, Lucien had grown severely cautious and paranoid when it came to security in recent years, especially after the Greys had ambushed and attacked Lana, leaving her on the brink of death.

Inside the massive, translucent Golden tent, the party was afoot. There was a canary yellow light hovering all around the dancefloor as though it were cast by an ornate lamp. But it wasn't a lamp. That too was none other than Lucien's Golden energy at work.

Meanwhile, in the outer circle, roughly 70 members of the Golden court – the Osprey, as they were known – were gathered around, chatting under a haze of pipe smoke.

"Alright, children," Lucien rubbed his hands together like a show-magician preparing for a grand trick. "It's time to trip the light fantastic," he said cheerily before gliding across the party.

Junior made a face, "Huhhh?"

"I think he's referring to dancing," explained Lex.

Copying Lucien, she too dashed off to work the room. Junior watched as she drifted across the floor like 99 pounds of warm smoke.

"Why doesn't he just say that then?" Junior said to no one in particular. "Why does he always have to be so *old*?"

It was a black-tie event, so everyone was dressed in tuxes and floor-length gowns. Lucien donned a sweeping cape around his tux; it was adorned with long white-gold and rose-gold-colored feathers that curled up at the ends and arranged in a zig-zag pattern. He didn't how his Father got away with wearing things like that, but somehow the man made it look fashionable.

He may as well have come dressed as a giant golden peacock, Junior thought to himself. Even if Lucien had done exactly that, people would still have flocked to him the way they were doing now. The Gold King was 6 ft 4", with shoulders broad enough to take up the entire wingspan of an eagle, and cheekbones so sharp they could probably slice through steel. Saying that he stood out in a crowd was an understatement.

His sister attracted as much attention as Lucien, if not more. Lex wore a sparkling, gold-beaded number with minor cutouts across the torso; it was designed to embrace her body at specific points and then fall glamorously to the floor. And with a perfect face that was practically identical to their Mother's, Lex was pretty much set for life. The only thing holding her back in life was her job title.

Many hadn't taken too kindly to Lucien's decision to enter semi-retirement and promote his daughter to Regent. Lucien was still young (by valensmen standards), healthy and able. He had no ostensible need for a Regent to oversee all governmental matters of his realm. Nevertheless, he was an absolute monarch and his word was final.

And so, six years ago, Lex's résumé had changed from Golden Princess to Golden Princess-*Regent*. The difference was astounding. Almost overnight, she had gone from being universally adored to widely criticized. The public loved a beautiful woman. But that love quickly turned sour when said beauty began to make political decisions.

Then there was Junior. Lex and Lucien made it a point to dress him more conspicuously than the Osprey as a way of indicating his Royal status. His dark blazer had radiant golden sequins, shaped like feathers, trailing across the arms. He was still a growing boy, but there was a chance he could match his Father in height someday. He had already reached up to his sister's shoulders. As for his face, it wasn't quite as chiseled as Lucien's – not yet, at least – but he was still the most beautiful boy in the room.

Despite his Father's unwavering principle on dressing up to people's high expectations – and, more significantly, dressing up to *God's* highest expectations – the Prince still believed that it didn't really matter what the Golden Family wore. They could all show up wearing bath towels and still be hailed the diamonds of the ball. Divine beauty was in their bloodline.

Junior and his siblings had hit the genetic lottery, not only when it came to family fortune, but in the form and features they'd inherited from their parents. In ancient times, people often confused Lucien for Adonis. And not just being Adonis-like in appearance. They literally thought he was Adonis. As for their Mother, it was said that her beauty had made Helen of Troy seethe in jealousy. Lana had always denied it, of course, insisting that it was all hearsay. "*Oh no, that simply isn't true. Helen was long, long before my time,*" she would insist with a cheeky smile.

Tugging at the edge of his collar, Junior gave his companions a quick sidelong glance before refocusing his gaze onward. He and his friends – Meryl, Porki, and Terry – were standing a few feet away from the dancefloor. They watched as various members of the Osprey coupled off and waltzed around while a string quartet played from the sidelines.

The Prince grabbed two appetizers from one of the dozen or so members of the wait-staff who were walking around with full trays. Some of the trays had food, while others contained drinks. Three of the servers, however, were tasked with holding up velvet cerulean cushions that displayed a pyramid of King's Lucien's own hand-made gold bars.

Lucien's gold was considered one of the most precious resources within their galaxy. The King handed out his gold freely on special occasions. It was usually donated to various charities across his realm and to whomever was lucky enough to attend the King's birthday party.

Junior and Lex could understand contributions to charity; what they couldn't comprehend was why their Father felt the need to make the rich richer by gifting the Osprey with his gold. The aristocrats in Lucien's circle were far from impoverished. *Well, most of them, at least*, thought Junior as he eyed Porki's mother from a distance. Lady Porkina wasted no time getting her hands on the bars of gold and was currently trying to stuff three of them into her clutch like they were dinner rolls she wanted to savor for later.

Porki's family was the epitome of *land rich and money poor.* They were nobility by rank but had lost most of their wealth over the centuries and were now well into deepest of debts. They were so low on the Osprey ranking that they wouldn't have even finagled an invitation to the King's birthday had Junior not been best friends with their son.

Junior looked over at Porki to find his friend flushing with embarrassment. He too had been watching his mother's pitiful behaviour.

In an attempt to distract his friend, Junior held out an appetizer as an offering. "Sandwich?"

It looked like a tiny ball of shiny bread, but the waiter had declared it was a pureed macadamia spread paired with goat cheese and a grape relish reduction on sweetbread.

"It kinda tastes like peanut butter-jelly," said Junior.

Porki's lips twitched into a tilted smile, a deep dimple appearing on his right cheek. Junior desperately wanted to poke at that dimple even though he knew Porki would swat his hand away.

"I'm pretty sure it *is* peanut butter-jelly," said Porki dryly as he brought a flute glass to his lips and took a slow sip of a stallion's neck (a ginger-ale with a twist of lemon).

Like everyone else, Porki, Terry and Meryl were all glammed up for the night. Porki and Terry in tuxedos and Meryl in a modish evening gown. Out of the three, Porki stood out the most with his natural good looks. Junior didn't know where he got it from. It certainly wasn't in Porki's genes, especially when you factored in the way the rest of the Porkina men looked – it was one long ancestral line of stubborn cowlicks, hellacious facial warts, and discernable underbites.

Junior narrowed his eyes, inspecting Porki a little more carefully. Perhaps his friend had some work done on him? Plastic surgery was common among Golden courtiers. They were some of the wealthiest people in the world. They were also the most insecure people in the universe. They wanted so desperately to emulate their Golden monarch, but when it came to appearances, they lacked Lucien's natural beauty.

Looking around the room, Junior wouldn't be surprised if half the noses on the dancefloor were sculpted by the same surgeon.

Porki was the same age as Junior and thus, far too young to legally obtain any cosmetic enhancements. Even so, as his eyes fixated on Porki's doll-like features, Junior couldn't help but wonder…

Nah, not Porki, Junior shook his head internally, *He couldn't afford it.* Or maybe, all the Porkina men suffered from some sort of bizarre reverse-ugly-duckling syndrome, where they start off looking like swans and deteriorate into mallards with each passing century.

"What?" Porki shifted back a little, weirded out by the intensity of the Prince's stare. "Is there something on my face?" He ran a hand down his left cheek.

"Uhhh, no… it's nothing." Junior looked away sheepishly.

"Then why were you staring at me?"

"I wasn't staring."

"Except you were."

"Pfftttt, so what if I was?" Junior scowled. "You stare at me all the time."

"No, I don't!" Porki refuted heatedly.

"You do! All the time!" Remembering his Father's words from before, Junior said, "Quite frankly, it's rather mortifying being on the receiving end of your amatory attentions."

"My *what* attentions?" Porki's face flamed up at the accusation.

"Quit making such a fuss, will you!" hissed Junior. "I wasn't staring, OK?" he continued to deny. "I was only looking your way because... because you look hungry."

"But I'm not hungry."

"You look it though," said Junior. "So, how about we grab some of those mushroom stuffed capons?" he suggested. "It tastes just like chicken."

Porki sighed as he explained, "Capon *is* chicken, my Prince."

"It is?"

Taurus Reed III, a.k.a Terry, nodded in agreement as he said, "Capon is a rooster that's been castrated to make it's meat more tender."

"Ewww, I didn't know that," Junior grimaced. "How come nobody told me? I've eaten five of those suckers already."

Porki shook his head. He suspected someone had told the Prince exactly what he was being served in meticulous detail. Junior, most likely, hadn't been paying attention.

"That's nothing," said Terry. "I've read that in ancient times, they used to bring live animals – mostly lambs – to Royal parties and have them killed and cooked right there on the spot."

"Riiightt... well, best stick to the caviar then," Junior suggested. "Our chef got the eggs from a rare albino sturgeon in the Silver Sea."

"No thanks."

"Don't worry, Porki, the caviar's Beluga," Terry assured him. "His Majesty would never think to serve Osetra to his guests."

"It's not that," said Porki, "I'm just not hungry right now."

"Speaking of lambs to the slaughter," Meryl piped in with a question she had been itching to ask for awhile now, "Has the Regent selected a wife for Phantom King Michael yet?"

"Pfffttt, of course she hasn't," snorted Junior.

"It's already been five years," said Porki. "Is it really so difficult finding a suitable match?"

"Five years is nothing for our kind, Porki," Terry reminded him. "It wouldn't even take up a spec of sand in an hourglass."

Junior internally agreed with him. Lex could stretch out the hunt for her ideal sister-in-law for another six hundred years and it wouldn't make a lick of difference. For their class of humankind, for valensmen, centuries could slip by unnoticed.

"She says she's waiting for the right one to come along and thaw Michael out," Junior explained.

That's what Lex had said. But Junior knew that despite her efforts, she was in no hurry to get Michael tied up in matrimony. He could tell she was still afraid of losing Michael's attention and affection to another woman.

"He'll still be our brother, Lexie," a nine-year-old Junior had tried to comfort her. Just as she could easily detect his lies, he could see right through her as well. "And you'll still be his favourite sister."

"I'm his only sister," Lex had said with an amused smile. A beat later, her eyes dropped to the ground, her grin disappearing. In a soft, sad voice, she said, "But it won't be the same after Michael marries. He'll be entering a different era of his life, and I won't be able to rely on him as much. His devotion will be redirected to his wife."

Junior doubted that would ever happen. He couldn't picture Michael devoting himself to anyone. True to his title as the *Phantom* King, Michael often behaved like a ghost – heartless and lifeless – both in personality and appearance. Junior had never seen his eldest brother display any type of emotion. The man had one face where everything was set permanently in place. Even his silver eyes resembled dead diamonds created from the ashes of human remains.

A quick side glance toward Meryl, and the ridiculous smile striking her features, made Junior realize why she had asked. "Don't get any ideas, Meryl," he sneered at her. "It's never gonna be you."

"It could be me." Meryl crossed her arms. "I'm too young for him now… but in another century or two—"

"You'd *still* be too young for him," said Porki. They all knew Michael was fast approaching his Second Millennia of life.

"Even so," huffed Meryl. "By then, I could certainly be a contender for the Phantom King's heart—"

"You could if he had one," muttered Junior, thinking back to all those times he'd witnessed Michael throw people away like a used toothpick.

"—and, I think I'd be exactly his type," Meryl said over him.

"So what? He's your *boyfriend*, now, is that it?" Junior curled his lip in disgust.

"I don't get you, Meryl," said Porki, "Are you saying you actually *want* to be a lamb to the slaughter? Because that's what you'd be signing up for with King Michael. You've heard the rumours … They're not even rumours, really. A lot of it is historically documented … The things he did back when he was the Golden Prince. Not to mention the things he's been doing since he became the Phantom King—"

"He did it all for his country! It's perfectly patriotic! … And even if he is a little horrible, so what? He's still the most beautiful man in the world." Meryl's gaze swerved across the floor to Lucien. She quickly amended her words. "Well… maybe not the *most* beautiful. He's second to His Majesty the Gold King, of course."

Junior wondered if she was saying such things to stir up a storm of jealousy inside of him. If so, it was working.

"Meryl, I swear I will retch capon on you and your tacky taffeta if you don't stop talking like that," Junior said threateningly.

"Tacky?! Shows how much you know, Junior," she hissed, clearly affronted. "This dress is a mixture of ivory and satin gazar."

Junior rolled his eyes. He had nothing to worry about. Meryl definitely wasn't Michael's type. There was no way his eldest brother would ever tolerate someone snapping back at him like this, especially not over something as mundane as an outfit.

Then again … it wasn't as if Michael was allowed to choose his bride. That decision was entirely up to Lex.

Snatching another look at her from the corner of his eyes, Junior suspected Meryl could someday grow up to be exactly what his sister was searching for in an in-law.

The fifth daughter of the Duke of Lark, Meryl DiLaurentis was a bit of a powderpuff wrapped in barbed wire. But most of the time, she was fun. And, she checked all of Lex's requirements:

- Someone with a respectable familial background.
- Someone who'd take up a footnote in their family's history, but never an entire chapter.
- Likeable to their subjects, but not lovable to the masses.
- Very pretty but not supremely beautiful.
- Smart but not shrewd.
- Compliant but not spineless.
- Aspirational but not influential.
- Not too extraordinary but none too ordinary.

In that sense, he supposed Meryl would make a decent candidate for Phantom Queenhood in a few centuries time. A tremor of unease came across Junior at the mere thought of

Meryl marrying Michael. *Ugh*. He could feel the capon coming back up his throat.

"But you know," Meryl said, "Arranged marriage is soooo last millennia. I'm surprised it's still happening. I mean, it certainly doesn't make for a great romance, does it?"

"What's your idea of a great romance?" mocked Junior. "Love at first sight? Going all daft and dotty at the first turnip-head who winks your way?"

"No, that's not what I meant," she said soundly, "… Not entirely, anyhow… Perhaps love at first sight is improbable, but it's certainly not impossible. I think there's something to be said about an instant connection between two people. Perhaps even two strangers."

Junior pulled a face. "Spare me."

"Meryl might be right," Terry said, not one to disregard any probability. "If a butterfly flapping its wings can lead to a hurricane, then surely one chance encounter could potentially alter the course of a person's life forever. So, yes, I think it's possible for two strangers to be intrinsically drawn to one another for reasons beyond logical understanding."

"That sorta thing never happens in real life," grumbled Junior.

"It does so! It happened with your parents. His Majesty even said so, remember?" Meryl nudged him lightly, reminding him of what he had forgotten.

A filmstrip flashed across his mind. An old black-and-white clipping of his parents…

Meryl had found it in her father's archival room when she was nine-years-old. She had shown it to Junior, Porki and Terry soon after.

Lucien had all imagery and traces of Lana removed from the Cage long ago, after they had separated. And, while his brothers kept portraits of Lana in Talon Towers, this would be Junior's first time seeing actual video footage of his Mother – back when she was the Gold Queen, when she was alive and healthy and happy-ish.

Junior had felt completely floored while watching it. His parents were side by side, glancing slightly away from the camera. Visually, they looked equally beautiful. And yet, somehow, their respective energies came off as strangely mismatched.

Griffins and Swans were the creatures that symbolized Lucien and Lana in their respective coat of arms. A perfect beastly representation of who they were as people. But they didn't come across as either of those creatures at that very moment. Instead, it was more like watching a golden retriever standing next to a black cat. One was vociferous, dramatic and demanding attention. The other was taciturn, aloof and alluring.

"Was it love at first when you first met, Your Majesties?" The interviewer behind the camera had asked the Golden Royal couple.

"Of course!" Lucien boomed, no trace of doubt in his voice. "It was as though destiny sprang to attention at last. Like night and day melding together in delight."

Lana said nothing.

"Can you elaborate, sir? For your subjects who have yet to experience love?"

Lucien appeared thoughtful. "Well, I suppose, upon first glance at my future Queen," he nodded leftward at Lana, "It was as if we had already known each other. As if we had said hello and goodbye to one another a million times over. Perhaps even loved one another a million lifetimes over... I felt as though God had showed me the entire story of my life in three seconds, and the mere glimpse of it all, left me with the biggest smile on my face."

Lana blinked up at her Husband-King. The black cat's cool demeanour trying desperately not to crack.

"You never told me this before," she whispered, her voice delicate yet melodic.

"You never asked me," Lucien shrugged down at her. "I would have said had you asked."

"And you, Your Majesty?" The interviewer had turned to her. "Was it the same for you, ma'am?"

Lana shot her head back over to him, slightly alarmed. It was obvious she had forgotten there were other people in the room.

It took Lana a moment to answer. She appeared torn. It was as Lex had said: Lana was never one to inflate Lucien's ego. Still, in front of their subjects, she had to play the part of the doting Queen.

She didn't rush into an answer the way Lucien did. After taking a moment to collect her thoughts, she finally said, "I can't recall everything about our first encounter seeing as it happened many centuries ago. But I do remember, I was in a slump, feeling out of sorts, but then I saw Lucien—the King... in that one brief moment, it was like a wonderful spell had been casted on me...and the world suddenly felt a little more kind...a little more beautiful."

"Ahhh, thinking about it makes me want to eat five bowls of noodles!" chirped Meryl, oblivious to the darkness that had come across Junior's features.

"Er, Meryl," Porki cut in, sensing the Prince's emotional downturn, "Let's not—"

"The Queen didn't say much after that," Meryl kept at it, "But the way the King finished the interview by saying he'd give up all the gold in his possession just to re-experience the moment he met his wife all over again... Ahhh, it was so irrefutably romantic! Like a fairy tale—"

"Yeah, and look how that turned out?" Junior snapped at her.

Meryl went quiet.

All three of his friends swapped uneasy glances.

Releasing a breath, Junior mumbled, "Sorry, Meryl. I didn't mean to—"

"It's OK," she said quickly. "I shouldn't have brought it up. Let's forget about it... Oh, look, there's Lady Hornbill. Rumours persist about her ex-husband's passing, you know."

"I heard he traveled everywhere with his own leather toilet seat," said Terry. "Just like me."

"What a coincidence," said Porki in a laconic tone. "Anyhow... I don't think she really 86-ed him. It was a car accident. I doubt she had anything to do with it."

Meryl shot him a look. "A car accident on her wedding night? Leaving him dead and her with all his money. How convenient."

"She already had *a lot* more money than he did when they married," retorted Porki. "Besides, she was in the car with him. Why would she put herself in danger like that?"

"That's true," Terry put in, "And if she really wanted to kill him, she could've simply blown up the yacht they were going to sail on. That would've been easier and far less messy."

"How so?" Porki asked.

"Think about it. All the evidence would've ended up at the bottom of the ocean..."

Junior tuned out as his friends continued to converse. He couldn't stop thinking about his parents. Lucien and Lana's first encounter had changed the course of their lives forever. But that didn't necessarily mean it changed their lives for the better.

Somewhere amidst their centuries-spanning marriage, they had drifted apart. By the time Junior was born, Lucien and Lana had been living and ruling in separate realms.

He had been their fourth and final child.

"Even if Queen Lana—"

"You mean, Phantom King Lana. That's her title now. She's not the Gold Queen anymore."

"Yes, well, she's a little too dead to be holding onto any title these days. Anyway, even if she had survived, they wouldn't have gotten back together," a Golden courtier had said to his group of friends. They were at a gala

hosted by the Regent. None of them had noticed Junior (then age 5) hiding under a nearby table, eavesdropping.

"Surely, they were on the mend," refuted another man. "They even had another child together."

The woman beside them released a cruel little laugh. "Yes, because every troubled marriage gets better after having a baby," she said mockingly, "Really, whatever were they thinking? It's the last thing they needed."

"I'm inclined to agree with you, my dear," said the first man. "That boy was born to be a band-aid for a marriage punctured with bullet holes."

Not everyone shared such sentiments. There were plenty of people who speculated Lucien and Lana would've gotten back together, but then Lana had been injured in a battle, and the pair had failed to reconcile before she had slipped into a death-like state.

His parents were obviously in love once. Two beautiful, powerful specimens getting married and having beautiful, powerful children in a majestic castle. They had started off as a fairy tale. But all that gold- and fairy-dust sprinkled around their relationship had been nothing but a spell to hide the true colours of their love story, which, in actuality, contained all the key ingredients for an Ancient Greek tragedy.

Chapter 7:
What's with all these Daddy issues?

"How come your brothers aren't here?" Terry asked as they continued to hang back while members of the Osprey whirled about the dancefloor.

"Huh? Oh… 'cause they hate him," Junior replied.

Lex had denied it. She had lied to his face when she told him the reason their older brothers, Michael and Gabriel, wouldn't attend Lucien's birthday party was due to a security protocol.

The Gold Kingdom and the United Phantom Realm bordered one another. This made it easier for one nation to oversee another whenever its monarchs were out-of-Kingdom.

"Mikey can teleport over here in the blink of an eye should anything unseemly transpire while we're away," Lex said cheerily as she packed a few last-minute items into her travel bag.

Junior sat at the large vanity area in her bedroom. He had no idea why his sister needed so many mirrors and lights to see herself.

"Uh huh, sure," he mumbled, examining a torture device Lex had out on display. She had insisted it wasn't a weapon, going as far as to call the heinous instrument an 'eyelash curler,' but Junior knew better. Lex had a way of sugar-coating everything.

'Should anything unseemly transpire,' was what she said. The subtext, however, was: 'In case some showboating supervillain tries to ambush and attack our homebase. I've given Mikey strict instructions to dismantle their bones and shatter their souls to the point where not even God can repair them.'

"And what about Gabe? What's his excuse?" Junior moved on to her selection of fragrances. He pressed one of her perfume atomizers to spritz

out a puff of her favourite scent. It smelled sunny and pretentious. It suited Lex perfectly.

"Gabby is Mikey's right hand. They can't be separated for great lengths of time—"

"It's only a few days."

"Mikey and Gabby have a deep spiritual connection. They need each other desperately, always have. Can't you sense their bond whenever they're in the same room? It's something that has undoubtedly taken different shapes life after life, but remains forever intact, forever renewed," she gushed, clutching her palms up to her chest in the semblance of a prayer.

Junior's reflection in the mirror blinked at her. Lex was more like their Father than she cared to admit. Both had a penchant for the dramatics. Both loved to make their presence known. And yet, they both knew when to stay silent and move like a spectre.

He never heard her coming. Her feet barely grazed the floor as she glided over to him. The next thing Junior knew, he was being spun around by the rotating chair. His cheeks were suddenly trapped between her hands as she cupped his face, demanding his absolute attention.

"Just like you and me, Little Wing. We'll never be apart." Lex grinned at him.

One could say Lex smiled like an angel. One could also argue she looked demonically possessed as she said, "I suspect you and I will be an entity for eternity."

"Uh huh, sure," repeated Junior, completely unfazed, "Say Sis, at what point across the span of eternity, are you gonna stop lying to me?"

Lex's smile stiffened. "Excuse me?"

"We don't really need Mike to babysit our Kingdom while we're off the grid," he said. "If anything goes wrong, Father can fly back here before Mike can even finish moving all his molecules over from the Phantom Realm."

Lex's grip on his cheeks tightened. "Junior—"

"C'mon, just say it. Mike and Gabe hate Father. They always have."

"They do not hate him!" Lex asserted, appalled by Junior's accusation. "Mikey and Gabby have been Father's children for much, much longer than we have—"

"'Cause they're old as the hills."

"Our brothers are not old."

"Gabe once hurt himself drinking water too fast, you know?"

"Oh, hush yourself, Junior." Lex shook her head. "Anyhow, as I was saying, Mikey and Gabby – while far from ancient, at least by valensmen standards – stood by Father's side during the early centuries of his Kinghood, and during that time, they developed a rather ... complicated history with our Father-King, but I assure you there's never been any outright hostility between them."

"Then how come—"

"That's enough questions for today, Junior." With a light slap to his cheeks, she cooed, "We must dash for the desert in an hour. So run along now and smack that grumpy-wumpy face of yours with another coat of sunscreen."

Junior snorted at the memory. Lex had been lying. He was so sure. But he didn't care. He was glad Michael and Gabriel weren't here. He didn't want to see Meryl fawning and slobbering over Michael's presence. He didn't want to hear Lex singing Gabriel's praises. Lex always lauded Gabriel as *"the Perfect Prince"* and would, no doubt, go on at length about his recent quest to cure a leper colony in an isolated peninsula by the Red Kingdom. Moreover, Junior didn't want to witness Lucien showering his older brothers with any attention.

Whatever *"complicated history"* Michael and Gabriel had with Lucien worked in Junior's favour. It meant he wouldn't have any competition when it came to their Father's affections. It meant he would remain Lucien's favourite son.

Junior swept his eyes from the dancefloor and over to his friends. Going by their glazed expressions, it was obvious they were bored rigid. He couldn't blame them. He was too.

The Prince could hear some of the conversations taking place behind him from guests who were lounging and drinking instead of dancing. In between sips of beverages that looked like potions – crème de menthe and dark chocolate liqueur, dirty blue cheese martinis, and flutes of champagne topped with shots of spiced honey liqueur and edible gold flakes – nothing of significance was being said.

It was all irrelevant matters that grown-ups liked to make a fuss about. Matters like "*how the Red King's wildfires were going to affect the global economy and contribute to inflation*" and "*why the average surgeon fee for aesthetic enhancements suddenly increased by over 20% in the Blue Kingdom.*" Unless any of those aesthetic enhancements included breast augmentations for women he knew personally, Junior couldn't care less.

This was the problem with Lucien's parties. He always invited the same dull people who fell into the same categories: uptight, aristocratic, and valensmen. There were a few exceptions here and there, like the Reed family. Terry's parents were also uptight valensmen, but they were commoners. Not a drop of nobility in their bloodline. Not that it mattered much; the vast amount of wealth Terry's father, Taurus Reed II, had acquired from running Grypus Tech, more than made up for their lack of title.

As a tot, Junior hadn't understood why Lucien hadn't granted Terry's family a noble title, but as he got a little older, he began to suspect it had something to do with the Reed's pagan ties. That was another unofficial requirement to being a member of

Lucien's court: you had to abide by a monotheistic denomination, preferably a Christian one.

The history books would tell you that Lucien was one of the few Chosen Kings who never persecuted people for their religious beliefs. That much was true. Those books also claimed he'd forged close alliances with Kings of other religious backgrounds. Also true. But what those books didn't mention was that despite his "*freedom of faith*" rule, Lucien still had his personal biases, which was very evident judging by the types of people who received his favour.

Since she had turned Regent a few years ago, Lex had been trying to change things up – both in Golden legislation and with the diversity of their courtiers. By the looks of things, she hadn't gotten very far with the latter.

Junior couldn't understand it. He knew his Father was prone to lengthy lectures and going off on wild tangents, but Lucien was still one of the most intriguing men you would ever come across. His Father-King could make a two-hour lecture on organizing socks sound dramatic and life-altering. So why was Lucien always hanging around these stiffs? Clearly, his Father needed more interesting friends… if any of these people could even be called *friends*.

Eyeing his own friends, Junior couldn't help but feel like he was to blame for their collective ennui. There weren't any other kids their age around, aside from his Secutor, Jeremiah, who had slunk off miserably to a dark corner. Junior's three best friends were here only because of him, to keep him company, and how had he repaid them? With jam sandwiches and castrated chickens.

The Prince knew he had to do something to spice things up. As a Valenta, he had a reputation to uphold. The Golden Family were the most famous and glamorous royals this side of the universe. Never let it be said that any of them threw a dull party.

Undoing the obnoxious bow-tie Lucien had made him wear, Junior said quietly but with authority, "C'mon. Let's get out of here."

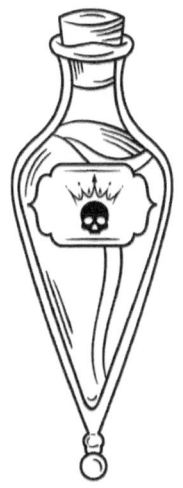

Chapter 8:
The Tree of Queens is just a myth...
isn't it?

"For-get. It." enunciated Porki, when he realized what Junior was up to.

Junior and his friends had squeezed their way out of the circle and found themselves closer to the semi-transparent Shielded barricade. A little beyond the Gold King's Shield, they could see the makings of a dark forest.

The King's party was a mile away from a human-made jungle, Godshoots Forest. Porki had caught the adventurous gleam in the Prince's eyes as they wandered over at the place that looked like a green refuge by day and an ideal spot for a horror-story chase sequence by nightfall.

"C'mon Porki. This is a golden opportunity," said Junior keenly. "My Father's given everyone access to come and go through this Shield tonight … the forest is only a 15-minute walk from here, maybe 10 if we're fast enough. We'll be back before your mom can stuff another gold bar between her breasts."

"Keep your voice down," whispered Porki, glancing over his shoulder. They were still close enough to the crowd of partygoers; not to mention, there were Volucris Knights patrolling the perimeter. "And don't talk about my mom's breasts."

"Fine," said Junior. "You coming with?"

"No," hissed Porki. "We'll get caught."

"Not with this we won't." An infernal grin began to grow on Junior's face as he pulled out a small colourless vial of liquid. "You know how my brother Michael can go invisible?"

"His *Unseen* ability," said Terry with a nod. He had read a few things on Phantom King Michael's powers.

"Mike doesn't like to call it that, but everyone else does… so yeah," shrugged Junior. "Anyway, he's been working on charging consumables and devices with his Unseen ability for months."

"So that liquid is charged with all three of the Phantom King's energies? Black, white, and silver?" inquired Terry, intrigued.

At Junior's nod of confirmation, Meryl pondered, "But why? Phantom King Michael can already turn himself invisible whenever he wants. Why would he create this?"

Before Junior could answer, Terry piped in with his postulation, "Probably so that his Knights can use it. I hear they're not very adept with the Phantom Gift, so they rely heavily on items and weapons charged by King Michael for defense and combat."

"Riiggghht," Junior hadn't even considered that possibility, but it made perfect sense now that he thought about it. "Anyway, I snatched this from Gabe's lab the last time I went to the Phantom Realm. It's in beta stage and I hear it wears off quickly, but it still works. I'm sure it'll give us plenty of time to sneak off."

"We're not allowed to use anything charged with a King's energy here," said Porki. "You know that."

"We're not using it, we're consuming it," said Junior. "There's a diff."

"Hardly," said Porki. "Even if we weren't on Neutral soil, minors can't have any traces of Divine energy in their system. It's illegal."

"Actually, Porki, you'll find there's no hard rule against it," said Terry. "It really depends on any given King and whether or not he—"

"Or *she*," added Meryl, accounting for all the female Kings, past and present, throughout history.

"Or she," Terry nodded at her, "decide to Gift a minor. Though there have been some studies to suggest it's dangerous for minors like us to have a King's Gift since our bodies haven't fully developed yet."

"Pfffft, that's a total crock and you know it," snorted Junior. "My Father gave Lexie the Golden Gift when she was a kid and she turned out perfectly normal," and then with a cough, muttered, "For the most part."

"Well, I suppose that is true," acknowledged Terry as though Junior had provided a fair point.

Porki didn't agree. Nothing about the Valentas were normal, and Porki got the feeling they probably preferred it that way.

The Princess-Regent, in particular, had a reputation that seesawed between two opposite ends of the moral spectrum. Some people claimed she was like a saint; others had warned she was Satan in gold silk chiffon. Porki was more inclined to believe the latter, especially after hearing about how Princess Lex had started electrocuting people with the Golden Gift at the tender age of 8. She wasn't the best example of a *normal* person.

"No one's gonna notice we've gone," insisted Junior, when it looked like Porki wasn't going to budge. "Look at them," he said, loosely waving a hand toward the crowd, "They're all too busy waiting for my Father to exhale."

Practically all the women, and half the men, looked like they'd keel over and die if they took their eyes away from King Lucien. It was always like this when it came to his Father-King. Junior was positive the man was made entirely of gold, blood, bone, and contradictions – in that order.

Lucien was intense and intimidating, but he was also affable and approachable. He knew when to rule with a Golden fist, and he knew when to show compassion and mercy. He loved the sound of his own voice, but he was also very good at staying silent and listening to others. For all these reasons and more, people gravitated to him wherever he went.

Lex was no different. Those who didn't orbit Lucien usually had their sights set on the Golden Princess. Junior had noticed more than one man dash toward her with a lit match in the hopes of lighting her cigarette, only to be disappointed when Lex revealed she didn't smoke.

Normally, Junior detested anyone who made outward advances toward his sister, but he made an exception for tonight. When it came to sneaking away undetected, the Prince always had two insurmountable obstacles in his way. The first were his Father's Shields, which – conveniently enough – wouldn't be a problem tonight. The second was Lex.

Junior knew his Father would become sizably distracted by the sound of his own voice once his speech came along. The only person liable to notice he was gone was Lex.

Luckily for the Prince, Lex was going to be too preoccupied with all these dopes vying for her attention, hoping to become the next consort of the Golden Regency era.

As for his other caretakers, the Prince wasn't worried. He had already become quite adept at bypassing his guards. Many of the Volucris couldn't even tell the difference between Junior and Jeremiah since they looked so much alike; it was like having a stunt double around. And, as an extra stroke of luck, his nanny wasn't in attendance either. She had declined the invitation, citing the need to take a couple of mental health days. For reasons Junior couldn't quite fathom, all his nannies seemed to require ample access to mental healthcare.

"You lot can't possibly want to go along with this?" said Porki, who was now looking to Terry and Meryl.

"I've never been to Godshoots before," said Terry, his interest piqued. "If we go, we might be able to spot a vulture or two."

"What's the appeal in that?" Porki raised a brow.

"They're an endangered species and one of the most trafficked animals in our world," explained Terry. "I saw it in that documentary, *The Various Virtues of Vultures*. It was on the UnEarthing Channel last month. Apparently, vultures are a hot commodity for witch-doctors over in the Indigo Kingdom. They use their bones and skulls to see into the future... It's a tragic life for such noble creatures, really. To think, they might not even be around in twenty years time."

"Neither will we if they rip us to shreds out there," said Porki blandly.

"If we drink this," Junior held up the vial again, "They won't detect us."

"You just said that stuff wears off easily," Porki reminded him. "And, even if they don't see you, it doesn't mean they can't smell you or hear you, does it?"

"Errr...well..." Junior fumbled for a response. He wasn't entirely sure how it worked.

"Vultures won't hurt us," said Terry matter-of-factly. "They're scavengers, not predators. They never attack living things. In fact, they're the only carnivores kind enough to wait for you to die before eating you."

"That's considered a kindness, is it?" said Meryl.

"Sure," said Terry with an eager nod. "I mean, it's what we do, isn't it?"

A look of puzzlement formed on Meryl's face. She would never have thought of it that way, not until Terry had pointed it out.

"Forget it," repeated Porki. "We're not going birdwatching in a dark forest located smack dab in the middle of the desert—"

"Birds aren't the only appeal," Terry said. "Godshoots is home to more than three million trees and some of them are the most unique ones in the world, like Dragon Blood and Blue Jacaranda. And, sometimes, the committee that maintains the forest tucks away natural crystals for people to excavate."

Junior held up a hand. "We're not going for birds or rocks."

Terry's face drooped in disappointment. "We're not?"

"No, but you're right to mention the trees," said the Prince. "Because I have it on good authority that the Tree of Queens lies in that forest."

Meryl rolled her eyes. "The Tree of Queens is a myth."

"Is it though?" smirked Junior. "I heard my Father and Lexie talk about it last night when they thought I was asleep. It's real and rooted right there in those woods."

"Wait … are you serious?" Meryl tilted her head, inspecting his features for any traces of prevarication. "This better not be one of your tall tales, Junior."

"Would I lie to you?"

"You would and you have." Meryl cut her eyes at him. "Repeatedly."

"I'm not lying about this, OK?" he assured his friends. "It's the genuine article."

Meryl bit down on her lower lip as she mulled it over. Junior's ideas usually led to some degree of trouble. But just this once, it might be trouble worth enduring if it meant she got to experience the Tree of Queens. Half of her wanted to say yes. The other half didn't want to succumb to Junior, especially not while he was giving her *that smile*. She hated it when the Prince smiled at her like that. It was a grin that looked akin to an evil child with a mad crush, staring at you from across the nursery school playground.

"Well…" Meryl mumbled with a frown. "I dunno…What do you think Porki?"

This time, even Porki looked tempted. The Tree of Queens was a legend. People across the world had been debating about its very existence for more than a century. No one knew what type of tree it was, but its taxonomy made no difference. No one cared about the tree's natural properties. The mythos around the Tree of Queens was that it bore fruit that carried supernatural abilities.

As legend would have it, all the Chosen Kings of Earth had blessed a specific tree (no one knew which) with their respective Divine energies. It was said that consuming its fruits could grant you absolutely anything you desired in the world. All you had to do was visualize your desires while eating the produce. The trick, however, was that you couldn't simply *wish* for it. Whatever you wanted, you had to picture it in your head like it was a persistent memory – something you had already experienced. If you grew up poor and wanted money, you would need to see yourself immersed in a state of wealth as though you were born rich. Same goes for anything and everything else: fame, happiness, good health, romance, etc. By consuming the fruit, you would be revising the entire story of your life.

All the Kings of Earth had denied the tree's existence. Some of them had laughed off the theory as a silly fable. But there were plenty of conspiracy theorists out there arguing the Kings had created this tree and were purposefully hiding it from the worldwide- and universal- public.

Originally, Porki hadn't thought there was any truth to those theories. But if King Lucien had acknowledged its existence, then that meant—

"Forget it." Porki repeated thrice-over, headshaking off the impulse to follow along with the Prince's plan.

Tempting as it was, it wasn't a risk worth taking. Mankind had a mutual agreement to remain peaceful on Neutral soil. Nevertheless, going into a jungle at this hour was pure lunacy.

"We're not going," Porki said firmly.

"I don't recall you being the leader of our group," said Junior, his dark eyes now narrowed.

Porki narrowed his eyes right back. "Neither are you."

"I'm the Prince of the group."

"You're also the Idiot of the group." The way Porki saw it: Junior's proclivity for stupidity cancelled out any profound impact his friend's Royal status would've had on him. "We were invited here for His Majesty's birthday, not to—"

"You weren't invited," Junior cut him off coldly. "I sent for you."

Their gazes clashed, filled with aggravation.

Porki decided he wasn't getting roped into Junior's antics tonight. He was still in trouble for what went down last week when Junior had insisted on making prank calls to members of the King's secret security team, the Covert Royal Operations Wing (C.R.O.W).

Ignoring Junior, Porki turned to face Terry and Meryl. "If you two want to get involved in his harebrained schemes again, then that's on you. Don't come crying to me when it inevitably backfires."

Porki could tell Terry and Meryl wanted to go with Junior. He didn't blame them. Junior had a magnetic shine to him whenever he got an idea in his head. It was a look that suggested the Prince was about to make your life infinitely more difficult and more interesting at the same time. Any other night, Porki might have entertained the Prince's whims and bended toward his light like a pathetic flower desperate for sun. But tonight, he was in no mood for it.

"Now, if you'll excuse me," said Porki, "I need to go stop my mom from being a national embarrassment."

"Fine!" Junior hissed at Porki's fast-retreating back. "Go on then! Go! Be a *capon*!" Then, muttering under his breath, he said, "That's what I get for wanting to show him a good time."

A loud gong suddenly went off – a call for attention and silence. The Gold King was about to address his subjects.

Chapter 9:
What more can a guy do
than say he's sorry?

Everyone cleared the dancefloor. With his entire frame now visibly glowing with Golden energy, Lucien levitated over to the heart of the circle.

There was a striking smile on the Gold King's face as he surveyed his subjects. "My dear friends," he began, "It brings me great joy to have you all gathered here tonight for my birthday. Mind you, no realm shall ever compare to our beloved Kingdom, which, to this day, remains the only place on Earth to shine brighter than Heaven."

"Here, here!" shouted one man in the crowd, raising his drink high in the air. "To the Gold Kingdom!"

"To the Gold King!" shouted another.

"To the Gold King!" chorused everyone else as they all raised their glasses.

"To our Eternal Monarch!"

"We love you, Your Majesty!!"

"Three cheers for His Majesty!!!"

"Thank you, you're all too kind." Lucien smiled politely but held up a hand for silence. "No one can ever contest the love I bear for our Kingdom. That said, I still consider this realm a home away from home of sorts. And I'm most honoured to stand here, alongside all of you, on Neutral soil. What one may call, The Midbar. The Garden of Allah," He waved his arm about in a flourish as though indicating to the entire scope of the desert. "For what better place to acknowledge the

Fatherhood of God and the Brotherhood of Man? Why, all the great men of Judaism, Christianity, and Islam entered the seclusion of the desert and returned with a most powerful message for their followers. As I reflected upon them today, I began to wonder what message I could deliver to all of you on this very night. What can I possibly say to inspire your souls and invigorate your faith …"

"My Father's sure to keep yapping for at least an hour or two," Junior leaned over to mutter quietly to Terry and Meryl while the Gold King's speech carried on. "Now's our chance… So, how about it?" He waved the vial over their faces as though he were trying to hypnotize them with it.

"I'll go," said Terry with a shrug. "With respect, I must say, I feel like His Majesty has recited parts of this speech before."

"He has," Junior nodded, deciding not to tell Terry that his Father was improvising. Terry would undoubtedly want to stick around if he knew Lucien was delivering new material.

"How about you, Meryl?" The Prince jutted his chin in her direction.

"I don't know," she said apprehensively. "Porki will be upset."

"So what?" said Junior snidely at the mention of Porki. "He's your *boyfriend* now, is that it?" And then, in an accusing tone, "I saw you poking at his dimples earlier on and – and I saw him *let* you poke them too. Don't try to deny it."

Meryl rolled her eyes. They had been friends since nursery school, but in the past year, things had begun to change. She didn't understand why Junior suddenly had an issue with the state of Meryl and Porki's friendship. Sometimes, like now, he sounded downright jealous. Even more frustrating, she couldn't figure out who he was jealous of. Did Junior have a problem with the idea of Meryl being *boyfriend-girlfriend* with Porki? Or was it the reverse? Did he take offence to Porki being with Meryl? It was hard to tell.

Refusing to respond to his childishness, Meryl kept her eyes on the Gold King.

"… Some of you here may remember how it was in times of old, when the desert was considered a place of meditation, where men realized that with God, all things are possible," continued Lucien. "That realization is manifestly true for here we are today, several millennia later, in a world that runs on Divine energy, where nothing is beyond our grasp … No other place in this universe has what we have. No other planet can compare to Earth's special brand of magic…"

"Meryl…" said Junior, this time in a more polite tone that sounded, for anyone knowing the Prince, too sweet to be true. "Merrrryyyllll," he whined softly to get her attention. "I'm sorry I snapped at you, OK?"

Terry, who kept his face calm and inscrutable, was starting to wish he had stood somewhere else. Anywhere other than where he was now, sandwiched between Junior and Meryl. The Prince quarreled with Meryl almost as often as he did with Porki. Terry was sure his ears would start bleeding if they decided to go a few rounds right then and there.

"C'mon Meryl," Junior tried again. "I said I was sorry, didn't I? What more can a guy do than say he's sorry?"

Meryl didn't respond.

"Come with us," the Prince persisted, "You know you want to."

"No," Meryl bit out in a whisper, trying her hardest to refrain from giving the Prince any more attention.

"How come?" said Junior, the sourness returning to his voice. "Is it 'cause of my Father? I saw you staring at him earlier on. You're just like all these other women. You probably want to marry him too, don't you? Don't try to deny it."

"… Now I know birthdays are a time for personal celebrations and gifts. But I don't want anyone here to commemorate me with words and material trinkets. Far from it… Looking around me now, it uplifts my heart to see so many of my subjects living lives of great abundance. So tonight, I want us all to rejoice in our many blessings and praise He who gave us everything. Let us never forget that we freely walk this earth thriving in Gold because it is God's will," said Lucien proudly. "For we can not spell Gold without God…"

Meryl sliced her eyes over to the Prince. "Look at what I'm wearing, Junior."

"What about it?" He eyed her from head-to-toe, from the soft waves in her hair, to the puffy dark evening gown on her body, and the kitten heels beneath her feet.

"Unlike you, I didn't just run a hand through my hair and pop a mint in my mouth before coming here," she whispered angrily. "My hair, my dress, my makeup," she waved a hand down her frame, "All of this is *art*, and it took a lot of time, work, and energy to put everything together."

"So?"

"*So*, it'll be ruined the moment we step out."

"Who cares? You always look great no matter what." The Prince said those words with so much genuine honesty that Meryl's anger dissipated. Or at least, it would have, had he not added, "Except for the time you got that perm. That was *not* good."

"You told me you liked it!" she whispered tensely.

"Er…did I?" Junior winced. There were two severe drawbacks to lying: getting caught and having so much to remember.

"Yes, you did," she gritted out, returning her attention to the Gold King.

"... Every moment should be a celebration of our lives and of the energy that courses through us – for that energy is God ..."

"Last chance, Meryl. You in or not?" Junior held out the vial in her direction. "Look, I promise we'll be back before my Father can make a reference to me and Lexie coming out of his loins."

"...While we're here in this place of peace, prophets and paragons, let us all take a moment to remember that life is God's gift to us and what we choose to do with it is our gift to God."

It didn't take long for the *Unseen*-tonic to kick in. Three drops on the tongue per person and they were hidden from the world in less than three seconds.

The first thing Junior felt was a tightening in his gut. It was like someone had thrown a lasso around his stomach and hauled him across space before finally deciding to land on the moon.

Junior looked around. They were still at the party, but much further away from the crowd. His Father, bless him, was still speaking. But now, there was a surrealness to Lucien's voice, as if it were echoing inside of a tunnel.

"Did it work?" asked Terry.

The Prince whipped his head back to Terry and Meryl. They looked the same. They appeared unstirred by the Unseen.

But then he blinked, and their features and garments were gone. They were no longer people with faces, but living shadows and moving silhouettes sprinkled with stardust. It was like having x-ray vision, only instead of bones, Junior saw big blots of white and silver inside his friends. They looked like nebulas trapped in the shadows of bodies.

He blinked again. Terry and Meryl were back to normal.

"Well?" Meryl tilted her head like a confused puppy. "Did it take? I don't feel any diff."

Without answering, Junior strode past them to perform an initial test run. Ever so slowly, he stalked beside the Volucris Knights patrolling by the eastern edge of the dome and slid through the semi-transparent wall of Gold as easily as a poltergeist. No one tried to stop him. No one even noticed he was there.

"It works," he said nonchalantly when he got back to Terry and Meryl.

His friends nodded eagerly at him. Their eyes were turning glossy, but they appeared unbothered.

The trio were completely concealed yet they could still see one another. Junior chalked this up to the fact that they had the same Divine energies in their system and those energies could sense its own presence.

"I need to grab my bag before we go," said Junior.

He had left his satchel full of essentials – which included a torchlight, a compass, and a camera – behind the open bar area. Lex had thought it was silly of him to bring it to the party, but Junior had been adamant about it, even going as far as to call it a *precautionary measure*. For the remainder of this trip, he was going to have his satchel within his reach. Leaving his bag behind last time had cost him a great photo opportunity with those women. He wasn't going to make that mistake twice. For all he knew, there were bare-breasted pagan priestesses out there, howling and dancing under the desert moon, just waiting to be immortalized through his profound photography skills.

"You already got it." Terry nodded down at his satchel.

Junior's eyes dropped to the leather messenger bag hanging across his body. For the life of him, he couldn't remember sneaking over to the bar to fetch his belongings. Nor could he recall walking back to his friends after retrieving said bag. He figured it all must have happened at some point, but when?

He flashed another glance toward the open bar. A second ago, he was certain Lady Hornbill had been standing there, taking her first puff of the night from a bejewelled cigarette holder longer than her own arm. Now, the cigarette was reaching its butt.

"We better get going," whispered Meryl excitedly. "The forest won't wait for us forever."

Junior stared at her. There were glitches in his vision. Every now and then, he caught blotches of white and silver radiating from within Meryl and Terry's frames. It reminded him of those heatmaps that provided a color-coded study of pain and pleasure in the human body.

"Why are you giggling, Meryl?" asked Terry.

"What are you talking about? You're the one whose caught the giggles. You've gone mad," she chortled, "Wretched and mad."

Junior snorted, all swine-like. They were all laughing for reasons unknown. Drawing a finger up to his lips, he whispered, "Staph! Staaapphhh! Shhh, shhh, guys! I think they can still hear us. You must staaaappphhh."

Their moods had flipped 180 degrees. The sense of detachment was now replaced with unstable giddiness. The trio felt full of vim and vigour. They were too young to realize it, but what they were actually experiencing was an aftereffect of adolescents consuming multiple Divine energies. The buzz they were feeling at that moment was the equivalent of a child finishing off their twentieth energy drink in one sitting.

"Let's get going," said Junior.

Together, they passed through the warmth of the Shield and out into the cold night air of the desert.

Thankfully for them, anything that made contact with their bodies went undetected as well. They certainly would've had a harder time getting away if people caught sight of their clothes and accessories floating around while they were invisible.

Junior could no longer hear his Father's speech. The soundproofing mechanism on Lucien's Shield prevented anyone outside the party from listening in. It also ensured the guests weren't disturbed by the rumbling of the dunes, the whispers of the wind, or any other external noises.

They couldn't have timed it more perfectly. The winds were gentle, nowhere strong enough to stir up a sandstorm. So, they didn't need to worry about getting dust in their eyes. And, the light breeze was enough to cover some of their footprints as well. This was ideal desert-wandering weather.

As they left, Junior shot a quick glance over his shoulder. As he'd predicted, all eyes were on Lucien. No one took notice of three pairs of footprints stomping through the sand. While everyone else was busy rejoicing in the Gold King's light, the Prince and his friends slipped away like little phantoms in the night.

Chapter 10:
Is *this* where God shoots and leaves?

"It's just a forest," Meryl said when they reached the area where the desert ended and the man-made forest began.

The forest won't wait for us forever. What was she thinking? Of course, it would wait. It had nothing else to do with its life but wait for people to creep on by.

She released a small sigh of disappointment. The mundaneness of the woods was a jarring return to reality.

The power of the Unseen tonic had begun to fade at the 5-minute mark, and by the time they reached Godshoots, Junior suspected they were no longer invisible. There were no more glitches in his vision. He could no longer see any shiny splodges of silver and white whirling inside his friends' chest cavities.

Meryl and Terry were now starting to look rather washed out and enervated. Junior reckoned he didn't look much better. The high they had experienced from the tonic had plummeted faster than a meteorite.

"What were you expecting?" asked Terry.

"Something a little more…enchanting."

"You don't need any more enchantment in your life, Meryl," the Prince jutted a thumb to his chest, "You've already got me for that."

"Because you obviously came straight out of a fairy tale," she said sarcastically, looking him up and down as one would a gremlin.

"Most girls think so."

"Yeah, sure," scoffed Meryl. "Stay delusional, Junior."

"Oh, but he has to. Junior doesn't have many talents he can put to good use. Delusional confidence is the only thing currently getting him through life," Terry said, his tone child-like and simple, like someone who couldn't differentiate between an honest remark and a put-down.

"Thanks Terry," the Prince said dryly.

Junior hadn't expected the effects of the liquid to wear off so quickly. He still had a few drops left in the vial. Hopefully, it would be enough for all three of them to sneak back into the party. Otherwise, he would have to think up some wild excuse to deliver to his Father-King and his Sister-Princess-Regent. Fortunately, he had plenty of experience coming up with alibis on the fly. Unfortunately, his family never believed any of them.

Meryl hugged her arms as a shiver ran down her form. "It's freezing."

The cold night air had been a slap in the face from the moment they absconded the tent, but none of them had felt it until now.

"Here, put this on." Junior removed his blazer and handed it to her.

Meryl thought Junior was being rather gallant. Little did she know, the gesture was more for his own benefit than hers. The chilled air made Meryl's nipples visibly protrude through her dress. Junior knew from experience she was likely to sock him if she caught him staring at her chest for too long. He had offered up his jacket to, quite literally, save face.

When they got to the earthed path leading into large, thick trees, Junior stopped to rummage through his bag in search of his torchlight. They would need it to navigate through the darkness of the forest. The moon provided some light, but it was more faded than full, looking like the edge of God's thumbprint.

The Prince nearly dropped his bag at the ear-piercing shriek that sprang beside him.

"AAAHHHHHH!!!!" screeched Meryl, latching onto Junior's arm. "WHAT IS THAT?!!!!"

"It's only a little insect," said Terry calmly. "A beetle, I think."

"Does that look like a *LITTLE* bug to you?!!!" she nodded her head fiercely to the two-foot bluish-black beetle crawling on the ground. The insect in question immediately fled at the sound of Meryl's hysterical voice.

"I didn't say it was a bug," clarified Terry. "It's an insect. There's a difference. You see, bugs are like beetles, but they're a completely different type of insec—"

"TERRY!" Meryl yelled in irritation.

In an effort to keep his eardrums intact, Junior tried to wrangle himself away from her grasp.

"Calm yourself, Meryl," Terry said in a soothing voice.

"I AM CALM!!!!!" Shoving Junior away from her, Meryl continued to bellow at Terry. "Did you see the size of that thing?!"

"It looked like a darkling beetle."

"I don't care what it's called! It's unnatural."

Terry couldn't deny that much. "It did seem unusually large. Normally, those type of insects only reach up to 19 mm in size... I wonder..." he drifted off, a curious look forming across his soft, boyish face as he stared up at the towering trees.

"What is it?" asked Meryl worriedly.

"If the Tree of Queens is here, then its fruit would be available to all the animals in residence," stated Terry, "Perhaps consuming the fruit is what caused such abnormal growth in that beetle."

"Oh well that's just terrific then, isn't it?!" Meryl said sarcastically as she threw her hands in the air. "There could be lions five times their standard BMI prowling about."

"I doubt it," Terry said, "The Convocation of Kings hired a committee to ensure most of the dangerous desert wildlife were segregated to the safari zone, far west of here. The lions would be hanging about over there. All we're likely to find in these woods are harmless birds, bugs and beetles...with an unconventionally large body mass." Eyes widening, he slapped a palm to his forehead as a sudden realization struck him, "Oh no—"

"What?" asked Junior.

"We're not likely to spot any vultures in these woods. There's not much for them to scavenge here. They're probably circling the safari region as we speak."

"Forget the vultures, will you, Terry?" Junior rolled his eyes. "I told you we're not here for birdwatching."

"Wait," Meryl said, looking around swiftly, "The Convocation had this forest made. So, wouldn't it be guarded the way the safari zone is?"

"It appears not," noted Terry. "Then again, this is Neutral territory. The most peaceful place in our world. They don't really have a need for security here, do they?"

"What was that?" Meryl jumped again, grabbing hold of Terry's arm this time around. "Did you hear that?!"

"Relax, Meryl." Junior was growing annoyed at her panicky behaviour. "I think it's water coming from a natural well."

"It's not completely natural though, since everything here is made by us," said Terry. "Not *us* us, that is. I mean to say, humans… though that's not entirely correct either, as labour from non-tellurian species was also used in the making of—"

"Ugh, ok." Meryl shook her head in frustration. "Whatever! Let's just find the tree, grab a few fruits, and head back to the King's party."

Meryl and Terry nodded at one another in agreement before turning to Junior.

"What are you two lookin' at me for?" asked the Prince.

"Which one of these trees is *the Tree*?" said Meryl.

"How should I know?"

"You said your family confirmed its existence," she snapped impatiently.

"Yeah, they mentioned it. I heard it myself. *I'm dashing off to assess the current state of the Tree of Queens, my dear,* says my Father to my sister," he mimicked Lucien's deep, debonair voice before switching over to a more feminine tone, "Then I hear his wings whoosh out as Lexie says to him, *OK Father, fly safe!*"

Meryl blinked, expecting him to expand and explain. "And then what?"

"Then my Father flew off," said Junior simply.

Terry and Meryl continued to stare at him, waiting for him to divulge more information. The type of tree. The type of fruit said tree bore. Where exactly in Godshoots it was situated. Any bits of useful information. But all Junior said was—

"That's it."

A beat of silence, and then—

"Are you freakin' kidding me?!" yelled Meryl, getting into Junior's face. "There are at least three million trees out here! How are we supposed to spot the Tree of Queens if we don't even know where to look?"

Terry gently placed a hand on Meryl's shoulder, pulling her back a bit, as if to discourage her from strangling Junior. "If the lore is true, then the tree is charged with the Divine energies of all the Chosen Kings. Or, at very least, it would contain energies from the Four Chosen Kings that make up the Convocation. Luckily for us, most Kings have very detectable energies that vibrate at specific frequencies and radiate in different colours visible to the mortal eye."

"So what?" snapped Meryl. "We need to be on the lookout for a tree glowing in all the colours of the rainbow?"

"Four of the colours, at the very least," nodded Terry.

"Why four?" asked Meryl.

"Because there are four member-Kings in the Convocation right now. So, we need to look for those four energies: Gold, Red, Blue, and Indigo."

"No way, that sounds too easy to be true." Meryl shook her head. "To start, there doesn't seem to be a sliver of light, Divine or otherwise, coming from anywhere in these woods."

"Well, there's still so much more to explore," reasoned Terry. "We're only in one area of the forest."

"Perhaps, but even so," said Meryl, "The Kings have publicly denied its existence, which means they're hiding it... maybe even hiding it in plain sight." With her eyes sweeping over the trees around them, she pressed on, "For all we know, the Tree of Queens could look like any ordinary tree. And if that's the case, how do we find it?"

Terry's face lit up for a moment. He suddenly remembered something. "The Tree of Queens is a female tree since it bears fruit." He snapped his fingers. "That immediately rules out all the male trees here which only produce pollen."

"Yeahhh," frowned Meryl, "But still, at 3 million trees, it doesn't narrow it down much."

"There are devices out there that can sense Divine energies, even when they aren't visible to the average mortal eye. We could use one of those," proposed Terry.

"Uh huh," Meryl made a grand show of nodding and pretending to go along with the recommendation. "We could. We could certainly use one of those. But I'm guessing we don't have one on hand." Throwing a sharp look at Junior, she said rhetorically, "Do we?"

"Errrr... no." Junior grimaced and pointed his torchlight her way as a defensive manoeuvre.

Meryl squinted at the sudden light on her face and shoved Junior's torch away from her. "Right," she scowled, "Because all you probably brought along was a camera to take high-definition pictures of naked pagan girls!"

"How did you kn—"

"Porki told me."

"That traitor," muttered Junior. "Look, that type of gear isn't allowed on Neutral soil. I couldn't bring it here even if I had it."

Meryl sighed in annoyance at Junior's lack of foresight. She should've known something like this would happen. Junior was horrible at preparation. This was the boy who hadn't even been able to obtain a single Merit Badge back when he was in the Griffin Cub Scouts of Gold. This was the little pervert who failed to pass a simple First Aid class because he kept asking his female CPR instructor to take off her blouse so that he could properly perform chest compressions on her.

What made it worse: this was the idiot Meryl *occasionally* had a crush on.

Meryl ran a hand through her hair, trying to compose herself. She was tired and sweaty, and she still had sand stuck in her shoes. "So, now what?"

"Why don't we walk around a bit?" Junior gave her a winning smile. "I'm sure I'll be able to sense the Tree easily enough."

Meryl didn't have any faith in Junior's abilities right now. "How?" she asked as she removed her shoes to release the sand.

"I can't detect the energies of other Kings, but I've been surrounded by my Father's Golden energy all my life. It has a certain… vibe to it." Junior wasn't sure how to properly express in words what Golden energy felt like. He supposed it was much like feeling sunlight on your face for the very first time. Warm, intense and full of love and life. "Even if the Tree of Queens is hidden, I'm sure I'd be able to feel it out if it's near enough."

Meryl took a deep breath. "Finnneee," she sighed out before strapping her shoes back on. "We'll stroll about for ten minutes. If we can't find anything, we leave."

"Sounds good to me," Terry nodded.

"Tree. Of. Queens! Tree. Of. Queens!" Junior chanted happily and threw his fists in the air as though he were emitting a caveman mating call.

With a bright smile, Terry stalked behind him down an open trail lined with dark trees.

With far less enthusiasm than the boys, Meryl frowned and followed them down the footed path.

"Why is it called Tree of Queens?" she said as they trudged on, "If it's charged with Kingly energy, wouldn't it have made more sense to call it the Tree of Kings?"

"Well, there is an allegory of intimacy involved," said Terry.

"How do you mean?"

"Both queens and trees are symbols of fertility and life. It's said that a King charging a tree and filling it up with their God-given essence is comparable to a man inseminat—

"OK, OK," Meryl held up a hand. "I get it, Terry."

Chapter 11:
Can't you see the Phantom fire?

As they trailed on, they talked about what they would manifest if they got to eat from the Tree of Queens. Godshoots was dark and, if it weren't for the echo of their voices, it would have been silent as well.

Meryl kicked things off by unveiling her wish list: the ability to teleport anywhere, her paintings going viral, being able to eat anything without gaining weight, universal peace, and a naturally high-bridged nose, to name a few...

Terry's desires weren't any less extensive, but he had narrowed it down to three key items: infinite intelligence, destruction of human greed, and conventional good looks.

Junior thought two out of three of Terry's wishes were unnecessary. Terry was already at the top of their class. He was highly knowledgeable. Sometimes Terry's intellect really took him by surprise, especially since this was the same boy who heated up his cereal every morning, designed a helmet for his horse to wear for their school's polo matches, and rubbed his mom's thumbnails on Sundays for good luck.

As for beauty, Terry wasn't on Junior or Porki's level, but he had enough boyish good looks to get by in life. Besides, Terry didn't really need any type of aesthetic appeal.

"Don't worry, Terry," Junior reassured his friend. "You don't need looks. You've got money."

"My dad has money. Not me."

"But he's not gonna be around forever, is he?" Junior refuted. He didn't feel bad for saying it either.

Terry Reed had once described his father as a "*formidable man ... with a strong personality.*" But Junior knew that was coded language for *asshole*.

Granted, Junior knew that wasn't an entirely accurate interpretation. His own Father-King and Sister-Princess-Regent were formidable figures. They were also strong-willed. But at least they weren't assholes ... most of the time. Taurus Reed II, by contrast, was dreadful, especially to his son.

The Prince remembered a time where Terry had accidentally tripped in front of the Gold King. Lucien hadn't minded. He simply helped the little boy get back onto his feet. The senior Reed, however, was outwardly embarrassed and internally livid. Afterwards, Junior had witnessed Mr. Reed drag Terry into a secluded room, only to slap him across the face. "*I do not suffer fools gladly,*" he had told his only son. "*And that includes the likes of you, boy.*"

That moment had cemented Junior's opinion of the man: a complete asshole through and through. Men like that were probably the reason someone had to invent the word *asshole*.

Instead of brain power and beauty, Junior thought what Terry needed to manifest more than anything right now was a better father.

"No offense Terry, but your old man is already on his Sixth Millennia of life. I bet he only has another six centuries left in him. Tops."

"That's not my dad. You must have him confused with my grandfather, *Taurus Reed I*," corrected Terry calmly. "My dad's only in his Second Millennia."

"He is?" Junior's left brow flew up in shock. "You wouldn't think it to look at him."

"What about you, Junior?" Terry tilted his head toward him. "What would you manifest?"

Junior thought about it as he waved his torch around to observe the trees in their path. They had passed by a variety of plants, like tamarisk, jujube, carob, eucalyptus, and acacia.

What did he want? From Day One, he was a boy who had the world handed to him on a golden platter. The universe was like a saltshaker to him – always within his reach, and he could order anyone to pass it to him whenever he pleased. He yearned for nothing, because he had everything… Well, almost everything.

Junior wasn't as pious as his Father-King. He didn't pray seven times a day the way Lucien did. But sporadically, throughout this past decade, he had asked God for one thing: his Mother, Lana.

History had already written Lana off as the former Queen to the Golden Empire and the former King to the Phantom Realm. But to the Valentas, her presence lingered painfully like a long scar across a beautiful face. She was the spectre that haunted their family. She was the missing link in an otherwise idyllic Princely life.

For now, his Mother was somewhere Junior couldn't reach, trapped in a place between life and death. His brothers had tried to resurrect her and had thus far, failed.

Junior wondered if he could be the one to do it. Could he bring her back? The Tree of Queens was said to bear the fruit of miracles. What would happen if he ate from it while thinking of a life where his Mother had never been taken from him? Would everything in the past revise and rearrange itself? His parents had already separated by the time they had Junior. If his Mother hadn't gotten hurt, he probably would've stayed in the Phantom Realm, under her custody instead of his Father's. And that meant… everything he had ever experienced with Lucien and Lex would be erased. Did he really want that to happen? Sure, he wanted his Mother back, but at what cost?

"Hellloooooo," Meryl sang out as she nudged him. "Your Royal Highness. Are you still with us?"

"Huhh?" Junior blinked as he exited the hazy fog of his mind and returned to reality. "Errr, yeahhh. I'm here."

It took him awhile to realize he had stopped walking.

Then, it took him another few blinks and beats to understand *why* he had halted.

They had reached a large fork in the earthed path.

"Actually, *we're* here," he amended, looking blankly at the empty patch of soil in front of them.

"What do you mean *we're here*?" Meryl furrowed her brows.

The two roads beside them were lined with trees, but the large triangular strip of land in between was bare.

"This is it," said Junior, pointing his light at the void.

Meryl and Terry exchanged a look.

"Junior," said Meryl slowly, "There's nothing there."

Logically, Junior knew this. He could very well see there was nothing in front of them. And yet, he could feel the unshakeable, unbreakable presence of Golden energy emanating from this area. It was immersed with something else. Another energy, perhaps multiple energies.

It was as though one energy was trying to set your heart on fire and the other one was ready to sweep right in to soothe the burn. What a weird and wonderful mix.

All these energies, merged together, was making Junior hungry. Desperately hungry. Even though he couldn't see it, he instinctively knew he was standing in the presence of Divine power, eternal love and infinite intelligence. It was as if all three ingredients were balled up into a celestial dough, and he wanted nothing more than to consume it raw and whole.

Junior's mouth was watering, his eyes were tearing up, and his knees were shaking. His body wanted to prostrate itself. This must've been what Moses felt like when he encountered a desert bush engulfed in flames. Miraculously enough, the bush was incapable of being destroyed by the fire. The flames were said to be radiating with God's life and power.

"There the angel of the Lord appeared to him in a flame of fire out of a bush," Lucien recited from the Bible, *Exodus 3:2.*

That's what this was. Or, at the very least, it was something akin to it. He couldn't see the flames, but he could feel its warmth. It was a phantom fire, hidden but high-octane.

"There's something here," the Prince kept his eyes on the spot. "This part of the forest is significantly warmer than the rest and...and I can feel my Father's energy here...More than that, there's—there's something really special here. Can't you guys feel it?"

Junior couldn't be sure, but he suspected whatever was here, it contained a combination of at least three Divine energies: Gold, Red, and Blue. He also speculated Michael's Phantom energies (Black, White, and Silver) were at work, keeping the tree unseen from unwanted eyes.

"This is ridiculous." Meryl rolled her eyes. "You hauled us all the way here like cows to look at grass."

"At least cows get to eat the grass." Terry's face soured as well. "I think we better head back lest anyone notes our absence," he said tightly.

"Let's go." Meryl clicked her tongue. "What a waste."

"No, don't go!" Junior pleaded, "There's something here. Honest! Look, I bet if I touched it—"

Junior froze in place. His torchlight fell to the ground in a clunk.

Suddenly, he was trapped. It was as though there were a phantom body wrapping its arms tightly around him from behind and a steely rod in front of him, pressing against his stomach.

"Bloody hell! Something's got me!" He shouted as he attempted to wrangle off what felt like an invisible guard.

"We're leaving," Meryl growled out, fed up with Junior's antics. "*Now.*"

She didn't look down. If she had, she might have noticed the empty space lingering between Junior's feet and the ground. An invisible energy did, indeed, have Junior in its clutches.

Forcefully pushing his head back, he rotated his body inward and shoved away from his unseen captor. He was immediately released.

With his feet now planted back on earth, Junior quickly picked up his torch and staggered away from the barren patch of land. His eyes might've been deceiving him, but for a hot second, he was certain he had seen two spectral silver figures, shaped like large, hand-drawn stars, standing guard over the area. For a moment, Junior was certain the triangles of their silvery arms and legs resembled the limbs of a real person.

They disappeared the second he called out to his friends.

"Meryl! Terry! Look!" Junior shot after them. "Wait! I'm telling you—"

"Knock it off, Junior!" Terry yelled.

"Terry, try to touch that spot," Junior motioned toward the Phantom tree, "I bet you can't do it. Because there's something there to stop—"

"That's enough." Terry leapt forward to yank the torchlight from the taller boy's grasp. "Your constant need for attention is redundant and tiresome. Now, you can either come with us. Or stay behind on your own."

Junior gaped at him. It wasn't out of character for Terry to snap at him. They had been friends for a long time. They were bound to grate on each other's nerves every now and then. No, that wasn't odd. What was unusual was Terry's unwillingness to test out Junior's theory. Terry was curious about *everything*. He never liked to rule anything out because to him, everything was in the realm of possibility.

Terry twirled the flashlight oddly. He moved it up to his face and then away from him like a Knight manoeuvring a sword. It was a swift motion, but it provided enough light and time for Junior to see the change in his friend's face – more particularly, his eyes.

Junior nearly screamed at the sight of it. The pupils and irises of his friends' eyes were completely gone. Their scleras were entirely black, and the skin underneath their eyes looked rough and bumpy like sandpaper.

The Prince's gaze swung like a pendulum, back and forth between his two friends. They didn't look mad. It was far worse than that. They looked menacing. They looked like they were ready to bury him alive out here in these woods if he didn't leave with them at that moment. From the corner of his left eye, Junior could tell Terry had tightened his grip on the torch and was ready to use it as a weapon, if necessary.

That's when realization hit him, a lightning bolt fracturing his understanding. This was the work of an enchantment. It might've been the Divine magic of Kings. Or… it could be ancient sorcery.

"A King's Divine energy is the only pure magic in this world, son," Lucien had told him once, "As it comes from God."

"What was there before Chosen Kings? What about the Witches of the Old Ways from the Old Days?" Junior, then age nine, had asked. "Where does their magic come from?"

With his shoulders drawn back and his lips pressed into a thin line, Lucien said grimly, "You don't want to know."

Either way, this was a very powerful brand of magic. Not only did it hide the Tree of Queens, but it also subconsciously discouraged people from wanting to go anywhere near it. And in the off chance anyone managed to break through the subliminal requisite to leave well enough alone – the way Junior had – then they'd be forcefully held back by phantom barriers. And if that wasn't enough, there was an additional layer of spiritual intervention in place.

Intervention was the polite way to put it. It was a lie. The more honest description would be *possession*.

After a lengthy pause, Junior gave in. "OK… you're right. You're both right. There's nothing there," he said uneasily. What else could he do? He was trapped. Invisible monsters behind him and demonically-possessed friends in front of him. He had no other choice but to go along with it.

Holding up his hands a little in surrender, he said, "Let's head back."

Chapter 12:
What's scarier –
a ghost or a real person?

The walk back was unsettling.

Terry was behind him, jabbing the torch at Junior's spine as though it were a warm gun.

The Prince felt like the protagonist in a gangster movie being led out into the woods by his treacherous best friend – "Babyface Terry" – to be *taken care of*.

It took Junior's heart a while to calm down. It took him even longer to finally drum up the courage to look back at his friends. When he finally did so, he heaved a sigh of infinite relief. Their eyes were back to normal. *They* were back to normal. Whatever dark energy had previously consumed them appeared to have completely vanished.

When he felt safe enough, Junior turned to reclaim the flashlight from Terry the way a guard would retrieve a weapon from an assailant – move in slowly and seize quickly.

Terry didn't even seem to notice he wasn't carrying the torch anymore, busy as he was rambling on about the origins of Godshoots and how the revegetation of deserts was important for biodiversity. Meryl had stopped once to examine a few Jacaranda flowers that were shining a vibrant shade of blue under bits of moonlight.

Both Terry and Meryl behaved as though nothing peculiar had happened. Junior wondered if a lapse in memory was part of the enchantment. So that people who came looking for the Tree of Queens would leave forgetting all about it. It was like when you couldn't recall what you were thinking about while you're thinking it. Much like going into a room and confessing, *I came here to do something, but then I forgot what I was going to do.*

But if that was the case, why hadn't he forgotten what had happened?

Junior shook his head. He'd force himself to forget if he had to. *Best to forget everything here,* he reasoned. Just thinking about what had transpired back there brought a chill to his bones. The invisible Tree of Queens was ablaze with Divine energy, but whatever had possessed Terry and Meryl was anything but godly. It must have been ancient sorcery, Junior figured.

He shuddered a little, remembering how the enchantment had rapidly turned his friends into fiends. *Friends to fiends.* How very easy it was to go from one to another. It was amazing what the removal of a simple R in a word could do.

"Look, it's a Dragon's Blood tree." Meryl leapt toward a thirty-foot tree whose branches and leaves formed the shape of an upturned umbrella. "You know why they're called that, don't you? It's because its sap resembles the colour of blood."

"It's a very rare type of tree," nodded Terry. "Endangered too."

"Junior, you brought your camera, right? Why don't we get a picture of us next to it?" proposed Meryl. "Something to remember the night and—wait, why did we come here?"

Terry scrunched up his face. For once, he couldn't deliver a clear answer. "I—I don't know... I mean, I remember us leaving the party and then we arrived here to—to—"

Junior made a grand show of clearing his throat. "Got my camera!" He wrenched the device out of his bag and hoisted it up in the air as though it were a trophy.

"C'mon, let's take a snap," he said, hoping to keep them distracted.

They gathered around the Dragon's Blood tree. Having the longest arms in the group immediately meant Junior had to be the one to take the shot. He positioned himself slightly in front of his friends and tilted the camera to the side to ensure his extended arm wasn't in the photo.

The trio went from grinning to flinching when the flash hit their eyes, leaving them seeing nothing but large white spots for a good thirty seconds.

Junior had brought along the camera Gabriel had bought him earlier this year for his birthday. His second big brother had demonstrated a way to adjust the settings to take nighttime photographs without the flash, but Junior hadn't been paying attention.

Once their visions returned, they carried on down the path.

Now that there was enough distance between them and the enchanted tree, Junior had thought they were in the clear. But he was quickly beginning to grasp how wrong he was.

There was another threat in the air. This time, he was pretty sure it wasn't a Divine, magical or spiritual entity. It was worse. It was a real person.

"Are you afraid of being alone in the dark?" Lex had asked him once, back when he was a tiny tot, terrified of sleeping by his lonesome.

"No," he had mumbled softly while pulling a blanket up to his chin. If he was truly alone in the room, he wouldn't have been frightened. The problem was, he was quite sure there were other…entities in his bedchambers, even if his mortal eyes couldn't see them.

"Oh, I see," Lex nodded, reading him easily. Sliding next to him under the covers, she pulled him close to her. "You needn't fear ghosts and spirits, Little Wing. Most of them mean no harm … Unfortunately, the same can't be said for real people."

Junior was still too young, but Lex was old enough to know that real monsters came with faces.

Someone else was here.

Junior had the distinct feeling they were being watched. It was practically more fact than feeling at this point. As a Prince of the most famous Royal family in their galactic postal code, he had plenty of experience being gawked at and observed like a rare bird in a cage.

If the eyes lurking within the forest weren't enough to set off alarm bells in his head, the faint sound of footsteps in the distance did the trick. He wasn't sure at first, but when the trio had stopped to rest on a large rock, Junior was certain he had heard the movement of feet, somewhere behind them amid the dark trees.

At first, he wasn't sure if it sounded more animal than man.

The second time the footsteps reached his earshot, they sounded more like a pair of walking shoes rather than two pairs of paws on the ground.

"Let's go." Jumping from the rock, Junior nodded his head forward, indicating they persist with their retreat.

Junior appeared to be the only one in his group to have heard it. Perhaps it was for the best. He didn't want to frighten Meryl and Terry, especially by letting on that he, himself, was getting rather scared.

Come to think of it, it was a crying shame his friends were no longer under any spiritual influence. Whatever possessed them could've driven away their prowler.

Real monsters came with faces. They pulled triggers, planned wars and plotted against their own kind. Junior understood that now. The unseen entities guarding the Tree of Queens had simply wanted to keep interlopers away. They meant no harm. They were daunting but not damaging. Junior wasn't confident he could say the same for whomever was following them.

Swerving his eyes away from the direction of the sound, Junior wondered if it was someone from the Forest Committee. Perhaps they had a security guard out on patrol? But that theory was quickly shot down when he remembered how the crime rate in the Neutral Realm was practically 0%. Apart from the safari zone and the borderlines of the desert, they didn't have any need for security here. Added to that, any prospective guard or committee member would've made themselves known and escorted them back to their parents. They wouldn't be creeping about in the shadows.

"Slow down, will you?" Meryl told Junior, frowning at the fast-paced steps the Prince was now taking. "Why are you in a rush all of a sudden?"

"Can we please take another rest?" whined Terry. "I'm feeling awfully bushed."

In the past half hour, both Terry and Meryl's adolescent bodies had been in contact with Divine magic and ancient sorcery. Such powerful bouts of energy had the ability to wear upon people twice their size. The fact that they could still stand upright was rather remarkable and a testament to their inner strength.

"No, we can't stop now!" Junior, on the other hand, wasn't tired in the slightest. His previous fatigue had instantly melted away. His mind, now acknowledging what a precarious situation they were in, had released a heavy dose of adrenaline into his bloodstream.

Meryl gave him an odd look, her brow rising at the edginess in Junior's voice and visage.

Clearing his throat, he said loudly into the night air, "I mean, we better get back now. My *Father, the Gold King,* is sure to take notice of my absence seeing as I'm his son! His youngest son... His favourite son... I suspect he'll show up any second now in a blaze of thunder, ready to scold and smite."

There. That did it. Name-dropping Lucien was sure to guarantee their safety... unless he had dropped them all in a bigger pit of danger by exposing himself as the Golden Prince, thereby making them targets for a kidnapping-and-ransom situation. Junior could have kicked himself. Maybe he should've left out the *favourite son* bit.

Oh well, thought Junior, *Father can just electrocute their would-be kidnapper and be done with it.*

Baffled by Junior's behaviour, Meryl stared at the back of his head as they walked on.

"Going by historical accounts, scolding people and smiting them do appear to be two of the King's favourite things," Terry conceded. "He does them both on a consistent basis."

Unlike Meryl, Terry wasn't rattled by Junior's conduct in the slightest. He was used to seeing random flareups from his royal friend. "But you know, I always thought Prince Gabriel was his favourite son," he added.

Junior's shoulders slumped a little. A few minutes ago, by the Tree of Queens, he had felt frightened. Now, he felt frightened and foolish. "Let's just go," he said quietly, helplessly.

They retreated, heading back down in the direction they came.

Meryl and Terry continued to chat, but Junior wasn't paying attention to the conversation being had. The only thing on his mind was getting them back to the campsite posthaste. His unease intensified as he shot a quick glance over his shoulder. He was quite sure he had seen the dark outline of a hooded figure among the trees.

Crap.

His mind was going haywire as he thought up a failsafe plan to implement in case their stalker – or stalkers, for all he knew there was an entire nest of them hiding in the woods – decided to make their presence known.

It was at times like these Junior wished he had already received his Golden Gift, but Lucien had been adamant about making him wait until his 18th birthday to get it. "*You don't need it right now… Besides, you're far too young for it,*" his Father had told him several times in the last five years. It was a bit hypocritical of him, thought Junior as he remembered how his sister had gotten the Gift at age 7… but, of course, Lex was always a *special exception* to everything.

As it turned out, his Father had been wrong, hadn't he? Junior clearly *needed* the supernatural powers that came with the Golden Gift right now. The Prince wagered he could take down any opponent within seconds if he were Gifted. Sure, it took most people decades – sometimes centuries – to properly learn how to utilize the powers from a King's energy, but Junior figured they were slow on the uptake. He was confident he could pick it up as easily as Lex had, if not better.

Everyone had labelled Lex as the Golden Prodigy, but just wait until he turned 18. Michael and Gabriel had been Golden Princes once, but neither of them had been adept at Lucien's Divine energy, and they both had their Golden powers revoked when they left for the Phantom Realm. Junior knew he was different. He would do what his older brothers never could. Someday, he'd show the world what it truly meant to be the Golden Prince…

Junior shook his head. If he wanted to make it to his 18th birthday, he needed to stay focused until they were safely back under the Gold King's Shield. *Think, think, think,* he silently commanded his mind.

To an extent, he already knew what to do. His family had prepared him for kidnapping- and assassination attempts. It wasn't even his first time dealing with such a situation. That was the downside to coming from the most famous Royals in the universe – there was always a target on your back.

The Griffin Scouts of Gold wasn't meant to teach him any real survival skills. It was merely for show. Something to keep Junior occupied and out of trouble. This had been his *real* training:

Run, hide, fight, was what they had taught him. Run away if you can. If it's not safe to run, then hide. If you can't hide, then fight… *"Try to stay calm and don't be afraid, Little Wing. You'll always be safe. The microchip inside your arm will tell us where you are if anything ever happens,"* Lex had told him while lightly massaging a hand down his left arm, where the bio-tracker had been inserted. *"And we'll be there right away."*

Junior sighed lowly, miserably. *Run, hide, fight. But most importantly: buy time and wait for your family to rescue you.* A solid plan, but not entirely flawless.

If only they had a phone with them to call for help. But Terry and Meryl hadn't brought along their devices. There was no point in doing so. It was impossible to get reception in the Neutral desert. They needed a device with a specialized signal booster in order to make calls out here. They needed the kind of top-of-the-line device Lucien had given Lex. It was the same model Lucien had once given Junior … The Prince might've had that device with him tonight … if only his phone privileges hadn't been revoked earlier this year, after he'd been caught making one too many prank calls to C.R.O.W agents.

Junior cursed himself for not anticipating the need for a phone. Lex had a few devices with her for emergencies. He should have swiped one of them from her clutch before leaving the party. Now, he was forced to improvise a solution. He still had his camera strapped around his neck and he knew he could use its flash to temporarily throw off any adversary that got too close; that would give them time to make a run for it. But running would be difficult in the darkness of the woods. This wasn't like the forest near Halkyon City (the Golden capital), which Junior had trekked every summer with Lucien and Lex. He was on unfamiliar grounds.

If he was by his lonesome, Junior might have taken the risk. But he had Terry and Meryl to consider. The Prince was trained to escape, but his friends weren't.

What if it came down to a fight? At least Junior had years of acrobatic training and the experience of a small handful of schoolyard fights under his belt. Terry knew nothing when it came to self-defence. Junior remembered how his friend couldn't even swat a mosquito away as it bit into his arm. Terry had kept holding out his limb, wailing, until Junior slapped the bug dead... And as for Meryl, aside from one or two occasions where she socked Junior for going too far and saying something supremely stupid, she wasn't one for physical altercations either.

As he kept silently asking himself what to do, the solution suddenly became a lot clearer.

"Hey, what's that?" Junior sped toward a nearby fig tree. It was right between the bark and the soil. There were a cluster of shiny crystals of various sizes. Some of the crystals were attached together at the end but shot up with spiky edges sticking out, resembling the towers of a castle perched on a rocky island.

The crystals were all arranged rather neatly beside the large tree as though someone had purposely set them there for display purposes. Junior didn't know why they hadn't spotted it before, and he didn't have time to care. He got to his knees and promptly began snatching up some of the larger crystals.

Terry came up behind him. Reclaiming the torchlight, Terry directed it toward a nearby sign.

"Those are Phantom Quartzes," said Terry, reading from the sign, which stated:

A Quartz is usually a clear crystal. A Phantom Quartz occurs when the growth of a crystal is interrupted by mineral deposits. As the quartz continues to grow, each mineral deposit grows within it as well... They're called Phantom Quartzes because they hold the appearance of one stone haunting another. These quartzes allegedly have many different spiritual properties. It's said they can help people recover repressed memories, undergo past life regression, and even take them between lives and realities... Please do not touch or take possession of these crystals as they're properties of the Godshoots Forest Committee ...

"How fascinating." Terry shifted the light back down to where Junior was crouched. "Look at those, over there on the right. Some of these have gold deposits in them ... I suppose you could call them *Golden Phantoms* then," he said with a silly little laugh as though he'd made the cleverest joke. "Do you get it, Junior? Golden Phantoms? Because your family is –"

"Yeah, yeah, I get it," said Junior. He wasn't even half-listening, focused as he was at commandeering the crystals. He put a few of them in his pockets and a couple others in his bag. Junior figured the phantom quartzes were sharp enough to make decent murder weapons. Not that they were aiming to *kill* anybody. The Prince simply wanted to be armed, just in case. He learned that from his training as well. He had to make weapons out of his surroundings should the situation call for extreme measures.

"We're not supposed to take those," said Terry. "They belong to the Forest Committee."

"So what?" said Junior dismissively.

"You're going to steal them?"

"I'm liberating them."

"But—"

"Look, it's perfectly fine. This whole forest pretty much belongs to my Father anyway."

The committee reported to the Convocation of Kings, which his Father led as a founding member. The way Junior saw it, Lucien practically owned this forest, and what belonged to the Father, belonged to the son as well.

"Why do you even want them?" Meryl's brows narrowed in suspicion.

"Oh… er… it's a gift for Lexie," said Junior. "She goes crazy for crystals." There was a tiny kernel of truth to his words. Lex did adore her shiny rock collection.

"Isn't her birthday months away?" Meryl could tell he was lying.

"Didn't say it was for her birthday, did I?" said Junior, a little irritably.

"It's probably one of his atonement gifts," Terry told Meryl.

"Atonement gifts?" echoed Meryl.

"You know, whenever he messes up and needs to beg forgiveness," explained Terry. "Junior always has an atonement gift at the ready… They're great. I once got a new thoroughbred after that time he shaved my left eyebrow while I was sleeping."

"It grew back, didn't it?" muttered Junior as he tapped on the tip of a phantom quartz and lightly tested its serration.

Meryl rolled her eyes at them. Only boys could play such ridiculous pranks on one another and remain friends. "I understand the concept," she said. "What I don't understand is how come I've never received one from him. I think I'm owed plenty of atonement gifts from you, Junior."

"For what?" frowned Junior. "What did I ever do to you?"

"What did you do? *What did you do?*" mocked Meryl. "Gee, I don't know, how about *my* birthday party last year? Remember that! You just had to bring a bunch of bows, arrows and matches, and make everyone play *flamethrower* tag—"

She didn't get a chance to finish as a loud hoarse screech and the flapping of broad wings blasted from behind. The three of them quickly shot up and away from the tree. Terry had dropped the torch in fright. But even in the darkness, the trio could easily make out the two birds of prey soaring several feet above them. They each had a set of angry golden eyes, a hooked beak, and a large chest of black-and-white-striped feathers.

Going by their intimidating appearance, they were clearly raptors.

"Don't scream." Junior acted quickly, pulling both Terry and Meryl behind him as best as he could. "Easy," he whispered, keeping eye contact with their two new problems. "Easy."

"They're goshawks," murmured Terry as he clutched onto Junior's right arm.

"I know," said Junior. Lex had taken him bird-watching last year during their trip to the Indigo Kingdom. They had seen a goshawk hunting in a forest. It had been an incredible sight. The bird wasn't that big – no taller than two feet and weighing no more than two pounds – and yet, it had managed to take down a buzzard twice its size for lunch in less than a minute.

These birds, however, were unusually large. At a glance, they looked around 4 feet, possibly weighing a little more than 10 pounds.

It was as Terry had said earlier on, *"If the Tree of Queens is here, then its fruit would be available to all the animals in residence. Perhaps consuming the fruit is what caused such abnormal growth in that beetle."*

Mankind was obviously barred from utilizing the Tree of Queens, but it appeared animals were given a free dining pass.

"They won't hurt us, right?" Meryl said in a hushed voice, her hands tight on Junior's other arm. "Birds don't hurt people," she added, even though the birds in front of them certainly looked like they were programmed to inflict the greatest of pain.

Junior wasn't sure whether to lie to her or not. If he lied to his friends, they might let their guards down and put themselves in even more danger. He couldn't risk that happening.

It would've been easier if these were normal goshawks. At their standard sizes, they wouldn't have been able to kill them. Unfortunately, whatever supernatural steroids these goshawks had guzzled down amplified their physical prowess. They certainly looked like they could scratch them all up and leave them worse for wear.

Junior tried to recall what Lex had said about goshawks. *"Fear not, Little Wing,"* she had told him as they watched the goshawk tear into its lunch from a safe distance. *"They're very tolerant of people, provided we're nowhere near their nests or their nesting trees. They're highly territorial and protective over such things."*

The Prince had a gut feeling that if he lifted his eyes upward at the large tree beside them, he'd spot a nest of goshawk eggs perched on a thick branch. *Crap*, he thought as he gazed up at the two enraged-looking raptors flying atop their heads. Junior had spent so much energy worrying about earthbound assailants that he hadn't considered all his surroundings.

"Listen to me," he said quickly and quietly to his friends without dropping eye-contact with the birds, "On the count of three, run. Don't look back, just run. Got it?"

He didn't have to turn around to know that Meryl and Terry were nodding in unison.

"One ... two ... three."

The birds shrieked as the flash went off on Junior's camera.

Meryl and Terry didn't waste time hightailing it down the path leading back to the sandy floor of the desert. As per their Prince's instructions, neither of them had looked back. If they had, they might have noticed that Junior wasn't behind them.

Chapter 13:
God, Allah, Yahweh, Buddha, Zeus...
What do the Hindus call God?

The Prince had taken a different direction. Knowing that goshawks preferred to hunt in the forest, he strayed from the earthed path and ran straight into the woods.

"They love to twist among branches and rumble through thickets in their pursuit," Lex had told him with an excitable, dramatic flare of her arms. Basically, like many raptors, they didn't enjoy an easy kill. They preferred to savour the hunt. They played with their food.

His friends would call him reckless and stupid for endangering himself in such a way, but he wasn't either of those things. Junior had made a very calculated and considerate decision. Birds of prey liked to single one out of a flock, didn't they? Junior was faster, stronger and more agile than his two friends. Making himself the target meant Terry and Meryl could get away unscathed.

It was his fault they were in this mess, so it was his job to get them out of it. Even if it hadn't been his fault, he would still be accountable for their safety. His Father-King had always insisted that the welfare of every Goldizen (Golden citizen) was their responsibility. The way Junior saw it, as the sole Golden Prince, he had a duty to protect his subjects, especially those who couldn't protect themselves.

As for protecting himself… well, he was already *Divinely protected*. Wasn't that what Lucien had declared earlier today? Junior was the first child to be born of two Kings and his Father was the most powerful monarch on the planet. No one would harm him. No one would dare—A vicious screech rang through the air once more.

"AHHHHH!" Junior screamed. Apparently these two raptors didn't get the memo that the Golden Prince was a special snowflake.

With his heart hammering away, Junior ran. He didn't linger at the towering trees that cast dark shadows across the forest floor. He didn't gaze up at the starry sky. He didn't look back. He most certainly did not look back. He'd seen enough horror movies to know how that turned out.

He could hear the flapping of wings behind him, fast-approaching. Still, he ran as fast as he could, dodging dark trees with long branches. Some of the trees ahead of him were fused together in inosculation; they had open spaces between them that looked like keyholes. Luckily, Junior was so slim he could easily jump through the gaps.

It was easier to run in a straight line instead of trailing around trees, but Junior wasn't sure if it was the right tactic. This was a flight response, but he couldn't remember the correct way to execute it. Was he supposed to run in a zigzag pattern? Or did that only work with one assailant? What was he supposed to do again if there were multiple attackers? The correct answer was sitting somewhere inside his mind. Unfortunately, his brain refused to present him with any solutions beyond the obvious, RUN!!!!!!!!

He knew he could go faster if he discarded his bag and camera. But he also knew the chances of him outrunning two ambush predators was slim. There was no way he could surpass two beings who could see through the dark and fly faster than he could run. He suspected the only reason was he was still ahead of them was because he was running on pure adrenaline.

If they caught him, he still had a good chance of deflecting their attacks with another flash or he could try to defend himself with some of the phantom quartzes he'd taken.

Now close behind, the goshawks were screeching away. *So loud and dramatic*, thought Junior, *They'd get on well with Father.*

Speaking of his Father, what would Lucien do in such a situation? Junior quickly shook his head. It was a dumb question because he knew Lucien would never flee from anything. He was a King. He never had anything to fear. If anything, *Fear* itself was probably terrified of his Father.

Junior remembered seeing footage of a time, long before he was born, when a group of assassins had tried to publicly execute Lucien. They had him locked in a circle with their weapons out, ready to fire. Lucien didn't move; he didn't so much as flinch. He stayed put, his eyes wandering around them in a vacant stare. He didn't do anything at all – yet it only took less than a fraction of a second for all the men to drop their weapons and prostrate themselves before the Gold King.

There were plenty of other instances similar, if not congruent, to that moment – like the time the Golden Family stumbled across a pride of lions on a safari, and they all bowed their manes and *kneeled* at the mere sight of Lucien.

The Prince didn't understand how his Father-King did it. It was like Lucien was doing nothing yet expecting everything to naturally fall into place for him. Miraculously enough, it always did.

Junior shook off his thoughts. Dwelling on his Father wasn't helpful right now. He wasn't like the man who sired him. He was nowhere near the Gold King's level, and he was quite sure the gruesome twosome behind him wouldn't be showing him a lick of deference anytime soon.

He had to think of another way to get out of this and fast, but what? *Lexie!* His sister was great at coming up with easy solutions to difficult situations. What would she do?

"Never underestimate the power of positive thinking," Lex had told him once during one of their conversations. Well, she had labelled it a conversation. Junior had seen it as a lecture. He knew the difference. Conversations were two-sided; lectures weren't. *"Our minds are our greatest gift, Little Wing. Our minds do whatever we tell it to do, and its job is to reflect the evidence of our thoughts in our reality. That's why it's important to always think good thoughts, especially about oneself."* Then, with a flip of her hair over one shoulder, she had added, *"Now, here are 222 easy-to-remember self-concept affirmations I tell myself every morning. Number 1: I am at peace with myself. Number 2: I am beautiful inside and out. Number 3: I trust my decisions. Number 4…"*

Junior had zoned out of Lex's lousy affirmations before she got to Number 5. Nevertheless, he understood the gist of it: all he had to do was think good thoughts. He could do that. His mind was required to manifest anything that was going on in his head, was it? Then so be it. *I'm safe. I'm safe. I'm safe,* he kept telling himself as he ran. *Yes, I'm safe. I'm Divinely protected, I am.*

Look at me. I came from my Father's loins, so I'm perfectly safe. I'm safe. I'm safe. I'm safe. I'm s—

Another series of rapid-fire bird-screeches echoed across the forest. Junior ran faster. *AHHHH, I'M GONNNA DIIIEEEEE!!!!!!!* His internal screams were manifesting nothing but tears on his face. *Your stupid affirmations aren't working, Lexie!!!*

Lex's voice suddenly shot back into his head, *"Of course, should all else fail, you can always stop and think of God instead. That's what Father would tell me when I was your age. He'd say, 'Lexie, thinking of God will help you withstand the world and bend it to your will. That's what He'll do for you, if you'll only let Him.'"*

Junior wasn't one for religion. Even if he was, he wasn't sure God would come through for him, especially if the Almighty was still holding a grudge over that time Junior (then age 6) had relieved himself in a fountain of holy water during church service. Still, desperate times …

God, God, God, God… God… God … God … Allah… Yahweh… Buddha… Zeus, Hades, Poseidon … Who the hell was out there? Who else was left? … What did the Hindus call God? Oh, they had multiple gods, didn't they? Or was it several gods that reported up to one big God? … Curses, he couldn't remember.

Immersed as he was thinking of God(s), he failed to catch sight of a massive tree roots sticking out of the ground and promptly tripped over it, falling face flat onto the earth.

Junior groaned in pain as he tried to scramble himself back upright. From the corner of his eye, he could see one of the goshawks coming right at him, talons gleaming under the moonlight.

This is so unfair, he thought miserably as he expected the worse. He was about to be disassembled by a couple of birds. Ironic considering his family had laws in place back home to protect birds of all varieties from being hunted – except for chicken and capon, apparently.

The Prince quickly ducked his head and covered his face as the talons drew near.

Luckily for him, what he expected to happen right then, didn't.

A long, raspy hiss rung through the air.

Junior slowly raised his head when he realized that not a single claw had touched his precious head.

He lifted his eyes to see the dark plumage of his saviour flying in the air. It was a bit larger than the goshawks with a broad wingspan of nine feet, if not more. In contrast to its large body, it had a rather short tail and a small head with a dark, curved beak. It was a vulture.

With the way it was spreading out its wings, Junior got the sense it was trying to protect him by blocking the goshawks' path. The dark bird made another drawn-out hissing sound. The goshawks responded with their own shrieks.

Junior decided not to stick around and eavesdrop on their argument any further. Rushing to his feet, he staggered back into a run.

He didn't have to look over his shoulder to know what was happening. He could hear the three birds duking it out, screaming and flapping about. He felt a little guilty. If what Terry had said about vultures was true, then there was no way his unforeseen rescuer – despite being bigger in size – would be able to overtake a bird of prey, let alone two of them.

Still… better him than me.

Junior ran and ran, and he didn't stop running until he stumbled onto another earthed path on the other side of the forest.

Chapter 14:
You wouldn't leave me here alone with nothing but faith and fear... would you?

The Griffin Cub Scouts proved useful after all.

In the absence of advanced technology, the Griffin Cubs had taught the Prince how to read a compass and the stars for navigation. Thanks to their lessons and the compass he had brought along, Junior was able to steer himself in the right direction. He took a few turns and continued down another footpath lined with trees until he saw it: sand!

Thank God.

Relief washed over Junior. Beyond that stretch of sand was the light at the end of the tunnel. Lucien's dome-shaped Shield was radiating over the party's campsite, glowing like a pot of gold beneath a rainbow.

The campsite was distant, but the Shield was visible. All Junior had to do was keep walking toward it. The path ahead of him was clear and he was starting to feel a sense of reassurance.

That wonderful sensation was short-lived.

In an instant, his knees hit the ground. The compass fell from Junior's palm. His hands flew up to his ears, clutching them in pain. A high-pitched shriek blasted into his brain. It sounded beastly and savage, like a mating call and a murder all at once.

Blinking rapidly, he peered up to find a flash of silver hovering above the path, a few feet away from him.

It was the same flare he had seen before sundown. The one Junior had mistaken for a comet. The same one Lex had dismissed as a cloud. It definitely wasn't cloud-like. It wasn't a comet either. It looked more like an unsteady silver flame.

Wincing, with his palms still over his ears, he got up and trudged forward. Upon closer inspection, Junior discovered it wasn't as polished or as shiny as he had originally thought. The flare had a darker, more muted tone. It was more grey than silver.

"Can you please cut that out?" said Junior, referring to the horrendous death whistle the entity was emitting.

The sound immediately ceased. The grey flare flickered under the moonlight. Junior got the impression it was apologizing.

Junior dropped his hands to his sides. As he stepped forward, closer to the flare, he heard a boot against a fallen branch. Wheeling his head to the right, he saw the hooded figure from before, standing next to a large oak tree.

Distracted as he was by the goshawks, the Prince had forgotten all about their pursuer. Junior instantly recognized the steely feline-mask on their face. It reminded him of the iron masks he'd seen in history books. The kind his Father-King used to make captives wear whilst travelling between penitentiaries.

And, if his eyes weren't deceiving him, the lurker was wearing the same lazurite-coloured ankle-length robe as some of the members of that cat-worshipping cult he and his family had come across earlier today. The stranger was dressed a little differently, with trousers to accompany his robe and a shabby pair of boots, but there was no denying that the person nearby was *that boy*.

Lex had insisted that particular pagan ritual was exclusive to women. No boys allowed. But Junior was certain she was wrong. Even though he had no proof, his instinct was telling him the person nearby was a boy his own age.

"Knowledge is important, but instinct... Instinct transcends all sense of reason and logic," his Father had told him once.

There was a moment where the two boys kept looking dumbly between each other and the grey flare. Neither one of them seemed to understand what was happening. The flare was molding itself, going from round to oval to other bizarre shapes, like it was a little kid who couldn't make up their mind on what they wanted to be for All Hallow's Eve.

It sculpted itself into a bird. Then a lion. Then a griffin. Then a snake...A butterfly. A dragon... A vulture. A lioness. A vulture. A lioness once more. A vulture again.

With another ear-piercing shriek, the flare returned to its discoidal form. It twinkled as though it were laughing at them before flying fast into the forest.

The hooded figure didn't hesitate. Neither did Junior. They both ran. The hunt was on.

This time, Junior could admit he really was being stupid and reckless. Had he kept going down the earthed path, he would've eventually hit sand and returned to his family. Instead, he'd sprinted back into to the blackness of the woods to chase down some weird grey-ghostly-puffball. He didn't know what it was or why he was chasing after it. All he knew was that he had to get to it before the other boy did. He had a feeling the flare would know exactly what it wanted to morph into, but it would all depend on which boy reached it first.

They ran for a bit, until the Prince caught up to his rival. Grabbing at the hood of the boy's ceremonial robe, Junior gave it a strong yank. "Back off, you cat-mummifying-culty-creep! It's mine!"

The boy's cowl flew back, revealing a short mane of dark hair. He nearly stumbled on his feet but quickly regained his balance.

The boy turned around and promptly socked Junior in the face.

Clocked on his chin, Junior was left briefly disoriented. It didn't hurt that much, but still—

"Hey! You hit me!" Junior snarled, rubbing his chin, appalled.

Junior could see the boy's thick brows and brown eyes through the large optical cut-outs on his mask. His eyes were soft and youthful with long, delicate lashes. They kind of reminded him of Porki's eyes.

The boy blinked at him. *Well... yeah*, his bashful eyes seemed to say. He appeared surprised at his own response, as if he hadn't intended to hit the Prince, but couldn't resist the instinctive urge to do so.

They stood opposite each other like mirror reflections.

The other boy was slightly bigger than Junior in size and stature. But that wasn't enough to deter him.

Like a prepubescent Spartan warrior, the Prince released his battle cry and charged. "BWAAAHHHHH!!!!"

The boy winced as Junior grabbed him around the waist and shoved him into a nearby tree.

The fight that ensued was clumsy and callow. They came at each other much like birds of prey, screeching and snarling with their talons clashing and clasping. Next thing they knew, they were free-falling into the earth. The boys lacked all finesse, coming across silly and unrefined as they rolled around the forest floor.

"I knew it!" Junior growled at him as they fought, chests colliding. "I knew your breasts were too flat to be a girl!"

Locked-in at close range, Junior was able to get a better look at the cat-mask that spanned across the boy's face, providing cutouts for the eyes and mouth.

143

The mask was made of metal. From a distance, it had looked like gold. Up close, Junior knew better. It wasn't real gold. It was likely pyrite, a.k.a *fool's gold*. He'd been around real gold all his life to know the difference. Whereas gold was shiny and solid, pyrite was far too brassy and brittle. Nevertheless, pyrite was a metal with some durability, which told Junior one thing: he couldn't go for the face.

Junior wasn't going to risk breaking his hands by punching his rival's metallic face. He couldn't even if he wanted to, not with the way their palms were locked together.

He was lucky the boy didn't attempt a head-butt. Maybe the boy was being nice. Or maybe he wasn't smart enough to consider it. Or maybe, he was nice and stupid at the same time, which was a highly unfortunate combination of personality traits. Whatever the reason, it worked in the Prince's favour. Junior knew he wouldn't have been able to recover quickly from a hit to the head.

Junior's satchel was still wrapped across his body. As the pair wrestled, the vial of Unseen, along with some of the crystals he had confiscated, tumbled out of his bag and rolled across the forest floor. If Junior's hands weren't latched on to the other boy's palms, he would've attempted to reach for one of the golden-phantom quartzes and use it as a weapon.

The Prince wished he could hit the boy's solar plexus. Body shots were no joke. A solid strike to the ribs would've left a mental imprint and ended the fight. But it was difficult for either boy to land a single punch with their hands clasped together. So, instead, they settled for kicking at each other's legs. This was accompanied with a lot of unnecessary teeth-baring, growling, and hissing.

In the future, when these boys shifted from awkward adolescence into awkward adulthood, their combative competence would be much improved. They'd still be two ridiculous men, but at least they'd be ridiculous men who knew how to fight. One man would expel rapid jab-hook-rear hook combos. The other would block and respond with a lethal jab-hook-upper cut. There would be painful punt kicks and bruising spin kicks. It would be a beautiful display of strength, balance, flexibility, discipline, and concentration.

But for now, they were kids. Two fetuses wrestling in the mud.

They left the flare no choice but to fire off another death whistle. This time, it sounded slightly less murderous, but no less furious. *KNOCK IT OFF,* was the screech-to-text translation Junior's mind had made.

The boys released one another with a groan and sprawled across the dirt, laying side by side like a pair of sleepy starfishes.

They didn't stay in that pose for long.

From his peripheral vision, Junior could see the grey flare floating around, taunting them, tempting them. Without hesitation, he grabbed a small handful of dirt and threw it over the boy's eyes. With his rival effectively distracted, Junior staggered to his feet and shot after the mysterious entity.

The chase resumed.

Junior was now in the lead, but much to his ire, his foe was hot on his heels.

The boys followed the grey light as it journeyed around tall trees and reached a body of water by the border between sand and forestry. It turned out, Junior and Terry had been wrong earlier. The water hadn't come from a well, as they had assumed, but from a natural spring.

After sprinting around the spring, they reached a muddy patch where the sand and water meshed. The boy ran around it. Junior, however, ran right into it, and quickly found that he couldn't go any further. He was stuck... even worse, he was stuck and sinking.

"What's going on?!" Junior shrieked in alarm. He couldn't move his legs at all. The ground had swallowed him up at the ankles and was devouring away.

The boy stopped in his tracks, returning to Junior. The grey flare shone behind the boy, encasing his entire head. It reminded the Prince of the halos in religious iconography where they had plain, round circles depicted behind the heads of saints, prophets, angels, and Kings.

They shared a look of mutual panic as they assessed Junior's dilemma. Before either of them could get a word out, the death whistle blasted on replay. Their eyes slammed shut in agony. The mating-murder screech felt like it had ridden a cue-tip into their brains.

The physical torment only lasted for a few seconds. What came after, however, was far more frightening. In that moment, neither of them could hear anything. Not the water from the spring, nor the insects and the birds. They couldn't even hear the ever-present rumbling of the dunes anymore. It felt strange and scary, experiencing the world without sound for the first time.

When they opened their eyes, all they could see was grey.

The round grey flare was glistening before them, taunting and tempting them all over again.

It made no sense. Logically, Junior knew he should be panicking. The earth was eating him, and he was pretty sure he had gone deaf. But his intuition was telling him – no, it was *commanding* him – to stop and pay attention to the flare.

There was a long, burning stretch of silence. Until finally, they heard it speak. Its androgynous voice was like a melodious representation of the biblical wilderness. Its tone was as enchanting as Eve, and as cool as the serpent in the Garden of Eden, as it told them:

You can have me forever
if you catch me here in the wild.
Oh, I know you well, lost child.
You were last in birth,
but I shall make you first by Divine right.
Present you with privilege and power,
I shall let you cast a grey veil in the direst hour.
Your enemies are blessed with great might,
But I shall leave them staggering without sight.
I shall make them cringe, cry, and cower,
but only if you win me here and catch my power.
Come to me now before I disappear
and leave you alone in this world with nothing but faith and fear.

With those devastating remarks, the voice left them.

The two young men blinked. It was like an enchantment had been lifted. The sounds of nature came back to them with speed and ease. Their ears were no longer bleeding. They could hear the song of sand dunes once again.

The grey flare began flying away, its light fading fast while Junior was sinking swiftly.

The voice was long gone, but even with its final flickers, the flare kept provoking them. Every dwindling blink of light seemed to say, *Catch me now or lose me forever.*

Junior wanted desperately to go after it, but he couldn't.

The boy began running toward the flare, ready to chase and catch, ready to leave his rival in the dust. But then he heard the terrified and chilling sound of Junior's wail as he sank further into the sand.

With a frustrated huff, the boy halted, made another about-face and dashed back to Junior, taking care to avoid the muddy area the Prince had stepped into.

"What's happening to me?" Junior's voice was panicky, but inwardly, he felt a little relieved that he hadn't been abandoned. The momentary relief vanished as the ground pulled him down again and started soaking up his calves.

The boy responded in an unknown language that Junior couldn't pinpoint. Was he speaking in one of those non-tellurian languages? Judging by his eyes, the boy appeared to be human, but perhaps he was from one of those planets where they merely *looked* human – human-passing, as it was called. That would certainly explain the strange language.

Then, Junior remembered the boy came from that cat-worshipping sect. Lex had told him they were paying tribute to an Ancient Egyptian god. If the boy belonged to them, then Junior suspected he was speaking one of the Old Earth Languages that civilizations used long before the Golden Bang. They were considered dead dialects, practically extinct for ages. Clearly, they weren't dead enough if there were people still using them.

"Sorry, I don't understand you," said Junior. "Can you speak the Earth Standard Sole?"

The boy scrunched his eyebrows in frustration. "Kwikzend?" he tried to explain.

"Kwikzend?"

"Kwikzend." The boy nodded.

"Kwikzend?" Junior repeated. "Kwikzend…Qwik? Quick? Quick-zend … quick-send…quick-sand …Quicksand??!!!"

The boy nodded vigorously.

"Pfftt, catch yourself on!" Junior shook his head outrageously. "There's no quicksand in the desert! That's nothing but a myth."

The boy couldn't speak Earth Standard, but it was becoming obvious that he could understand Junior well enough. He responded in his native language as he gestured wildly toward the natural spring and then back down at the sand.

"Oh … right," groaned Junior, suddenly grasping the situation.

A natural spring. Saturated soil. The granularity of sand. Put all three together and you get quicksand.

Quicksand wasn't something one came across very often in the bone-dry desert. It was rare, but it was possible, provided there was a source of upward-flowing water present. Water from the spring must have seeped through the soil and saturated the sand below.

Whenever water flooded into sand, it drove the sand particles apart, causing the ground to loosen. In due course, it would leave a soggy combination of sand and water that could no longer support as much weight; so, when you stood on it, you started to sink. Right now, Junior's weight was pushing water away from the sand, creating a vacuum around his legs and pulling him south.

"Well, don't just stand there gaping!" Junior shouted at the boy as he held out his hands. "GET. ME. OUT OF HERE!!!!"

The boy jumped to attention. He bent his knees in a squat, grabbed hold of Junior's arms, and began to pull. For the next few minutes, he tried with all his might to extract the Prince.

When that didn't work, they discarded the remaining contents of Junior's satchel. There wasn't much left inside after their wrestling match in the woods. Once emptied, the boy tried using the bag's handle as a makeshift piece of rope to pull Junior out. But the more effort they put into it the extraction, the more the ground continued to engulf Junior.

Chapter 15:
If I die, will you fly down and bring me back?

Five minutes in and they hadn't made any progress. If anything, things had gotten much worse. Junior could no longer see his knees; his legs were completely submerged in the muddy water.

The Prince couldn't understand it. Getting out of quicksand looked easy enough in movies where all one needed to do was grab a tree branch and wiggle out of it. In reality, wiggling provided the opposite result. It also wasn't enough having another person – in this case, a random, lanky young boy – try to yank him out. What neither boy knew was that pulling

Junior's legs free would require the same amount of force needed to lift a tractor.

The boy sat back on the sand, hugging his knees in apprehension, and panting in exertion. He still had his mask on. Junior didn't understand why he wouldn't remove it. He was sure the boy was sweating like the Devil's bathroom underneath that covering.

"You can take your mask off, you know?"

The boy shook his head.

"Suit yourself," shrugged Junior.

The boy had kind eyes, but that wasn't enough to judge his aesthetic appeal. Junior figured the boy must have the ugliest face in the world. Why else would he be so hellbent on hiding it?

The Prince released a long breath. He tried to remain as still as possible since the more he shook and squirmed, the further he sunk. Not that he could really move much anymore. His legs felt like they were stuck in concrete, and the pressure was starting to stop his blood flow.

"What do you think happened to that thing?" Junior asked, gesturing over to the spot where the enigmatic flare had disappeared. He didn't really care anymore, but he needed some type of distraction to keep his nerves at bay.

The boy said something with a mild shrug that Junior interpreted as a weary "*I dunno.*"

"Do you know what it was?"

The boy shook his head.

Junior lifted his eyes and gazed helplessly up at the night sky. He was trying his hardest not to cry.

Where were Meryl and Terry? They should've made it back to the campsite by now. They should've realized Junior wasn't with them and alerted his family. At this point, Lex would've sent out a rescue party. Better still, Lucien would've flown right over here himself to save his son. It would've taken him less than three seconds to get here with his flight powers.

He sighed. He was starting to wish he had stayed back and taken his chances with the raptors. Or better yet, he wished he had followed Porki's advice and never left the party.

Peering over at the boy again, he asked, "Can't you go get help? Isn't there anyone else you can turn to for help?"

Junior had considered telling him to run to his Father's party for assistance, but the boy couldn't even speak the Earth Standard Sole.

No one there would understand him, thought Junior miserably.

It wasn't true. Lex was well-versed in many languages, both global and galactic, modern and ancient. She might've been able to grasp the boy's words. But Junior wasn't aware of this. Not because Lex had never told him, but because he never paid enough attention.

"What about those pagan ladies?" Junior pressed when the boy didn't respond. "Aren't you here with them?"

The boy ran his hands through his hair in frustration. He looked as though he was racking his brain for a solution. Raising his eyes, he turned toward the Prince. He then gave a lengthy response, which Junior couldn't decrypt in the slightest.

Frowning at Junior's lack of comprehension, the boy irritably huffed out, "Far."

"Oh," murmured Junior. "They're too far, huh? I'm guessing by the time they get here, this place would've already had me for an appetizer."

Junior wasn't worried about sinking completely. Quicksand was far denser than the human body. It was impossible to be completely submerged by it. The concerning part was that he was nearly waist-deep in saturated sand; if he sank any further, it would cause more pressure on his heart, which would stop him from breathing altogether.

"Also," said Junior, "a wild guess on my part, but you're not supposed to be here anymore than I am, are you?"

The boy shook his head.

Junior remembered the people the boy accompanied. At first, the Prince had been cheered on by the cat-cult ladies after cartwheeling himself into their ritual. But their warm welcome had quickly turned into icy indifference at the sight of his Father. They all knew who Gold King Lucien was; his reputation preceded him. Their sudden change in demeanour reminded Junior how much of a polarizing figure his Father was outside of the Golden realm. He was a cherished King to many people, but also a cruel conqueror to numerous others. There was a fine line between monarch and monster, and Lucien was often teeter-tottering on the fence.

Even if the boy got to those priestesses in the nick of time, Junior wasn't sure they'd be willing to help the Gold King's son.

"You gonna get in trouble for this?"

The boy was now sitting cross-legged on the sand. Lifting a dark brow at the question, he eyed the Prince up and down. His eyes scrutinized Junior the same way Porki did whenever he felt like his friend was being an idiot. The boy's eyes were much easier to understand than his words, and this one clearly said, *You're the one who's in trouble, Idiot.*

Slightly offended by the unspoken remark, Junior said, "Well, you ought to get in trouble for this. It's all your fault, you know?" Then, at the boy's narrowed brows, Junior added, "I thought you were an assassin or a kidnapper... or a perv lurking about in those woods like that. What were you even doing out there? Taking a piss?"

The boy's eyebrows remained knitted together in irritation. He replied in his native tongue. Junior got the feeling the boy wasn't really answering him, but echoing his inquiry in a curt manner. "*What were you doing there?*" He seemed to say.

"Whatever." Junior snorted. "It still stands that if it weren't for you, I wouldn't have been anywhere near those crystals next to that nesting tree. Then I wouldn't have ticked off those blasted birds and ran into the forest and caught sight of that … thing… whatever it was. The way I see it, *you're* the one who knocked over the first domino in this series of unfortunate events … So yeah," and with a finger pointed at the boy for emphasis, "Your fault."

They both looked away from one another in annoyance.

Another bout of silence followed.

Junior sighed, acknowledging that perhaps he wasn't being entirely fair. It wasn't the boy's fault Junior had gone into the woods in search for the Tree of Queens. And whoever he was, he had stopped to help the Prince. He could've left him here to perish. But he didn't.

"Sorry," Junior said softly. "I know it's not your fault – not all of it, at least – and I'm sorry for throwing dirt in your eyes and calling you a cat-cun—" he coughed intentionally. "Cat-*culty*-creep. I know you're not really a creep. I bet you wouldn't look like one if you took that mask off. I bet you'd look like—"

Junior paused midsentence. *I bet you'd look like someone I'd be friends with*, was what he was going to say. The boy's energy reminded him of his best friends. It was something in the boy's eyes. There was a kindness that reminded him of Terry, a spark that was reminiscent of Meryl, and a wisdom that brought Porki back into his mind.

We could be friends, you know? If you want to? He was going to say it. Perhaps he should have said it. But he didn't.

"Anyway, I guess what I'm trying to say is … thanks … thanks for not leaving me stranded out here… Say, why did you come back to help me?"

The boy didn't answer, but in the privacy of his mind, he was thinking, *I know what it's like to be left behind.*

The Prince, of course, couldn't read minds. He could only assume the boy was regretting his decision to help him.

"Look… er…" Junior rubbed the back of his neck. "I want you to know I would've done the same for you."

The boy snapped his eyes back to Junior.

"OK, OK," huffed Junior, "I don't know what I woulda done, alright! No need to give me the stink eye! What? Have you been taking lessons from my family?"

Upon hearing the word *family*, the boy's eyes softened, turning a little apologetic as he said something to Junior. "*I'm sorry. I know you're scared… I'll try my best to save you. But if I can't… then I promise to stay with you until your heart stops beating.*"

It was a blessing the Prince couldn't understand him. The boy's words would *not* have been any comfort to him.

"Errr…. yeahhhh, I have no clue what you just said." The Prince shook his head. "OK, let's talk names. Names are easy. I never got yours. I'm Princ—My name's Lucien Justus Rex, but everyone calls me Junior."

He waited expectantly for the boy to say his name.

When the boy gave him nothing, Junior tried again. "What's your name?" Gesturing between himself and the boy, he said slowly, "Me, Junior…You?"

The boy offered up a lengthy response, but it didn't sound like a name. It sounded more like an explanation.

If only he had some type of translation device on hand, then Junior might've known the boy had said, "*I can not tell you. It's private. The declaration of a person's name is an invocation of their soul.*"

"Oookkkkayyy… how old are you then?" Pointing to the boy's face, he said, "I can't tell with that mask on."

With one long finger, the boy wrote a two-digit number on the sand beside him. Thankfully, numbers were a universal language that everyone understood. That's how humanity had originally communicated with the ancient aliens. They relied on numbers when words were meaningless.

"Oh," nodded Junior, unsurprised. "We're almost the same age. I had a feeling we would be." Holding up two fingers to represent a V, he said, "I'm a valensman. How about you?"

The boy nodded, copying his V hand-sign.

"Oh, yeah, I figured as much," lied Junior.

The Prince was mildly surprised to discover the boy was a valensmen. Junior had assumed that if he was human, he'd be a primigen. It was something in the boy's eyes, a sparkle of anxiety that revealed itself when they were fighting in close range.

Valensmen (homo vis) and primigens (homo sapiens) were two species of human that projected two very different energies. A primigen always had a heavy layer of hunger and impatience behind their eyes. Time was their enemy, and so they were desperate to achieve and obtain everything in the span of a few decades. Valensmen, by contrast, could wait it out. They could let centuries slip by with ease and make their mark over many millennia.

That said, valensmen weren't immortal. They could die with as much speed, absurdity, and abruptness as their primigenious counterparts.

How pathetic would it be for a valensman like Junior to die like this? He hadn't even completed his Second Decade of life yet let alone his Second Millennia.

Junior used to have nightmares about dying. Still did, on occasion. When he woke up, Lucien and Lex were always there to comfort him.

"You're not going to die, Little Wing," Lex would tell him after every bad dream. She'd wrap him in her slender arms and rock him back to sleep. "Even if you do, I promise to fly down and bring you back."

Junior frowned at her. "Don't you mean fly up?"

"No."

Lex had called it from the get-go. She knew her menace of a little brother was headed south.

How Junior wished Lex and Lucien were here now to save him, soothe him. He'd even be ecstatic to hear them scold him.

Looking helplessly at the sand bubbling beneath him, Junior asked, "So, where are you from?" At his silence, the Prince carried on, "My sister says your cult – errr, your coven – covenant is part of the Ancient Ones from the Ancient Gods back in the Ancient Days… Even if that's true, you can't be *from here*. There's no way. The Neutral Realm is not really a Kingdom. No one's allowed to live here permanently."

When nothing came, Junior glanced over at the boy to find him staring up at the stars, all dazed and glossy-eyed.

The boy's sudden change was a little disturbing. The fatigue in his eyes was now replaced with a hopeful gleam. Coming to a stand, the boy began speaking with his eyes rolled up so high, Junior couldn't see his irises anymore.

"What's going on?" demanded Junior, a nervous edge to his voice. "Who are you talking to?" Lifting his eyes up to the same sky, he couldn't see anything except the stars and the moon. There was nothing else there but air.

"Hey, snap out of it!" Junior loudly snapped his fingers at the boy's general direction. When the boy ignored him, Junior shouted, "What the hell is wrong with you? Why are you talking to the air?!"

The boy nodded firmly up at the sky. When his gaze plunged back down, Junior realized he might have been safer with the goshawks. The scleras and irises of the boy's eyes were entirely gone. In its place was a grey pattern that looked like static on an old television set.

Junior opened his mouth, intending to yell some more. His intentions refused to materialize as the boy removed his mask, arresting the Prince's attention. The mask landed on the sand-floor with a heavy thump. Junior stared open-mouthed at the sight of the boy's face, his eyes wide with wonder.

It was only when the boy made short, measured steps into the quicksand, the Prince found his voice again.

"What are you doing?!" Junior shouted up at the boy as he drew near. "Have you gone mad? Now we're both stuck in it like…like…" Failing to come up with an analogy, he yelled, "Like two people who are stuck in something!!!!" The Prince continued to shout.

He didn't know what else to do. Yelling was his only solace right now. Yelling was his only method for disassociating from the sheer terror coursing through his bloodstream. "Now, we're both sitting ducks! No, it's worse than that. We're sinking ducks! You—You—You're the Worst Rescuer EVER!!!!!"

The boy gently placed one hand over Junior's chest, running small circles over it. He could feel the Prince's heartbeat fluttering madly beneath his hand.

"*Hotep*, *hotep*," he said, telling the wide-eyed Prince to calm himself.

Junior, however, wasn't one for calm.

Calm wasn't how he functioned on the regular. Calm wasn't really his style.

"Are you—are you telling me to relax?!" Junior's left eye twitched. "You've got nerve! Don't tell me to relax!! YOU RELAX!!!"

The Prince squawked at the sight of the boy's eyes up close. In the back of his mind, he remembered how Lucien and Lex's eyes glowed golden every time they used their powers. The overall aesthetic was eerie and beautiful... This, however, was more of the former, and less of the latter. There was nothing beautiful about the dull, greyish, pixel-patterned eyes the boy was currently sporting.

The eyes weren't even the worst part. What was more concerning was the rest of the boy's face. The skin at his right cheek was starting to scrape away, as if someone had used a pumice stone to efface it. The boy's features were now half-erased, the skin grazed out to reveal the bones.

Junior's shoulders deflated, some of the anger leaving him as he looked up at the boy in equal parts fear and concern. "Sweet suffering Jesus, what's happened to you?" he whispered with a heavy quiver in his voice.

The boy didn't answer. His hands softly trailed up to Junior's shoulders. He placed his palms upon them. He touched them. Those young, calloused hands continued northward up Junior's neck until he was tracing the Prince's face like a blind man trying to feel a loved one's features.

"What—what are you doing?" said Junior quietly, nervously as the boy gently brushed a hand along the bruise on his chin.

Junior kept his own hands to his sides, not sure what else to do. There were rules against touching royals and Junior wasn't accustomed to strangers being so free with him. But it wasn't as though he could shrink away from the boy's touch, being stranded as he was. If he was being honest, Junior didn't want to push the boy away. His touch felt exceptionally warm and comforting. It was the same way Junior felt whenever Lex or Lucien hugged him after a nightmare, whenever Meryl latched onto his elbow for no reason whatsoever other than simply wanting to, whenever Porki threw an arm around his shoulder in a moment of delight ...

"Hotep," he repeated once more as he drew both hands up to cover Junior's beautiful face. His fingers hovered over the Prince's large, dark eyes. His palms pressed lightly against the Prince's soft cheeks.

Junior's heart stood still. He wasn't entirely sure what happened after that. The death whistle resurged, but this time it was accompanied by a ringing sensation that sounded like a lost lullaby. As the sound escalated, the ground began to shake. The went sand beneath them bubbled furiously as though they were inside a witch's cauldron.

The boy kept his hands over the Prince's eyes. It was probably a good thing he was blocking Junior's view, preventing the Prince from turning his face to behold the sudden sandstorm moving rapidly across the horizon. It was probably a blessing the death whistle was drowning out the howling of the wind.

"'God is faithful, and he will not let you be tested beyond your strength, but with your testing he will also provide the way out so that you may be able to endure it,'" his Father-King had recited from the 46th book of the Bible (1 Corinthians 10:13, to be exact). This was Lucien's idea of a bedtime story.

"What does that mean?" yawned Junior, then age 6. He wished his nanny was here reading to him instead. Her reverse-harem stories were far more riveting.

"It means you needn't fear anything in life, son, because God will never give you what you can't handle."

Junior probably wouldn't have handled this incoming situation well. That's why he never saw the way the dust particles swept through the air like an enormous fog cloud devouring everything in its path. He didn't get to see the sand mold and shape itself into a pride of lionesses charging at them.

He didn't witness any of it. But through the vertical gaps between the boy's slim fingers, the Prince caught glimpses of a blast of grey light erupting from the boy's body … right before everything turned dark.

Chapter 16:
What good am I, really?

Three years ago:

As the needle drew nearer to Junior's temple, the man looming over him sneered, "You useless boy, if you ever had a clever thought in this head of yours, it died alone and afraid."

The little Prince jolted awake with a gasp. He nearly cried out for his Father-King and his Sister-Princess-Regent. His eyes swept across the large room.

Right, he thought to himself as he noted the two neat rows of tiny cots occupied by nine-year-old boys. Two large bars of moonlight shot out from the windows and bled into the gap between their beds.

Lucien and Lex weren't here to console him. He wasn't in his bedchambers back in the Cage. He was in a cottage surrounded by his fellow Griffin-Cub Scouts for their summer camping trip.

Everyone was asleep. Everyone except for Junior and the guard sitting on a chair by the foot of his bed.

The Prince had a rotation of Knights and protection officers to stand guard over him. Currently, there was one in the room, and three patrolling outside.

The indoor guard made no move to comfort Junior, who was still breathing heavily from his nightmare. That wasn't the man's job. It was his job to protect, not to comfort. But the way

Junior saw it, comfort was a form of protection – mentally if not physically.

Some of his protection offers understood this and were gentle with the young Prince. Not this guard, though. It was obvious this man wasn't built for solace. He had a face that was positively reptilian. He silently stared at Junior like a snake ready to strike.

Most of Junior's guards had a few things in common: they weren't afraid of assailants, they barely batted an eye at bullets making a beeline for them, and they were terrified of their Prince. The ones who weren't afraid of Junior – like the officer before him – regarded him with disdain and distrust.

By the tender age of nine, Junior had already garnered a reputation for being a bit of a hell-griffin. He was prone to scaling walls, swinging on chandeliers, and sneaking away from his security detail whenever he so pleased. He ran about the halls naked, vaulting into priceless antiques, breaking them into porcelain breadcrumbs. He climbed the tallest of trees and proceeded to do cartwheels on the branches as though they were balance beams.

In short: he didn't make life easy for the people who looked after him. The Prince's wayward behaviour was a strain on all his caretakers – mentally, physically, and professionally. The aftermath was usually the same. His nannies ended up in therapy, and his guards ended up fired and replaced.

Practically everyone was replaceable in Lucien's eyes.

Sometimes, Junior worried Lucien would one day get mad enough to fire and replace him. It wouldn't be the first time the Gold King had formally dismissed a son. Lucien had already done it twice over.

"Oh, don't be silly, Little Wing," Lex had told him when he confessed his concerns to her, "Come here... Give me your hand."

Junior did as she requested.

163

"Now, you listen to me," she patted his hand gently, "Father would never do that to any of us. And he certainly didn't fire Mikey and Gabby. They chose to leave the Golden realm… Besides, you can't fire family." Bopping him on the nose, she winked. "Family is forever."

Junior blinked up at her. Lex was probably the only beautiful woman in the world who could make the word "forever" sound like a threat.

He remembered how his sister had tried to reassure him. A family member was irreplaceable. An employee was expendable. The former was a bond, the latter was business. But the Valentas were in a rather unique situation, being a family-owned business.

Junior was Lucien's son and his subject in equal measure. Failing to live up to Lucien's impossibly high standards, Junior couldn't help fearing that one day he'd be discharged as the Golden Prince just like his brothers.

With a sigh, Junior threw his bed covers off. His guard immediately shot to his feet, the chair scraping across the floor.

The Prince rolled his eyes. "Relax," he leapt off the bed, "I'm not planning on doing any damage." Then with a delightfully devious smile, he added, "Not *this time*, at least."

Under his guard's reproachful glare, Junior pattered over to the cot adjacent to him.

"Porki… Porki…" He whispered, shaking his friend's right shoulder. "Porki."

"Gwhuhhh?" Porki's head shot up from his pillow, his eyes squinting in the darkness.

"Oh good, you weren't sleeping," said Junior. "Budge over, will you?"

Porki sighed but acquiesced. He shifted leftward as Junior crept beneath the covers and curled into his bed. "I *was* sleeping, Idiot. Why aren't you?" he whined, slamming his head back against the pillow.

"I was…until I wasn't… and now I can't."

Porki side-eyed him. He looked like he wanted to thrust his fist through the Prince's face.

"Look, whatever's devilling your mind right now, I don't wanna hear it," Porki turned around and pulled the covers up to his chin. "Just go back to sleep. We'll have to get up soon."

Junior eyed the clock attached to the wall opposite to them. "We've got at least another two hours."

"Not even," Porki huffed into his pillow. "Terry's gonna get up any minute now, and he's sure to wake half the planet in the process."

"What for?" Junior shot a look at one of the cots on the opposite row, where Terry slept.

"Why do you think?" Porki pointed a finger toward the freestanding chalkboard beside the door. It currently contained the following text:

Terry's Thursday To-Do list:

- ~~Wash face and feet.~~
- ~~Finish reading book, *Why My Molecules Matter*.~~
- Go to bed.
- Fall asleep.
- Get up.
- Document dream journal.
- Wash face and feet.
- Perform morning calisthenics.
- Finish all ablutions.
- Write down Friday to-do list.

It was a mercy Terry never wet the bed. He would be shameless enough, or socially clueless enough, to put it on the list for all to see.

"Is he seriously gonna do this every day?" Junior recalled the morning prior. It had been their first day of camp. All the Griffin Cubs had been roused during nautical twilight by the sound of Terry fumbling around, eyes half-shut, smashing into cots as he searched for the chalkboard. "He's gonna wake up early just to scratch off '*fall asleep*' and '*get up*' from his precious list?"

"Yep," nodded Porki. "And to journal his dreams before he forgets them."

"Oh." Junior went quiet for a moment. Unfortunately for his friend, the silence didn't last long. "You know… I had a weird dream just now."

"That's nice."

Junior stared at Porki's back. "Don't you wanna know what it was about?"

"No."

"OK … That's fine. I get it."

A beat, and then—

"It was about Scout Leader Peregrine," Junior carried on. "I dreamt he stopped at nothing to kill me."

"I'm dreaming of the exact same," mumbled Porki.

"He said he was doing the Gold Kingdom a favour by getting rid of me. That I was a village idiot in my past life and had somehow miraculously reincarnated into a Useless Prince in this one. And by the end of it, he was trying to stab me in the face with a syringe full of poisonous chocolate. What do you think that means?"

"It means he hates you."

"How come?"

"'Cause you set him on fire."

"Not in the dream, I didn't. That only happened in real life … and it was an accident." In hindsight, Junior recognized that using a can of bug spray and a lighter as a blow torch wasn't the smartest way to start a campfire.

"And you spiked his water with salt during yesterday's hike," murmured Porki.

"I was giving him Elektra Lights." Junior still didn't know they were called *electrolytes*. Again, in hindsight, he might've gone a little overboard with the salt.

"A *pinch* of salt would've sufficed. You put in enough to dehydrate him."

"It's not like he got any of it down. He spat it all out right away ... And I tried to make it up to him. I even made him breakfast when we got back to the mess hall."

"You put five mosquitos in his pancakes."

"They flew in!"

"They flew around. You smashed them in with a spatula and tried to pass them off as chocolate chips."

"But I—"

"Oh, come off it." Porki finally turned around to face Junior. "What's this really about?"

Junior averted his gaze. "I think what he said was uncalled for, is all."

"What he said in the dream or in real life?"

"Both!" said Junior huffily.

Porki snorted a little as he remembered the way Scout Master Peregrine had snarled at Junior after yesterday's hike. The sneer of contempt was accompanied by the following statement, "*This great Kingdom of ours deserves far better than a Prince with only two brain cells. Both of which are fighting for third place!*"

"Maybe he was a bit hard on you. But can you blame the guy? Besides, you can't really hold what he said in a dream against him."

"Oh yes, I can," refuted Junior. "I'd send him to the stocks for it, if I could."

"His Majesty doesn't send people to the stocks anymore." Porki sat up in bed, now fully awake. "Why do you even care what Peregrine says about you?"

"I don't... I didn't ... but now I sorta do."

"Why?"

"He called me a Useless Prince."

"In a dream."

"He said it in real life too."

"And that bothers you because...?"

"He's not the first to say it." Junior examined his fingernails. "Just the first to say it to my face."

"I wouldn't take it to heart," said Porki. "It's like whenever I call you an idiot. It doesn't mean you're stupid. It just means you do stupid things, sometimes... a lot of times."

"It's not the same, Porki. I think he really meant it. And all those other people did too." Junior stared up at the ceiling, refusing to meet Porki's eyes. "What if they're right? That I really am a Useless Prince?"

Something twisted across Porki's face, flickering between irritation and fondness. It settled there, soft and cold like the winter sun. "Junior..."

"I'm not like my brothers, Porki. I can't do any of the stuff they did."

Both Michael and Gabriel had left their mark in Golden history before moving to the Phantom Realm. Michael as a great Warrior-Prince who won wars on behalf of their Father-King. And Gabriel as an innovative inventor whose creations helped Lucien weaponize his Divine energy. Gabriel's ideas were the reason their military now had arms that could blast Golden lasers straight through mountains.

Michael had the brawn; Gabriel had the brains. During their centuries-spanning tenure as Golden Princes, his big brothers had changed the world. Whether or not they had changed it for the better was debatable. Still, no one could deny they had played a significant part in molding the world into what it was today.

In comparison to his brothers, Junior couldn't even earn a merit badge for basic fire safety.

"Hey," Porki lightly thumped his forehead. "Get out of your own head, will ya? You can't do what they did because you're *nine*. You haven't even received the Golden Gift from the King yet."

"It wouldn't matter if I was in my Ninth Century or if I had the Gift. I still wouldn't be able to do it," said Junior reflectively. "Mike and Gabe fought battles and made Golden-powered nudes—"

"*Nukes*, you mean."

"Yeah, that's what I said. But I don't have the talent or the energy for that sorta stuff."

Porki suddenly burst into laughter. "You don't need talent to be a Prince," he snickered.

"I don't?" Junior poked at one of Porki's dimples.

"Not in this day and age, you don't." Porki swatted his friend's finger away from his left cheek. "Being a Prince means you can be as useless and untalented as you like and get away with it."

"I can?"

"Uh huh," nodded Porki. "You've got it easy."

"I do?"

"Our people don't want a Prince with any *real* talent. They just want someone with a cute face and a lot of money, who'll say nice things to them and make them feel good about themselves."

"That's it?" Junior's eyes bugged out. "I can do that ... I'm already doing that... I already have the cutest face, and I've got endless money."

"Your Father's got endless money. Not you."

"As his son, it's mine by Divine right... It's in the Bible...sorta."

"Sure."

"But my brothers—"

"I know, I know, they had actual achievements. But in the end, what good did it do? The Osprey hates them, and – luckily for you – I hear they're super unpopular amongst the Goldizens."

"How is that lucky for me?"

"Because it means you can use their unpopularity to make yourself popular."

"How?" pressed Junior.

They were interrupted by the sound of a creature scuttling across the floor.

Whipping their heads around, they discovered said creature was Terry, half-asleep and attempting to walk straight through the cot in front of him. When Terry found he couldn't glide directly past the bed like a ghost, he began climbing up and over it. In doing so, he had inadvertently woken up the bed's current occupant – Jeremiah, the Prince's Secutor.

Jeremiah groaned as Terry stomped over one of his legs. "Watch it, Reed!" the boy growled out before burying himself under his blanket once more.

Terry proceeded to do this with five more cots, awakening and annoying five more Griffin-Cub Scouts in the process, until he finally reached the chalkboard.

With his eyes still partly shut, Terry fumbled around for chalk. Upon finding a piece, he began making amendments to his list:

- ~~Wash face and feet.~~
- ~~Finish reading book, *Why My Molecules Matter*.~~
- ~~Go to bed.~~
- ~~Fall asleep.~~
- ~~Get up.~~
- Document dream journal.
- Wash face and feet.
- Perform morning calisthenics.
- Finish all ablutions.
- Write down Friday to-do list.

Porki and Junior watched in silence as Terry dropped the chalk and retreated to his cot to fetch his dream journal. He repeated his route, walking up and over a line of cots and cubs.

"Anyyyywayyy…" said Porki, returning to their conversation, "What were we talking about?"

"My brothers."

"Right. Goldizens hate them."

"Why?"

"Because they left," Porki said as though it were obvious, "They shifted their allegiance to another realm, another King."

"But that King was my Mother."

"That's neither here nor there. As far as our people are concerned, Gold is all that glitters and matters. Your brothers made a huge mistake moving to the Phantom side. But where they've failed, you can prevail."

Junior blinked owlishly. "I still don't follow."

"You have to show everyone you're not like your brothers. That you'd never turn your back on the Golden realm the way they did," explained Porki. "As long as your loyalty stays Golden, our people will love you… Everyone except Scout Master Peregrine, that is. He's always gonna hate your guts …

But you'll have everyone else's favour. All you have to do is live here, *stay* here."

"That's it?" Junior couldn't believe it was that easy, but Porki seemed certain of it. "That's all I have to do to outshine my brothers as a Golden Prince?"

Porki wasn't one to sugarcoat a situation, especially for Junior. Most days, the Prince had an ego that stretched for miles on end. But right now, Junior's face was about as tender and vulnerable as a boy of their era could risk revealing. The sight of it made Porki pause to think up a response that fell somewhere between telling the truth and giving Junior the lie he wanted to hear.

In Porki's opinion, it had been a bit redundant to call Junior a "*Useless Prince.*" It was like calling a blank sheet of paper empty. It was pointless. All Princes were pointless. The world had no use for any Prince – let alone Junior – who would most likely never inherit the throne.

Michael and Gabriel were special exceptions. They came in at a time when the Golden realm was still in its diapers. The Kingdom needed them; they needed their strength, their minds, and their contributions. Junior, by contrast, entered the scene much later when the realm was mature and thriving. He could never be the Prince the people needed, but he could be the one they wanted.

"Think of it this way, Junior. Maybe you're not the right guy for the job. But you're in the right place at the right time without ever knowing it. Not everyone can do that, you know? That's your special talent, my Prince."

Chapter 17:
I'm still alive.
That means you can't eat me, right?

The Prince woke up to a chorus of dunes amidst a swine's song … at least, it sounded like a swine. He wasn't sure.

He was dizzy and disoriented and could barely see anything beyond the flashes of light against his eyes. He felt very much like one of those cartoon characters who – having been hit by an unexpected falling anvil – was now lying half-dead and cross-eyed with stars circling his head.

For a while, Junior stayed put, with his entire body laid back against the sand. He didn't rise, not until the shimmering lights in his vision disappeared entirely and he was able to make out actual stars in the sky.

Snippets of him, Porki and Terry at a Griffin-Cubs Summer Camp from over three years ago lingered in his mind. He had been dreaming of a memory. But before that, he had been— wait, what had he been doing?

When the grating pig sounds resurfaced, Junior groaned, "Lock it up, will you?"

Blinking rapidly, he slowly sat up and looked to his right.

It wasn't a swine.

"Oh, it's you," he said, coming face to beak with a vulture. And not just any vulture. It was *the* vulture, the one that had saved him.

Now, he remembered what he'd been doing.

The vulture's golden eyes blinked back in confirmation.

"You sound like a pig, you know?"

The bird blinked once more. Then it bent its long neck and narrowed its eyes. It didn't make a noise, but Junior got the impression that it was thinking, *So do you.*

Junior shuffled away and got to his feet as the bird's beak edged closer. "Watch it! I'm still alive, so you can't eat me."

Terry had assured him vultures were harmless, but it was hard to believe. They certainly looked rather lethal.

He was a little put off by how the bird's face resembled the colour of blood. Back in the forest, he could have sworn the vulture's face had been entirely black, not red. The Prince was too young to put it together. He had yet to be exposed to grave amounts of violence and brutality. But someday, far in the future, he would know firsthand that blood looked black in the moonlight.

Even though the creature looked a little different up-close, Junior had a gut feeling this was the same bird that had rescued him.... And, speaking of rescuers. "Where did *he* go?"

Junior spun in a circle, once, twice, thrice, searching for the boy, but he was nowhere in sight. It was then that he realized the boy wasn't the only thing that was missing. His bag with his belongings was nowhere to be found. And the ruthless patch of quicksand – that was gone as well.

Biting his lip, Junior slowly, hesitantly placed a foot on the spot where he had been trapped, silently praying his leg wouldn't sink in again. It didn't. The muddy area where the sand and water melded together had vanished. In its place was a cool spread of mineral grains that easily blended in with the rest of the sand floor.

Now that he had a chance to move his legs again, a series of oddities grabbed his attention. To start, there was no grime on his pants or anywhere else. But how? Junior had been waist deep in quicksand. He should have been completely drenched in mud. There should've been grit in his clothing. There should've been a lot of chafing going on in his nether regions, which could've led to a nasty infection. There should've been a few bruises on him, courtesy of the fight he'd had with the boy. But there wasn't any of that. The Prince looked as pristine as he had when he'd first entered his Father's party. There were still bits of sand in his clothes and hair from the little catnap he'd taken, but that could easily be wiped off.

"Did you see him?" He asked the vulture. "There was this boy... he was about my age ... and he looked... he looked like..." Junior stumbled on his words. For some reason, he could no longer pull up a memory of a face, even though he was certain the boy had removed his mask at one point.

The vulture looked away from the Prince. For a moment, Junior thought the bird seemed a bit remorseful. He quickly dropped the notion. It was ridiculous. Animals weren't like people; they didn't have a vast range of expressions and feelings. Did they?

"You're an odd bird."

The vulture's eyes cut back to him. *So are you*, it seemed to say.

"Why did you help me out back there?" He inched closer, now feeling more relaxed in the bird's presence. "If you hadn't put the razzle-dazzle on those goshawks, you could've had my carcass for dinner."

The vulture made a grunting noise, its blunted talons kicking at the sand. *Yeah... well...*

"Thanks," said Junior with a small smile.

Another grunt. *Whatever.*

The vulture made a movement with his wings as if to take off – only to drop them back down and hiss in pain.

"Your wing's a little broken." Junior came closer and bent down to take a closer look. The vulture's left wing was sticking out slightly at an odd angle. "Those goshawks must've hurt you."

They held each other's gaze for a moment, enjoying the velvet calmness of the desert.

"Well, looks like it's my turn to save you," Junior sighed. "C'mon, let's go."

If Junior had thought it was impossible for a bird to display facial expressions, he was quickly proven wrong. The vulture's eyes nearly bugged out of its head in astonishment and apprehension as Junior proceeded to pick it up and carry it like it was an oversized teddy bear. Never held in such a manner by anyone before and far too shocked to react, the vulture went completely still and silent in the Prince's arms.

"You can come home with me," Junior said airily as he strode deeper into the desert. No longer in possession of a compass, he relied on the stars to steer him back to where he belonged.

"Don't worry. My family will fix you right up. They adore birds, especially my sister. She'll be thrilled."

Chapter 18:
Did it make them cry harder?

Lex was not thrilled.

She wasn't thrilled when Terry and Meryl had pulled her aside to alert her that Junior was nowhere to be found. She wasn't thrilled to step lightly through the party, the picture of complete calm and serenity all the while having an internal panic attack. And she certainly wasn't thrilled to step out of the barricade of the campsite to find Junior stomping through the sand with a bizarre bird in his arms.

It wasn't like any of the vultures she had seen before. It was thrice the size of a white-backed vulture, but it was black with a red face like a turkey vulture. It was a rather unique specimen. Too bad, it sounded like a swine.

When Junior had caught sight of Lex a few feet outside the campsite, the golden dome-shaped Shield shining behind her, he knew he was in for the *longest* lecture of his life to date. Lex was flanked by two Volucris Knights. Junior recognized them as the ones she trusted the most, and possibly the only guards among all their sentry who were more loyal to her than their Father-King. Both Knights looked relieved to see him. Lex, however, had a much different reaction as Junior approached.

In lieu of an explanation, Junior held out the vulture in his arms and said sheepishly, "Got you a gift, Lexie… You like?"

Lex's eyes narrowed down to the vulture before swinging back up to Junior, unimpressed.

All traces of the usual warmth in Lex's large, brown eyes had vanished. And, with a wall of sheer gold flashing behind her,

Junior couldn't help but think she looked very much like an angel guarding the gates to Heaven, ready to deny him entrance.

"I named it Alexandra, after you," he offered again when Lex didn't respond.

"It's a male," she said flatly.

"We can call him Alex then," said Junior, still holding out the bird as a peace offering. "His wing's fractured. Can you help him?"

"In a moment," said Lex softly, sternly. "Put the bird down for now, Junior. We have much to discuss."

Junior sighed and did as he was told, gently placing his new friend down on the sandy floor beside him.

Discuss. She said *discuss.* If he was wondering how much trouble he was in before – on a scale of grounded for a week to never seeing the light of day until he reached his Second Century of life – then that certainly confirmed it. It never ended well for him when Lex said the D-word.

Out of the corner of his eye, Junior could see Meryl, Terry, and Jeremiah through the semi-translucent Shield. They were coming his way, speeding right through the barrier with ease.

Junior held out his arms, expecting at least one of them to embrace him. But the fury on all their eyes, especially Meryl's, made it clear they hadn't rushed out to give him a warm welcome. He dropped his arms and hands, but quickly brought them back up again in time to cover his face as Meryl threw the golden blazer he'd lent her at his head.

"YOU!" Meryl shrieked, her cheeks stained with mascara tears. "WHERE THE HELL DID YOU GO?!"

Meryl and Terry had done what Junior had instructed back at the forest. They had run and they hadn't looked back. Not until they were safely inside the campsite. Imagine their surprise to realize their Prince was not behind them or anywhere else in sight.

"I'm sorry. I had to tell someone," was the first thing Jeremiah the Secutor had said to them once they were back inside the confines of the Shielded-dome. He had quickly ascertained the Prince and his friends were missing. At first, he had kept this information to himself, but then, "You lot were away for over an hour. I was getting worried."

"Have you told the Regent or the King?" Meryl was still panting heavily from the run. Her head kept swinging back expectantly as though Junior would magically appear.

"Not yet. I saw these guys patrolling the perimeter just now and told them what happened," Jeremiah indicated to the two Knights behind them, "They're the Princess-Regent's personal bodyguards."

"Good," wheezed Terry, who had his hands to his knees. He was also trying to catch his breath.

"Good?" Meryl mimicked.

"Better we tell the Regent than the King."

"Tell her what?" said Jeremiah, looking between them, then around them.

Their panic levels collectively rose as they witnessed a massive dust storm swept around the party. For all the guests under the King's Shield, the storm was perfectly harmless. It was even entertaining to watch through the semitransparent layer of Gold surrounding them. But what about those outside of the barrier, exposed to all the elements?

There was a tremble in Jeremiah's voice as he asked, "... Where's the Prince?"

The storm hadn't lasted long. It was the memory – along with all the feelings of fear and dread that came with it – that lingered in Meryl's mind.

With a furious face, she waited for Junior to provide a proper explanation. Unlike Meryl, Terry and Jeremiah weren't shedding any tears, but they both looked three seconds away from demanding an explanation as well.

The longer Junior remained silent, the more irritated they became. The three kids were so focused on Junior that none of them – not even Terry – had taken notice of the vulture quietly observing them.

"Do you have any idea what you put us through?!" Meryl yelled. "Do you even care?"

Junior stepped back a bit and glanced nervously over to his sister. His eyes were pleading for help. Lex, however, did not appear to be paying the little scene any mind. She had pulled her Knights aside to have a private word with them. She had no interest in getting involved in whatever ridiculous bout of pre-teen angst that was currently playing out before her.

When no response came, Meryl stomped one foot heavily into the sand. "Well, do you?!!"

If Meryl was only shouting, Junior could've dealt with it. He could handle a spot of yelling. If someone shouted at him, he could always shout right back, provided it wasn't Lex and Lucien. It never ended well for him when he barked back at those two. He learned that the hard way … But Meryl wasn't only shouting. She was shouting *and* crying. Or was she shouting *while* crying? *Same difference*, thought Junior with an internal shrug.

The Prince was rather fond of girls with bad tempers. He could deal with their tempers. He couldn't deal with their tears.

"Uhhhh…." The Prince stuttered. He didn't know what to say. He wasn't great with crying girls. He never knew what to do when they cried. Then, in a flash, he thought of his Father. Lucien was accustomed to people crying around him. Or were they crying *over* him? *Same difference*.

Whenever Lucien flew, walked, glided, or drove by in a procession, there were always hordes of people screaming and sobbing – especially women – with salty tears flowing out of their eyes like waterfalls. They never held back as they wept away, losing valuable electrolytes at the mere sight of the Gold King.

His Father always knew what to do in such a situation. The man always knew what to do in *every* situation. *So, what would he do now?* Thinking back, Junior recalled how Lucien would respond with a kind smile and a subdued waving gesture whenever there were crying women calling for him at a distance. But if their faces and tears were up close, he'd give them an endearing compliment to calm them down.

Right, thought Junior with an internal nod, *A few nice words always perked them right up... or did it make them cry harder?* The Prince couldn't remember. *Oh well, best give it a go.*

"Gee, Meryl," Junior pulled out his most winning smile, "I never noticed before, but you sure have the most beautiful eyes when they're full of tears."

That got her to stop crying. But it was the wrong thing to say.

From the side of his vision, Junior could've sworn he had seen the vulture cover his head with his uninjured wing – the avian equivalent of a human facepalm.

Meryl looked even more livid. A second ago, she had only wanted to yell at him. Now, after that ridiculous remark, she was tempted to wring his skinny little neck, maybe smack him around a bit for good measure as well. But she didn't do any of those things. Not because Junior was the Prince, but because Meryl figured he was just enough of a perv to enjoy that type of treatment.

"What's happening here?" Porki inquired as he shot past the Shield and into their little gathering.

"And *you*!" Meryl whipped toward him accusingly. "Where have you been?!"

"I've been *here* this entire time," Porki remarked coldly as he gestured back toward the party.

"You certainly weren't anywhere to be found when we got back," Meryl crossed her arms.

"What are you getting angry with me for?" demanded Porki. "You three were the ones who went swanning off into a dark forest in the middle of the night to find— to find—" His brows knitted together. "Why did you guys go there?"

Junior was a little taken aback. He knew Meryl and Terry had been magically forced to forget the Tree of Queens, but why couldn't Porki remember their reason for ditching the party? Had the enchantment extended so far that it touched anyone who so much as suspected the Tree of Queens lived in that forest? If so, why hadn't the enchantment affected Junior?

Meryl frowned. "I'm not sure either." Swiveling back to Junior, she sniped, "All I know is that this is ALL HIS FAULT!"

Unable to cope with Meryl's ire any longer and dreading the "*You're-an-Idiot*" look he was sure Porki had reserved for him, Junior decided to set his attention on Terry. "What took you guys so long to get back?" He asked as he threw his blazer on, getting both arms in. "I coulda finished off my First Century back in that forest, waiting for you lot to rescue me."

"What do you mean?" said Terry, giving Junior an odd look. "It's barely been ten minutes since Meryl and I returned. We finished explaining everything to the Regent just now. Her Royal Highness was on her way to get you."

Junior blinked dumbly. Everything he went through, did it all happen in the span of a few minutes? It had felt like an age.

"Got lost in the forest, didn't you?" Porki crossed his arms. "Told you not to go, didn't I?"

"Yes, I know you told me!" Junior snapped irritably. Then, with a sigh, he decided there was no point stewing over what had happened too much. The worst of it was over now. "Oh, well, you can't say it's ever a dull party with me around."

Jeremiah shook his head at him disbelievingly. *Damn rich kids*, he thought to himself. "I'm parched. I'm gonna get some water," he said tightly before going through the Shield and re-entering the party.

"I can't believe you." Meryl scowled at Junior. "Is that all you have to say? Are you even the least bit sorry about what you put us through? Not to mention poor Jeremiah in there. I felt so bad for him…"

Meryl had seen the way Jeremiah's beautiful olive complexion turned completely fish-belly after discovering the Prince was missing.

"Pfffft," Junior scoffed at the mention of his Secutor, who hadn't shown him so much as a speck of attention in recent years. "As if he cares what happens to me."

Meryl threw her hands in the air. Her expression suggested their Prince was a lost cause. "You're right," she said to Porki, "He's an idiot."

Porki dropped his chin and eyed him warily. "You don't know why Jeremiah's *really* here, do you?"

"Sure, I do," said Junior. "My Father hired him to be my travel companion … gets paid a fat lot of gold to do nothing but be my shadow. If you ask me, he's got the cushiest job in the world."

His three friends exchanged a look.

"What?" Junior gazed between them, wondering what he was missing. "What is it?"

"Junior…" Terry bit his lip, unsure how to explain. "*Secutor* means companion, but that's not what the job entails … You see, Jeremiah … Well… he's a valensmen too, and he's the same age as you, and from what I've heard, his blood and tissue type matches yours…"

"So?" said Junior, failing to understand where Terry was headed with this. Terry was usually blunt and direct to a fault. It was odd to see him fumbling over his words like this.

"He's your organ donor," Porki blurted out.

A pause.

"MY WHAT?"

"Don't worry, you're perfectly healthy," said Terry quickly. "Jeremiah's around in case anything ever happens to you and you're in need of a blood transfusion … or a kidney, or a pancreas … or a heart … that's what he's here for…"

"All this time and you really didn't know?" said Porki.

Junior stared at them, aghast.

"Alright children." Lex clapped her hands lightly as a call for attention. "It's time for you to return to the party, lest your parents wonder where you've gone."

Despite her words, Lex doubted that would happen, especially considering their guardians had failed to take any notice of their missing children throughout the course of the night. Not that she had any right to judge them. Afterall, neither she nor Lucien had detected Junior's departure from the party. None of them would be winning any parenting awards anytime soon.

"My brother shall provide a formal apology to you all at a later time."

"Um… Your Royal Highness," Meryl's voice turned subdued and uneasy as her eyes fearfully darted up at the Princess-Regent. "Will you be informing them about what transpired?"

"Which part, dear?" replied Lex tersely. "The part where you all snuck off unattended? Or the part where three minors illegally consumed a concoction charged by the Phantom King's energy?"

Porki opened his mouth. He wanted to point out his nonparticipation in the matter, but before he could get a word out—

"You told her about the Unseen tonic?!" Junior shouted accusingly to Terry and Meryl.

"She made me tell her," said Terry.

The Prince scoffed in an exaggerated manner. He knew his friends had to inform Lex that he'd gone missing, but they didn't have to tell her everything. What were they thinking? They had been friends with Junior long enough to know how lying by omission worked.

"Oh yeah, '*she made you.*'" Junior would've believed it if they were adults. Lex had the prowess to mentally – and perhaps even physically – torture someone into squealing. But she wouldn't harm a bunch of kids. "How? How could she possibly *make* you tell her?!"

"She looked at me!" Terry nodded repeatedly. "With her eyes."

"Enough." Lex snapped her fingers once. They all went silent. They all turned to her.

The hard expression on Lex's beautiful face was perfectly aligned with her tone – both veneer and voice were soft and icy. Junior thought those three simple words summed up his sister perfectly. Lex ... not Lucien's powerhouse Princess-Regent-Lex, not the Golden-beauty-Lex who always had a camera-ready smile in place for the public... but the *real* Lex, the one that Junior knew in a way most others never would, was *soft and icy,* like snow melting in your bare palms.

"Seeing how it's my Father-King's birthday and he's not too fond of anyone upstaging him nor does he care for anything that sounds remotely scandalous attached to our family name... I shall give you all a one-time courtesy and turn a blind-eye to this matter." Her dark eyes slowly swiveled between the four young valensmen. Sensing their relief, she added, "However, should such a situation ever repeat itself, you'll answer directly to our King *and* the Phantom King."

They all glanced apprehensively at one another at the mention of Phantom King Michael. For all his faults, Lucien was still known to be merciful and generous King to his subjects. Michael, however, did not hold such an amenable reputation, not with his own subjects, and certainly not with non-Phantom citizens.

Pleased with their collective discomfort, she finished with, "Your Regent's mercy is not something you should test any further than you have tonight. Understood?"

"Yes," said Porki, Meryl, and Terry in unison as they dropped their heads in deference. "Thank you, Your Royal Highness."

Feeling as though they were properly reprimanded, Lex nodded to her Knights, a gesture instructing them to escort the three children back inside.

"Wait a minute, is that a vulture?!!" Terry's jaw dropped.

"C'mon, Terry, let's go," said Porki.

"But I want to see—"

"It's only a bird." Porki threw an arm around Terry and began dragging him away. "It's nothing special."

Junior watched as his friends ghosted through the Shield, heading back into the swing of the party. Meryl forged on without looking back. Terry kept turning his head to gawk at the vulture. Only Porki had glanced over at Junior, giving him a brief nod to indicate that everything was going to be fine.

"Is it true?" he asked when it was just the two of them. Three, if they counted the vulture. "About Jeremiah?"

"We'll discuss that later," said Lex. "For the time being, you'll be answering my questions."

"But you never told me he was—"

"That's enough," said Lex curtly. "You're in no position to be talking back to me, especially after all the unnecessary grief you've caused tonight."

"I wasn't aware there was such a thing as *necessary* grief," he shot back.

Lex's large eyes narrowed into slits. "Don't be facetious, Junior," she said warningly. "I may have granted your friends immunity to any punishment, but such courtesy does not apply to you."

Junior glared up at her. He hated it when his sister chided him like this. He hated having to look up at her while she chided him. Someday that would change, he was so sure. He had already reached her shoulders in terms of height. If he was lucky, he'd become even taller than Lucien. Someday soon, he'd be the one looking down on his big sister. See how she liked it.

"Come off it!" he shouted up at her. "You can't punish me! You're not my mother!"

"Precisely," Lex said calmly, coldly. She was entirely unbothered by his remark. "I am nothing like our all-suffering Mother, which means I don't have to tolerate your stupidity or make any exonerations for it." And with a small sneer, she added, "You're not an obligation to me, brother dear, you're an irritation. One that I can send packing to the Phantom Realm at any time."

Normally, irritation on his sister's face was one of his favourite things. The fact that he was the one to inspire such an emotion in Lex usually made him very happy.

It didn't make him happy right now.

Junior dropped his head in shame and regret. He shouldn't have made that comment about Lex not being his mother. Sure, logically, he knew his sister was not his mother. But with this real mother dead…or rather half-dead, temporarily dead, a little dead, comatose … Whatever Lana was, she wasn't around, and in her absence, Lex was the closest thing he had to a maternal figure.

Junior had always assumed it was an unspoken agreement between them that Lex was a mother-substitute of sorts, at least until their actual Mother stopped being dead. To hear Lex shut him down so quickly and refute that sentiment left a sour feeling in his stomach. A mother's love was supposed to be unconditional, wasn't it? Here, Lex was practically declaring she didn't love him unconditionally.

Seemingly oblivious to Junior's inner turmoil, Lex went on, "Now," she took a breath, "You're going to answer all my questions with honesty. No lies, no false alibis, and no asinine excuses. If I so much as detect a trace of prevarication, I shall alert Father right away."

Junior's head sprang back up at the mention of their Father-King. "But I—"

"Let me make it very easy for you to comprehend, Junior," said Lex. "You can either answer to me or to our Father-King. Take your pick."

Lucien was still inside, surrounded by his subjects and admirers, and enjoying his birthday. Junior didn't want to ruin his Father's good mood, nor did he wish to be on the receiving end of Lucien's bad mood should he discover what his youngest son had been up to.

Junior hung his head once more. Even the vulture, who was now close beside him, had bent his neck down and practically dropped his beak to the ground, as though he too were being properly admonished.

The Prince sighed in defeat. What a fool he had been to think, a second ago, that physical height would've made a difference between him and Lex. Even if he did tower over her, she'd still find a way to cut him down to size and then some.

"Did you really think you could beat me, Little Wing?" Lex had said teasingly after she had checkmated Junior for the seventh time.

It was a rainy weeknight in where the three members of the Golden Family had gathered in one of the drawing rooms of the Cage. Lex and Junior were by the fireplace playing rounds of chess while Lucien was at a nearby desk, editing one of his poems.

Junior knew it was a trivial game, but he still felt bitter over his loss. He couldn't help it. It was in his veins. The Valentas were sore losers and horrible winners.

Gazing angrily at the black, fallen King before him, Junior wanted to throw the entire game overboard in anger. He was even more tempted to do so when Lex had leaned over the table to ruffle his hair.

"Oh, you silly creature," she had cooed. Golden sparkles flew out her left eye as she winked. "Greater men than you have tried to best me and look where they all are now."

The Prince wasn't entirely sure to whom she was referring, but he got the feeling she wasn't talking about chess. He didn't know the history of all of Lex's adversaries. Still, he knew his sister was a force of nature. There were even rumours about her facing off in a duel – and practically winning – against the former Grey King. An astonishing feat since most Kings could only be bested in battle by other Kings.

Lex's smile widened as Junior's glare persisted. Satisfied with her winnings, she got up and left, her stride easy and confident like someone with the inherent knowledge they were better than everyone else, especially pesky little brothers.

Blinking away the memory, Junior lifted his eyes once more. Lex already knew he didn't fancy taking this up to the higher authority that was their Father-King.

"Tell me everything that happened," she said. "*Now.*"

Junior frowned. Meryl and Terry had likely told her a great deal already, which meant she only wanted to hear his account to see if their stories matched. He knew he had to be meticulous with his words. Lex was just as good as Lucien at sniffing out a lie, maybe even better.

So, he confessed up to a certain point. Purposely omitting everything regarding the Tree of Queens, he talked about taking the Unseen tonic, sneaking off to Godshoots, being stalked by someone, being chased by the goshawks, and being saved by the vulture.

"So, you went in search of the Tree of Queens," she said when he finished.

His eyes went wide. "How did you—"

"There's no other reason for you and your friends to want to go into that forest," she clipped out.

"So… it's real then? It's hidden, but it's there, isn't it?"

"Its existence is irrelevant," Lex shrugged with indifference.

"Ahhh, I get it. Our Father-King wants to keep it all on the hush-hush," nodded Junior, tapping at his nose. "I still think the demonic-possession trap was a bit overdramatic. Even for Father."

Lex raised one perfectly plucked brow. "Excuse me?"

"Terry and Meryl," explained Junior. "Pretty sure they were possessed for a few minutes when we got too close to the invisible Tree."

A pause.

"I see," Lex said slowly. Changing the course of the conversation, she asked, "Speaking of invisibility, why didn't you take the vial again?"

"What?"

"You said there was enough Unseen left in the vial for one person," she said. "Had you taken it, you could've bypassed the goshawks' notice."

Junior could have slapped himself. Why hadn't he thought of that? It was such an obvious solution. Eyesight was a bird's greatest advantage. If he had only drunk it while running into the forest, the Unseen-tonic would've rendered him invisible and given him enough time to quietly sneak away. Everything that happened afterwards could have been avoided.

"I … I…" Junior didn't know what to say. "I don't know … I guess I didn't think about it in the moment." That was true enough. At the time, the only thought blazing through his mind had been: *RUN!!!!*

"You were frightened."

Junior nodded. "Yeah, I was."

Lex's face was still a glacier, but Junior noticed it had softened a smidge at his admission. "We can't think properly under fear," she said. "You must learn to calm yourself whenever you're afraid, Little Wing. The smartest and simplest solution can only be found with a sound mind. Do you understand?"

Junior nodded again. He could always count on Lex to throw in a life lesson with every lecture.

"You want to know the best way to stop being afraid?" She asked with a small smile.

Junior nodded once more.

Her smile instantly vanished. "Stop putting yourself in danger to begin with, you foolish boy," she gritted out.

Junior frowned. He had walked right into that one.

"What happened next?"

"What do you mean? That's all—" he had started to stay, but stopped at Lex's firm gaze, warning him not to lie to her. That look was the equivalent to a sword being unsheathed and held up to his throat. *She made me tell her… She looked at me,* Terry had said, *with her eyes.* Junior acknowledged his friend may have had a point. "OK, that's not all…"

Chapter 19:
Silver or Grey,
what difference does it make?

Lex went very still and silent after Junior had finished telling her about the mysterious grey flare and the equally enigmatic boy who had tried to help him out of the quicksand.

After a cold, lengthy lull in the conversation, she said firmly, "You said it was silver before."

"What?"

"You said it looked like the same flare you saw earlier today." Lex stared at him. She wasn't blinking at all. "Back then, you said it was silver... but now you're saying it's *grey*. Which is it?"

"I dunno," shrugged Junior, unsure of where she was going with this. "Grey. Silver. Grey … what difference does it make?"

Lex said nothing. Her face gave nothing away. Without another word, she glided across the sand.

Junior and the vulture turned their heads and watched as she swept past them. A woman who always seemed to float, rather than walk, through every moment of life.

The Golden Regent looked reflectively out into the desert, toward Godshoots Forest.

It was then that Junior noticed the minor changes in Lex's wardrobe. She had the same gown as before, but over it, she had donned a very light, thin wrap consisting of translucent tendrils of gauzy fabric. When the wind suddenly picked up, her long wavy hair flew off her shoulders. The strands of fabric from her wrap mimicked the motion, trailing behind her in a dramatic train.

Lex exuded an aura that somehow managed to come across as both calm and intense at the same time. *Soft and icy.*

At her best, Lex was poetry in physical form. Looking as ethereal and untouchable as she did now, Junior began to wonder if maybe those men back in the party hadn't been after her because she was the Regent. Maybe it was simply her they desired.

Now that he was growing up, he was beginning to understand. It was a very masculine type of energy that came with such a desire: the allure of wanting something that seemed so out of reach and the courageousness to chase after it anyway. It was how he felt sometimes when he saw girls he fancied or when he was around boys he wanted to impress. Strangely enough, it was also how he had felt when he'd seen that flare.

Junior headed over to stand beside her. Lex still hadn't said anything or even looked his way, and he didn't know what to do. He didn't like silence. Much like calm, silence wasn't really his style. But he felt like he had to be quiet right then, if only for Lex. It was obvious his sister needed a moment to collect her thoughts and categorize them in a way only her mind could understand.

Several minutes flew by where Lex remained as still as stone.

Slowly, tentatively, Junior reached out to grab her hand. "Lexie?"

"How did you get out of the quicksand?" Lex's eyes remained fixed ahead at the forest, her expression still unreadable. "Why is there not a trace of grime on you?"

"I dunno," said Junior, "When I woke up, it was like the quicksand wasn't even there."

"What about the storm? How did you avoid it?"

Junior furrowed his brows. "What storm?"

"We encountered a dust-devil a little while ago. Mind you, it didn't last long. A minute or two. We were protected from it thanks to the King's Shield… but you…"

"I didn't see anything like that." Junior shrugged. "I guess the storm didn't reach the forest."

"Hmm… And what about the boy?"

"He was gone too." Junior spotted the slight clench in Lex's jaw after he said that.

"This boy… Did he see the flare as well?"

"Yeah."

Lex finally turned her head to the side to face him and asked, "What did this boy look like?"

"He looked—well, he had his mask on, but he took it off for a sec and…and he looked…He was rather… I think he was… I… I don't know."

Assuming that her brother was lying, she suddenly tightened her grip on his hand with her talon-like nails practically digging into his epidermis. "Junior," she said warningly.

195

Junior roughly retracted his hand and stepped away from her. "I really don't know!!"

Snapshots of tonight's events coursed through his mind. He recalled the goshawks, running through the woods, the vulture saving him... There was some sort of argument...No, it wasn't an argument. It was a fight...The birds were fighting while Junior ran off ... Then he was stuck in muddy waters. But there was also a boy there with him... wasn't there? *Of course, there was a boy.* He had just told Lex about the boy's existence a few minutes ago. So why couldn't Junior remember him?

The boy had been Junior's age, only a bit younger. No, that was wrong. He was older, wasn't he? Junior couldn't put a face to him anymore, but he remembered how the boy's eyes had been grey— silver— grey... He shook his head. No, that was all wrong too. The boy's eyes were warm and dark, like oak and chestnut honey ... weren't they?

"Lexie, Lexie!" panic rang through Junior's voice. He ran a shaky hand through his hair, stopping mid-way to grab the side of his head. "Something's not right... I-I can't remember..."

He couldn't make any sense of it. It felt as though someone was deliberately pulling memories from his brain and extracting it through his earhole like string from a floss dispenser.

"Lexie ..." he cried, looking to his sister for help. "What's happening to me?"

Lex went silent again. She stared at him, her eyes inflating.

Junior flinched, shutting his eyes and crying out in pain as the back of his head began to throb. He tried to hold onto threads of memories, but it was like clinging on to a cat while it was resisting. It was too aggravating to handle, leaving him with no choice but to release the metaphorical cat. And, suddenly, everything that had transpired after his run-in with the goshawks and the vulture had turned fuzzy and warped.

Strangely enough, he felt much better after that. The stinging pain in the back of his head was completely gone. Taking a deep, relaxing breath, Junior opened his eyes to find Lex and the vulture staring at him, twin flickers of fear and concern in their eyes.

"What?" he said, perplexed. "Why are you looking at me like that?"

Lex regarded him carefully. All the ice in her features had suddenly thawed. Her voice turned quiet and delicate as she said, "Junior... I want you to repeat everything you told me, verbatim."

Junior thought it was a rather odd request. Nevertheless, he obliged her. "We took Michael's Unseen-tonic and went to Godshoots, and then those crazy birds came after us for no reason at all. They went gunning for me while Terry and Meryl got away. That's when this vulture saved me."

It didn't escape Lex's notice that he had omitted the boy and the flare from his retelling. "And after that?"

"Then I brought him back here," Junior said plainly, motioning to the vulture. "That's all."

"And you went to the forest in search of the Tree of Queens?" said Lex, still testing him.

Junior's eyes lit up. "You know about the Tree! It's real then? It's hidden, but it's there, isn't it?" He said, entirely unaware that he was reiterating his previous statements. "I knew I felt something there."

Both of Lex's eyebrows shot up when she found no trace of deception and evasion on her brother's face.

"You OK, Lexie?"

"Junior... Little Wing, do you remember that strange cloud you saw on the drive back to the campsite?"

"What cloud?" Junior raised a brow. He hadn't the faintest idea what his sister was talking about.

At his response, Lex's face went completely glacier, going from golden to ghostly in less than a heartbeat.

Squaring her shoulders, she made an about-face and gazed pensively toward the forest once more.

The Golden Regent had a theory as to what had happened, and for the first time in her life, she hoped she was wrong. Because it sounded like her brother had encountered a Totem. More specifically, he had witnessed the Grey Totem.

It wasn't out of the realm of possibility for a Totem to select a child as the next Chosen King. It had happened before, but it was by no means taken as a welcomed opportunity. Female-Kings were bitterly tolerated, but Child-Kings were considered aberrations.

Most Child-Kings couldn't cope with the physical strain of containing Divine energy in the confines of their underdeveloped bodies. They ended up exploding like supernovas within their first month of Kinghood. As for the one who managed to endure the symbiosis… well, it hadn't ended well for them either.

Lex still remembered a moment in her sixth-grade history class where her instructor recounted the story of the last Child-King the world had ever known. The child had been selected by the Blue Totem in the year 1333. He had been nine years old. And, he had been brutally murdered by his own subjects. Mind you, this was long ago, before there was a hard-and-set rule proclaiming it was the gravest of sins to kill a King.

Self-combustion or death by murder. Lex didn't desire either destiny for her little brother.

Lex let out a deep breath. Fortunately, it appeared that Junior had evaded a Divine decree. Hence, the sudden stroke of amnesia. There was a saying that any Kingly candidate who failed a Totem's test were stripped of their memories of said Totem.

Michael had seen this play out with their Mother. Many years ago, Lana had mentioned seeing Three Totems – Black, White, and Silver. But only the Black and White Totems had deemed her worthy of leading; the Silver Totem had rejected her. After her Kingly conversion, Michael had been surprised to find she had little to no recollection whatsoever of the Silver energy.

Taking in another long gulp of air, Lex told herself it was best that Junior had forgotten everything. If a Totem rejected you once, then you weren't likely to see it ever again. It was as though Junior had dodged a silver bullet … or rather, a grey bullet.

Junior was at her side once more, reclaiming her hand. His sister had been silent for far too long. Her face was no longer frustratingly devoid of emotion as it was earlier. Her eyes gave everything away. They looked sad and stricken.

"Lexie?" he spoke hesitantly.

"You can't name him after me," she said, her forlorn eyes still glued to the forest ahead.

"What?" Junior blinked. Of all the possible words Lex could've used to break her silence, he hadn't expected her to say that.

"Your vulture," she explained. "No creature that looks like *that* shall bear my namesake."

The vulture, who had been quiet up until now, grunted loudly at the implied insult, indicating that he had understood her perfectly.

"Wait—*my* vulture?" Junior's eyes lit up. "You're letting me keep him? Really?"

"Father gets the final say on that," she said as a reminder. That's how it worked in their little Golden Family of three. Lex wielded plenty of power as his Sister and Regent, but Lucien still held absolute authority as his Father and King.

"So… you're not going to tell him what happened tonight?" he asked, smiling hopefully.

Lex finally turned her head to look at him. Would she tell Lucien? Should she tell him? Junior's mind was already in the dark about being a Grey candidate. Perhaps it made sense to leave Lucien in the shadows as well?

The Regent wasn't sure how her Father-King would react to the discovery that Junior had been a contender for the Grey energy. He certainly hadn't been supportive when his wife had been chosen as the 1st Phantom King, nor had he been thrilled to see Michael becoming the 2nd Phantom King after Lana's "*death*." And, given all the bad blood between the Gold King and the last Grey King, Lex decided that staying silent seemed to be in everyone's best interest.

She knew Lucien would be furious with her for keeping this from him. But her Father had also entrusted her with his beloved Kingdom. It was something he had never done for any of his sons. That meant he had more faith in her than anyone else – the only exception being God Himself.

You'll have to trust me on this, Father, she thought, *It's for the best… I think.*

"It's his birthday," Lex said softly. "Let's not ruin it for him."

Junior's smile expanded across his face. "I highly agree, why ruin it for him?"

When Lex narrowed her eyes and pressed her lips together sternly, he decided to throw in a compliment to keep her disdain at bay. "Uhhh… you know, Lexie, you're really beautiful out here at night when it's too dark for anyone to see you properly."

Wait, that might've come out wrong, thought Junior as said compliment echoed lightly in his head. Maybe he ought to give her a hug… though she didn't look very huggable right about now.

Lex refrained from rolling her eyes. "I stand by what I said to your friends, Junior," she reminded him gravely. "My mercy is not something you want to test."

"Right, right. Thanks Lexie. My most merciful Sister-Princess-Regent-Tyrant. I appreciate it!" Junior nodded solemnly as he tried to maintain his glee. He couldn't believe he was going to get away without penalty.

The Prince had already endured plenty of punishments over the years. Like all those times he messed up and his Father made him sit alone for hours on end by the bluffs near their castle to contemplate "*the true meaning of life*" – whatever the hell that was. Or the time one of his teachers had reported him for repeatedly disturbing class. In response, Lucien had decided to teach his youngest a lesson by following him around school, going from class to class. Junior still remembered the way his Father had sat in the back of every class and stared him down *all* day long. Junior, along with every single person in attendance at Our Golden Lady of Fatema had been on edge that day. Lucien had even sat with him during lunch, death-stare perfectly intact throughout Junior's pink pear and kohlrabi tricolore salad. *So embarrassing!* … Then, there was the time when… Well, the list was rather endless. Best not get into it now.

"Alecto," said Lex.

"What?"

She nodded down at the vulture beside them. "That's what we'll call him."

"But that's a girl's name," he whined.

"You were about to name it Alexandra."

"That was before I knew he was a *he*."

"Come up with something else then," she shrugged.

Junior thought about it for a moment. No other name really came to mind. None that he liked, anyway. And it wasn't like the vulture looked like any of the commonplace male names found on Earth. He didn't look like a John or a Joseph or Zayan or an Asmodeus… The more he thought about it, *Alecto* didn't sound so bad.

"Alecto it is then," he said.

"We'll have to explain him to Father, though," said Lex.

Junior nodded in agreement. He certainly couldn't tell Lucien he had come across Alecto in the forest at this hour. "I can say I spotted Alecto earlier this morning while I was out sunbathing, and… and he followed me …and then…" Junior bit his lip as he tried to whip up a story out of thin air. "And then we decided he'd make a great birthday gift!"

Lex pursed her lips again. "I suppose Father's grown accustomed to subpar presents," she muttered, recalling the time Empress of the Planet Marnixia had gifted Lucien with a sword made of shark's teeth and a golden box of mud taken from the battlefield of a war she had exacted back in her home planet.

"Listen carefully, Junior," Lex's voice turned serious again, "I'm going to release a Gold Swan to investigate the forest. Let's see if it can find any of your belongings."

In the privacy of her own mind, Lex added, *See if it can find this mystery boy as well.*

"Oh… right," nodded Junior. He hadn't even noticed his bag was no longer in his possession until now. It struck him as rather odd since he couldn't recall removing his satchel from his person. He could've sworn he had kept it around his shoulder all throughout his venture.

"If it's still there, my Swan will find it."

"But wait, Lexie," another thought hit him, "You're not allowed to use your powers here. It's illegal and when Father finds out—"

"I'll deal with that," she said, brushing off his concern. "All you need to do is follow along with whatever I tell him … and remember, the second the Swan's out, this conversation never happened. Understood?"

Lex waited for a nod of confirmation before proceeding. Junior was too young to comprehend the full extent of Lucien's Kingly powers, but Lex knew how it worked – for the most part. Presently, their Father was still inside the party, happily oblivious to what was happening out here, because he *chose* to be.

As the Gold King, Lucien had enhanced eyesight and hearing capabilities, which allowed him to see and hear things from well over 100,000 feet away. The only reason he hadn't overheard his children's current conversation was because he wasn't tapping into those specific abilities right now.

Many people thought Lucien was constantly accessing the powers that came with his Divine energy. But that wasn't true at all. It was ludicrous to think Lucien was spying across vast distances and eavesdropping on everyone's conversations all the time. All that would do was deplete his energy and leave him with a monumental migraine.

So, Lex wasn't worried about Lucien earwigging on their conversation. But she knew the second she used her Golden Gift, everything would change. As the proprietor of the Golden energy, Lucien could detect traces of it from anywhere in the world. The second Lex summoned said energy, Lucien would know it and he'd be on high alert.

When Junior slowly nodded in confirmation, Lex straightened her already perfect posture and let out a deep breath. She wrote out a cursive S in the air as though her index finger were a gold-inked pen, and the sky was a piece of paper.

The Prince watched in awe as a large translucent golden swan quickly formed itself and leapt out of the S. The Swan let out a deep trumpeting call as it soared toward the forest.

Junior had seen Lex wield the Golden Gift many times and it never ceased to amaze him. He couldn't wait until he was old enough to be Gifted as well.

Lex hadn't bothered to look back at the Swan as it flew past her. She didn't need to provide verbal instructions either. The Gold Swan was her creation, linked directly to her thoughts. It knew exactly what to do.

She then closed her eyes and silently counted to three.

One.

She hadn't even made it to *two* when the wind ceased completely and —

"What's happening?" snapped Lucien.

"Father!!!" screeched Junior as he staggered back in shock. Lex had warned him that Lucien would be alerted the second she used her Gift. Even so, Junior hadn't expected to see their Father so suddenly.

"Junior." Lucien stood, towering over his children, his expression hard and stoic. His arrival shifted the atmosphere between the two siblings. It was as though they were back in a highly formal setting with their Father-King's entry commanding attention and respect. Junior dreaded those type of settings. It was during those moments where Lucien came off as less of a Father and more of a King.

"Er…Father," Junior repeated dumbly, unsure of what to say.

"Son," Lucien responded coldly, one pristine eyebrow on the rise.

"Father," said Lex.

"Alexandra."

"Father," Junior parroted thrice in a ridiculous attempt to delay the inevitable.

"That's enough, Junior." Lucien kept his eyes on his daughter while shutting down his son's nonsense. "Explain yourself."

"Ummm…." Junior stammered for something to say. It was his fault they were in this mess. It didn't seem fair that Lex was getting the brunt of their Father's ire. He had to come up with something to appease the man. "You know, Father, you look really handsome out here at night when it's too dark—"

Lucien cut his eyes at him and suddenly Junior found himself unable to speak. A glowing golden sash instantly appeared around his lower face, completely covering his mouth and preventing any sound from escaping his lips. The sash looked like liquid silk but felt like steel.

Junior's eyes widened at the realization that his Father had Shielded his mouth shut. Once again, Lucien had exhibited his powers without so much as a lift of his finger.

"Alexandra," Lucien said impatiently as his hard gaze returned to Lex, "Tell me why you used the Gift out here. Now."

Lex's poker face was already on. She hadn't even flinched at Lucien's appearance. She kept calm with a polite smile perfectly in place. Junior didn't know how she did it. Sometimes it felt like he was on a boat that was constantly on the verge of tipping over while Lex was observing him cooly from dry land.

"I had to, Father," she said smoothly, not even a tremor in her voice as she lifted her eyes and stared dead-on at the intimidating, imperious face of their Father-King. "I came out here after the dust storm dissipated. That's when I felt an unknown and unique energy coming from the forest. My Swan is investigating as we speak."

Junior didn't say anything. He couldn't say anything, literally. Nevertheless, he tried his hardest to visibly show that he was in complete alignment with Lex's explanation. But of all the lies she could have come up with, this one sounded rather odd. Apart from the Tree of Queens, which Lucien was already aware of, what other *unique energy* could be out there in the desert at this hour?

The Prince thought someone as clever as his sister could've come up with something far better than that. Of course, what Junior no longer knew was that Lex wasn't lying. There had been an additional source of Divine energy at work in the forest tonight – a Grey-coloured one, to be exact – and Lex was being meticulous with her words, providing Lucien with the bare minimum amount of truth to get by.

"You should have brought this to my attention straight away," he said admonishingly.

If Junior could move his mouth, he was sure his jaw would have dropped to the sand. He had never seen Lucien scold Lex in such a way. Lucien usually looked at Lex like she was his pride and joy, his greatest creation. But right now, he looked ready to punish her, both as Father and King.

"It's your birthday," said Lex. "You were having such fun. I didn't care to disturb."

"It's illegal for anyone to use a King's Gift in the Neutral Realm," said Lucien, his voice on the verge of splitting into an echo. "As the Golden Regent, you of all people know that doing so is an act of malfeasance."

"As the Golden Regent, I shouldn't have," she nodded, conceding to a certain degree, "But you forget, Father, I'm also the Phantom Princess."

Lex was the Gold King's daughter, but she was the Phantom King's sister. Regardless of her devotion to the Golden Empire,

Lex still maintained a title as Princess of the United Phantom Realm.

Junior's face beamed as though a lightbulb had gone off above his head. He understood where she was going with this. Their eldest brother, Phantom King Michael wasn't part of the Convocation, which meant he hadn't signed the agreement that prohibited the use of a King's Gift on Neutral soil. Technically, Lex had broken the law as the Golden Regent, but as the Phantom Princess, she also had immunity.

It was a good excuse, acknowledged Junior. He wished he had remembered to use it on Porki when his friend had chided him for illegal use of the Unseen-tonic. Junior always prided himself on being the sole Golden Prince, but technically, he was a Phantom Prince too, right? That meant he had immunity to do as he pleased here as well... didn't he?

Lifting his head, Junior found that Lucien didn't look mollified in the slightest by Lex's reasoning. If anything, the controlled anger that had been properly maintained on his Father's face thus far, now looked ready to explode on them.

"You foolish child!" He yelled at her, his voice rumbling across the desert. Thankfully, the Golden Shield behind them prevented their guests from eavesdropping. "You realize you're only avoiding trouble because of the protection that comes with being my daughter. Anyone else would have faced serious consequences."

"But I'm not anyone else, am I?" Lex kept her composure, not even flinching at Lucien's domineering tone. "As you said, I'm your daughter."

Lucien shook his head. "I expect better from you Lexie... You're a Regent now. You're supposed to lead by example. What would the world think of our realm if they witnessed your actions tonight?"

Lucien had always been a man who kept up appearances, and as a King, he believed in the Golden Standard, which meant absolute perfection in every aspect of life. It was something Lucien had drilled into all his children at one point or another. His realm wasn't like other realms. *This is the Gold Kingdom – the Golden Empire – where the higher standards prevail.* You had to be better than everyone else, and more importantly, you had to *show* them you were better than them every day and in every way. Never let them forget who you are. Never let them forget their place beneath you.

"You're right." Lex dropped her eyes to the sand and curtsied deeply in deference. "Forgive me, Father."

Before Lucien could respond, a familiar trumpeting sound blasted between them.

They all turned their heads to face the Gold Swan. The creature – well, it wasn't so much a creature as it was a swan-shaped bout of Golden energy – focused on Lex and shook its head in the negative before diving into Lex's chest and disappearing completely.

"It appears I was mistaken," said Lex as she whirled back to Lucien. "My Swan found no unusual energies."

Junior pouted a little and gave Lex a look as if to say, *What about my bag? What about all my stuff?*

No bag. No belongings. Lex gave him a faint, subtle head-shake.

No boy, either, she thought to herself.

"Alright Junior," Lucien said, now ready to interrogate his son, "Your turn."

The steely sash immediately disappeared. Junior finally managed to open his mouth and released a deep exhale.

"Wklweklaahhhhhh," he screeched, testing out his voice again. His Father had never silenced him with a Shield before. It had been rather petrifying.

"What are you doing out here?" Lucien asked him, and with one long finger aimed at the hideous being hiding behind his son, he demanded, "And what is *that*?"

"It's… That's Alecto. He's your birthday present," said Junior, purposely opening and closing his jaw as a way of exercising his facial muscles. "My gift to you, Father. You like?"

Lucien did not look impressed.

Alecto shifted behind Junior, trying to conceal himself as much as he could from the Gold King's disapproving gaze.

"You still haven't explained why you're out here, Junior. And on top of that, you'll need to explicate how you acquired an endangered bird," said Lucien.

Junior tried to recall what lie he and Lex had agreed upon. "The first time I saw him was this morning while I was out sunb—er," he paused, knowing Lucien didn't take kindly to his son disrobing in public, "while I was contemplating the meaning of life. You know, like all those great men of God you're always goin' on about… guys like, like Jesus and… all those other old guys that hung around Jesus … anyway … tonight, when I saw Lexie leaving the party, I decided to follow her out here … and that's when I saw Alecto again. I figured it must be destiny! Don't you think, Father?"

Lucien stared at his son throughout his ridiculous attempt at a believable explanation.

They're lying to you, Lucien, the Golden Totem inside him whispered bluntly in his head.

Really? You don't say? Lucien internally snarked back. Honestly, sometimes his own Totem treated him like he was a village idiot instead of a Chosen King.

Lucien knew perfectly well when his children were lying to him. The two of them were clearly concealing something of consequence from him. It was only a matter of whether he was going to let them get away with it or not.

I don't suppose you're going to tell me what actually happened? He asked his Totem through his thoughts.

The Golden Totem, who was allegedly omniscient, went radio silent.

Thought not, scoffed Lucien. He respected his Golden Totem as a Divine entity but still acknowledged it could be a right bastard at the best of times. Lucien suspected the Totem kept more secrets from him then all his children combined.

"Well?" said Junior softly, nervously, entirely unaware of the internal conversation his Father was having with the Golden Totem.

"*Well* what?" countered Lucien.

"What do you think, Father?" Junior stepped away to pick up the vulture and present it to him like it was a puppy or a kitten. "Do you like him?"

Like wasn't the word Lucien would use. But as far as presents ago, it wasn't the worst he'd ever received from Junior. The worst being the time Junior, then seven-years-old, had snuck into one of the kitchens in the servant's quarters to make Lucien breakfast in bed for Father's Day. It would have been a touching moment had Junior's idea of an ideal breakfast not been a tin of processed meat, a bunch of grapes, and a bottle of root beer. Even so, Lucien suspected all the nutrients (or lack thereof) in that vomit-inducing meal was of greater use than this obscene bird.

During the Dark Ages, the vulture might have made for a suitable gift. It did look rather lethal, and Lucien could have used it for dramatic effect. A ruthless-looking animal that could soar beside him into the battlefield made for a great entrance. In these modern times, however, he had no need for a hideous flying beast … and a broken, cowardly beast at that, judging by its wounded wing and the way it squirmed and avoided Lucien's gaze.

"This is what you consider a suitable gift for your Father-King, is it?" said Lucien.

"I thought you'd like a pet." Junior's chest deflated at his Father's apathetic tone. "And Lexie wouldn't let me buy you a girlfriend... Please, can we keep him?"

Lucien knew he shouldn't allow any of this. He shouldn't let his daughter get away with whatever she was concealing. Nor should he reward his son with a pet for whatever part he was playing in this. But he knew he would end up doing both because when it came down to it: he always went easy on his kids.

Correction: he went easy on his two youngest kids.

No one could argue that Lucien was gentle, loving, and patient with Lex and Junior in ways he had never been with Michael and Gabriel. Maybe it was because Lex was his Golden prodigy. Maybe it was because Junior didn't have his Mother around. Or maybe it was because Lucien remembered and regretted how he had treated Michael and Gabriel in the past. His two eldest children rarely ever spoke to him these days. He didn't want that to happen with Lex and Junior.

"He'll be your responsibility, Junior," he said stiffly.

That prompted surprised eyes and a wide smile from his son. "Really? We can keep him?"

"There is no *we* in this situation," Lucien gave him a pointed look, "That bird will be under your care."

"Thanks Father!" Junior sprang towards him.

Lucien lifted one palm in the air to cease the boy's movements. "Do not embrace me while you're holding that unsanitary creature," he said. "Lord knows where it's been."

"Shall we return to the party?" suggested Lex.

Lucien sighed and ran a hand tiredly along the side of his face. "Well, we certainly can't stay out here forever, can we?" he said dryly. "Yes, yes, let us go before our subjects begin to spread rumours as to why we've abandoned the celebration."

With his vulture in tow, Junior followed Lucien and Lex through the Shield and back into the party. He didn't care about whatever idle gossip the Osprey were spreading or the strange looks they had given the Prince when they caught sight of his newfound pet.

Obviously, he couldn't tell them he had absconded to Godshoots, got into a bind, and was subsequently rescued by a vulture. He would have to feed everyone the same lie about how he had met Alecto while he was sunbathing or meditating the meaning of life ... or something of that nature.

It was another lie. Another thing to remember. But Junior didn't mind. He was happy. And why wouldn't he be? Everything worked out in his favour. Lex hadn't squealed about him sneaking off to the forest. Lucien was letting him keep Alecto. Sure, Junior's friends were still miffed at him, but he knew that wouldn't last long. They always forgave him in the end.

All things considered, the Golden Prince found it to be a memorable night. Little did he know, he had forgotten the most memorable parts of that night.

Chapter 20:
What sort of sorcery is this?

It was a cold, beautiful night in the Neutral desert.

All the nights here were cold and beautiful. The desert, at this late hour, didn't know how to be anything else.

The party was over, and the Valentas had retired to their private campsite. Certain that Lucien and Junior had dozed off, Lex crept out of the tent, ghosting through the Golden Shield surrounding their lodgings.

The Volucris Knights currently on watch dropped their heads in deference as she passed.

Without looking behind her, she raised a hand to the air. It was a silent command to her guards: *Stay put. Stay out of my way. But stay close-ish.*

Lex swept through the seemingly endless spread of sand. She stopped at a seating area Lucien had created with his Divine energy. As with nearly everything Lucien made, it was glowing and golden. It looked like a large inflatable sofa.

Lucien had made it especially for her. He had ordered everyone to refrain from disturbing his daughter while she was seated here.

In the confines of his mind, Lucien could admit that he and Junior expected and demanded far too much of Lex's time and attention. This was his way of giving her a pinch of privacy whenever they traveled together.

Lex shivered. The wind felt like a whip against her tender skin. She had strapped on a coat before departing the tent, but it wasn't enough to fend off the night air. If only she could use her powers here. She could easily have created a Full-Body-Shield around her entire frame to protect herself from the elements. But she couldn't risk it. Not again. The Golden energy currently belonged to her Father, and using the Golden Gift would set off alarm bells in Lucien's mind, rousing him from his slumber.

Hugging her arms, she settled herself on the sofa and gazed out into the distance. There was nothing but sand for days.

"Look at all this. Take it in," Lucien had told his kids when they first arrived, *"The stretches of sand beneath us. The mystery and magic all around us."*

"What's so magical about it?" said Junior, unimpressed.

Lucien pulled Lex and Junior to his sides so that they were bracketing him. He squeezed them tightly as though he'd never let go. Gazing out into the raw beauty of the wilderness, he said with his usual dramatic flair, *"This, my son, this is where we shed our humanity and discover our immortal souls."*

She hadn't realized it until now, but her Father-King had made a good point.

Lex certainly felt like she had left her bodily existence behind at the borders separating the Neutral Realm from the rest of the world.

Daughter. Sister. Princess. Regent. Out here, all those manmade labels felt as distant as the stars shining above her.

The desert was anti-human. All worldly desires and ambitions were abandoned. Left outside the front door as though they were nothing but a pair of dirty shoes. You weren't allowed to leave the stains of human frailty here.

She loved the Gold Kingdom. Truly, she did. But as the Regent, she also knew the second she got back home, it was back to business in the very stifling world of politics, surrounded by men with vengeful egos and appetites for destruction. Knowing this, she savoured this quiet moment to herself.

The desert was the perfect backdrop for relaxation and solitude.

Like many beautiful women, Lex was a lonely girl. But even though she often felt lonely, she was never truly alone.

"Mikey," she said cheerily, seemingly speaking to nothing but air. "This is a nice surprise. What brings my favourite brother here? Have you missed me? It's been too long."

Crackles of Black energy shot through the atmosphere as Phantom King Michael materialized before his sister.

Michael had the appearance of a tall, youthful man in his 20s, but as a valensmen, he was well into his Ninth Century of life.

"It's been three days," Michael said in a deep, toneless voice.

He didn't bother addressing her other remarks. Lex fed the "*favourite brother*" line to all three of her siblings amid private conversations. Only Junior was dumb enough to eat it up. And, even if Michael had missed her, he'd never admit it. Lex's ego could drive to the edge of the universe without ever once stopping for fuel. He refused to contribute to the rapid inflation of her own sense of self-worth.

"Which gives you more than enough time to be missing a most beloved sister," Lex nodded at him.

"You knew I was here?" Michael was mildly impressed, though he'd never say it or show it.

As the Phantom King, Michael held proprietorship over the Black, White, and Silver energies. Whereas other Divine energies were loud and easier to detect, Michael's powers were elusive. Even an experienced King like Lucien had trouble sensing Michael's presence at times.

"Oh Mikey, you silly beast!" From her perch, Lex smiled up at him like a canary taunting a cat creeping around the bird cage. "Your Phantom energies are as sly as ever. It's your personal aura that gives you away. It's massive and unavoidable, much like the meteor that killed all the dinosaurs."

Michael merely grunted in response to her commentary.

Lex continued to grin at him. Michael looked so much like Lucien. They were both such strikingly beautiful men. But unlike Lucien, there was no trace of softness in Michael's eyes. No warmth in his aura. Whereas Lucien was loquacious and animated, Michael was a man of few words and even fewer facial expressions.

Trained by warrior monks throughout his adolescence, Michael could do more damage to a person's soul with a straight face and a slightly lifted brow than most people could with their entire bodies and an arsenal of weapons at their disposal.

"Junior and Father are asleep," she told him.

"I know."

"The guards probably can't hear much past the dunes, but they are watching."

"Only you," he said. "They can't see me."

For the time being, Michael had given his energies strict instructions to render him invisible to everyone except his sister. Before he became the Phantom King, he had been a Golden Prince and a General. He was a man who was accustomed to being obeyed. He expected submissiveness from everyone, even from the three Divine energies dwelling inside his body. Especially from them.

"Ah, the perks of your Unseen ability. I suppose they'll think I'm out here droning on to desert ghosts." With a shrug, she added, "Oh well, I doubt it'll rattle them. They're used to seeing Father talking to himself. They'll assume it runs in the family."

"He's not talking to himself."

"*I know*," she said pointedly. "But they don't know that."

"They don't need to know."

"Quite right," she agreed. "Anyway, you're here for the Tree of Queens, I take it?"

Michael gave a brief nod. There were several security measures in place to guard the Tree of Queens from unauthorized persons. Michael's Phantom-wardens, which he'd recently created and was currently testing in the beta stage, were merely one layer of protection. A few hours ago, those wardens he'd positioned around the blessed tree had released an alarm – one that only he could hear.

He would have come sooner had he not been preoccupied with business back in his Home-Realm. Besides, he knew Lucien and Lex could've handled any exigencies without his help.

"I figured you'd drop by to check in on it." Lex was surprised that Michael had agreed to help protect the Tree of Queens, especially since he outright refused to join the Convocation. It was odd to see him willingly engage with his fellow Kings on a project. No one knew his reasoning for it. But that was her eldest brother for you: big reputation and zero explanations.

"You needn't worry," she said reassuringly. "It was only Junior, having a bit of fun with his friends."

"I gathered." Michael assumed that was what his Phantom-wardens had tried to tell him when he investigated the tree. *Brother… brats…* were the only two words he was able to make out. He wasn't entirely sure if he had interpreted that correctly.

Michael expected absolute subservience from his three Totems and anything he created with their Divine energies. But much to his frustration, he didn't always get it. He still struggled to properly interpret the sounds they made in his head into actual words. Most of the time, their messages sounded like nothing but radio static in his ears.

It was irritating beyond reason. Lucien could create thunderbolts, unleash them across the planet, and get them to report back to him. The man didn't just make lightning out of thin air. He made it and he *spoke* to it. Michael, by contrast, could barely get a single word out of the ghostly soldiers he had created with his Phantom energies.

"Speaking of," said Lex, reclaiming his attention, "Mikey, I understand the need to be thorough with your safeguards. But is it really necessary to include spiritual possession as a means of protection? It's a mercy I didn't have to hire an exorcist for those kids."

"What?"

"Junior mentioned something had possessed his friends to stay away from the Tree. He implied they were hexed."

"That wasn't my doing."

"It wasn't?"

"Not entirely," said Michael. "Such mediumship isn't done with a King's energy."

"But you—"

"I outsource that type of work."

Lex paused. Understanding hit her. Upon reaching the Tree of Queens, Junior had been hindered by Michael's Phantom-wardens, but the temporary seizure of his friends' faculties had been someone else's handiwork.

"You recruited the Antaolia Family?" She nodded knowingly.

"Mother trusted them." Which meant Michael trusted them as well. Or, at the very least, he had found them reliable enough to keep around.

The Anatolias were sorcerers for hire. Hailing from a long dynastic line of witches, they employed ancient forms of magic using Earth's natural elements for manifestation, but much of their work was contingent upon finding and binding powerful spirits to obey their commands.

Witchcraft was a contentious practice in their world. Some realms outlawed it entirely, stating that the only true and trustworthy source of magic stemmed from a King's energy.

Under capable hands, magic from the Divine worked instantaneously and miraculously. Under a skilled spellcaster, magic from ancient sorcery could take anywhere from hours to years to manifest. But the one main benefit of sorcery was that it was as invisible as a ghost. There were no colourful bursts of energy lingering in the air when it came to old-world witchcraft.

Think of it this way:

- Killing a person with Divine energy was fast and easy, but it meant the cadaver would carry traces of said energy for days, sometimes months after decomposition. It was the equivalent of an assassin leaving their fingerprints all over the body.
- Killing a person with a hex took a lot more time and work, but it was possible to perform and impossible to prove. When done correctly, it created the perfect murder.

During her tenure as the Gold Queen, and later as the Phantom King, Lana had frequently employed the Anatolias to complete highly classified missions – ones which left no Divine fingerprints behind.

If Lex recalled correctly, the Anatolias were very learned when it came to hexes. And, if her assumptions were correct, then the Anatolias must have installed a curse: any persons without authorized knowledge of the Tree of Queens, who came to the desert in search of the very thing, would leave forgetting all about it. It certainly explained why Junior's friends didn't carry any recollection of the tree's existence. Lex wouldn't be surprised if Junior himself forgot all about the tree by the time they left the desert.

"I see," Lex whispered. "Well, don't tell Father. He's sure to pop a neck vein if he finds out there's witchcraft at work around his blessed tree."

Michael nodded.

"What?" he asked, noting the concern and curiosity that briefly flickered across her dark eyes.

"What do you mean *what*?"

Michael glared down at her for making him utter more than one syllable. "What's wrong?"

"Wrong? Whatever makes you think something's wrong?" Lex laughed lightly.

The Phantom King cut his eyes at her. He didn't say anything. He continued looming over her like a shadow, waiting her out.

It didn't take long.

"Oh, very well," Lex rolled her eyes. She didn't want to bring it up now. It felt inappropriate to talk shop in such a sacred place. The desert would have to forgive-and-forget her for it. Write off her discourtesy as that of an ignorant foreigner visiting its land.

"Look, about the Tree of Queens," she started, "I know it already contains quite a few Kingly energies… Gold, obviously … and the Red- and Blue Kings provided their contributions, as well… But, did you happen to sense any *other* Divine energies in that forest tonight?"

"No," he said tightly. "Why?"

Lex sighed. "I was going to wait until we got back home. But since you're here, I may as well tell you."

With all the warmth of a glacier, he narrowed his eyes and bit out, "Tell me *what*?"

Chapter 21:
What are *they* playing at?

Michael stayed as silent as a graveyard. His face looked as though it had been carved from stone. He remained standing as Lex recounted everything.

It was only several minutes after she finished speaking that he inquired, "You're certain it was the Grey Totem?"

"I can't say with absolute certainty, no. My powers couldn't detect anything off-kilter in the woods. Neither could you, apparently," she remarked. "But you know how evasive Grey energy can be."

The Grey energy vibrated at a very similar frequency to Black, White, and Silver. It was highly spectral and nebulose, making it difficult to sense.

"And no trace of the boy Junior encountered?" Michael said.

"I couldn't find any." Lex shook her head. "Junior said he was the same child from the sect of pagan priestesses we ran into earlier." Sensing what Michael was about to ask next, she said, "But I can't run a search for them without using my powers – thereby, alerting Father."

"I'll do it then." Michael moved his head sharply leftward to the point where it sounded like he had snapped his own neck. His face then split itself three ways as a trio of apparitions shot out of him. Three ghostly eagles in three different colours, black, white and silver. They spread their wings and waited.

Michael forced his face back into place and gave the eagles silent instructions to find a coven of Ancient Egyptian cat-worshippers.

With a synchronized shake of their beaks, the Phantom-eagles sped off. Michael and Lex watched as the eagles rode the current, changed directions and scanned the landscape until they were no longer within close range.

Now, it was their turn to wait.

"If my theory is correct," said Lex, still gazing heavenward, "Then that boy – whoever he is – may be the next Grey King."

"There's no proof of that."

"Not *yet*, you mean." Lex dropped her eyes back down to him.

"I doubt it."

"You're not worried?"

"Junior wasn't chosen, but that doesn't mean the other boy won the Grey crown," said Michael. "Not that it's anything worth winning."

"But that boy—"

"—is nothing more than a child. Even if he is chosen, it wouldn't matter. His body will self-combust within two weeks."

"Fine, let's say the boy poses no threat. Regardless, the Grey lands haven't had a monarch in over a decade. The fact that its Totem is looking for one now…" she drifted off. "I believe that means we need to prepare for the emergence of a new Grey King. And if that happens, what will we do, brother?"

We was what she said. *You* was what she meant.

What will you do, brother? Will you make the same mistake twice?

The Greys and the Golden-Phantoms had been on bad terms for ages, but everything came to a standstill twelve years ago, when Michael had killed the previous Grey King.

He had no regrets, despite knowing fully well the murder of a King always came at a huge cost. So far, Michael hadn't been met with any karmic payment demands. Not yet.

Lex believed the energies governing the Universe were biding their time with her eldest brother, waiting for Michael to have one very bad day. At which point, *The Powers That Be* would come sweeping in to make things infinitely worse for him.

"There's nothing to do," he said, completely unbothered.

"Mikey—"

"You've seen what the Grey Kingdom is like these days."

Currently Kingless, the Greys were now managed by a chamber of corrupt politicians. Michael knew that whomever the Grey Totem chose – boy, man, or otherwise – would inherit nothing but a scrap of land crippled with political instability and poverty.

"They're no threat to us, sister," Michael said severely.

Lex disagreed with that sentiment but kept it to herself. Unlike the Golden- and- Phantom realms, the Greys had nothing left to lose. That alone made them dangerous.

The Golden Regent believed her brother had made two major mistakes all those years ago. The first had been killing the Grey King. The second had been refusing to invade the Grey realm after killing their King.

The Greys didn't have any seemingly valuable resources that made them worth all the effort that came with a full-scale invasion, but acquiring them would've made it difficult for a new Grey King to sweep in and run the land.

Acquiring a land was much like fostering a child. You'd have to provide for its citizens and their welfare, at least to a certain degree. But Michael had never forgiven the Greys for what they had done to his Mother, and he would sooner walk barefoot through a sea of broken glass than accommodate their civilians in any capacity.

The brief silence that came between them was broken by the return of the phantom-eagles. Without so much as a screech, they flew back inside Michael's head.

"Well?" said Lex. "Did they find them?"

Michael's lips merged into a flat, grim line. "No."

"So, the boy's nowhere to be found, and neither is his congregation."

"Doesn't mean anything."

"Doesn't it?" countered Lex coldly.

Michael glared at her again. Much to his advantage, he had a stare that could easily shame and break a person's soul. Much to his dismay, he had a little sister who was immune to his intimidating presence.

Averting his gaze, Michael asked, "You're certain Junior doesn't remember what the boy looked like?"

"Positive."

"He's been known to tell tall tales."

"If he was, I would've caught him. He's not that good of a liar," said Lex. "I suspect the Grey Totem must have been wiped it from his mind."

Michael whipped his head back to her.

"What?" Lex frowned up at him. "What is it?"

"Junior doesn't remember. But *you* do."

Lex's expression was raked with confusion... until it dawned on her. Memories had been erased from Junior's mind, but not before he got the chance to tell her everything. Why didn't the Grey Totem wipe her memory as well?

"It wants me to remember what Junior saw," whispered Lex. "But why?"

"What are they playing at?" Michael growled out into the air.

By *they*, he was referring to the Totems.

When a Chosen King's body merged with the Divine powers of a Totem, it formed a symbiotic relationship. However, a King's beliefs and schemes didn't always align with whatever their respective Totem was planning.

Totems had their own private agendas. They gave Kings free will to do as they pleased, up to a specific point. It was said that a King's energy contained limitless power, but the truth was there were certain times where Totems purposely held back their Kings.

This was why their Father had never been able to conquer the entire world. Lucien had obtained a large portion of it, to be sure, but he would never become the sole King of Earth. Because the Golden Totem inside him would never allow it.

It also explained why the Neutral Realm was Kingless. It wasn't because all the Chosen Kings acknowledged the region's holiness and history. Plenty of them had wanted to conquer this desert for themselves. But when it came time to plot and dominate, they found themselves much like impotent dogs – entirely unable to perform.

To this day, the Neutral desert remained undisturbed by the power-hungry folly of men because all the Totems willed it so.

"Perhaps…" started Lex.

"Perhaps what?"

"We don't know if a new King was chosen tonight. Perhaps we won't know for a while. But one thing is clear, the Grey Totem was here and it's looking for its next mortal host," she said. "Maybe they left my memory intact so that I could relay that bit of information to you … as a warning."

Michael mulled it over. Was that what this was? He had ignited the wrath of a Divine entity. And, this was the Grey Totem telling him, warning him, threatening him. *I'm back, you bastard, and I'm coming for you.*

A lesser man might have cowered in fear, but Michael was on another level. He had long ago conquered all his fears – to the point where they wouldn't dare make a reappearance in the confines of his psyche.

The Grey Totem was nothing worth fretting over, in Michael's opinion. That's why he wasn't afraid. If anything, Michael was merely a little miffed that said entity had used his little brother as bait to grab his attention.

Of course, Junior was nothing but bait. A boy like that could never be Chosen, Michael thought scornfully. Was he wrong about his brother? Doubtful. Michael had once seen the boy remove his left shoe, bring it to his lips, and attempt to eat it. Junior had been around three years old at the time. An unimpressive child, who was currently growing into an equally unimpressive man.

"Do you still believe there's *nothing to do*?" mocked Lex. She could sense Michael was on the verge of dismissing their current situation as an empty threat. "We made the mistake of underestimating the Greys once before," she said sternly, "Remember how that turned out."

An ambush … The previous Grey King and his troops attacking their Mother… Lana left broken and dying in the snow… Phantom King Lana's Totems leaving her body and choosing Michael… Michael using his newfound powers to punch a hole straight through the Grey King's face.

The memories pierced him like thorns inside his bone marrow.

They stared at one another. There was nothing but sand and silence between them.

Finally, Michael yielded to her concerns. "What would you have me do?"

Lex was seven centuries younger than him, but Michael wasn't too proud to turn to his sister for guidance. There was a reason everyone called her the Golden Prodigy.

As the former General to the Golden Armed Forces, Michael had extensive experience winning wars. In a battlefield, he knew how to defeat 100,000 enemies with only 1,000 troops. Lex lacked such military prowess, but she had more than enough creativity in her mind to make up for it. She knew how to win a fight without fighting. She knew how to play the long game.

Michael used weapons and brute strength to break a person's body. Lex used her knowledge and imagination to break their spirit. Throughout the course of their lives, Michael would keep the Valenta-Empire running on a day-to-day basis, but Lex… she would be the one to make it last to the end of eternity.

"You needn't turn to me, Mikey." Flashing him a row of ivory-white teeth, she said through a tight smile, "You'll know what to do in time, I'm sure."

"Alexandra—"

In a venomously polite tone, she asserted, "Your Totems are listening, are they not? Perhaps they can offer some guidance?"

Michael immediately nodded, a sharp jerk of his head to indicate he understood her perfectly.

It had nothing to do with turning to his Totems for advice, and everything to do with the fact that they could see and hear everything.

This was Lex's coded way of telling him, *Yes, I have a plan. No, I can't tell you what it is because your Divine energies might thwart us.*

There was a fine line between symbiosis and para-symbiosis. The Totems were meant to work with their Kings, but sometimes, it felt like they were purposely working against them.

What are they playing at? It was a question applicable to all Totems.

"Anyway, let's put a pin on this, shall we?" Lex feigned innocence and pretended to backtrack. "You're right to a certain extent, I'll admit. There really is nothing we can do for the time being, except keep an eye out for the Grey energy."

Michael nodded. "It's late. You should get some rest."

"Oh, but I'm not sleepy. Far from it." Just like that, Lex's voice changed back to its usual shade of sweetness. "Won't you sit with me? You've been on your feet this entire time."

"I need to get back. I left Gabe in charge."

"But we haven't had a chance to catch up. You've been all business from the moment your molecules shot into the scene. Don't you want to hear about how Father's birthday party went?"

"No."

"What about me, then? Aren't you curious as to how the better part of my night fared?"

"No."

Lex rolled her eyes. "Oh Mikey, for once, can't you pretend to take an interest?"

"No."

Undeterred, Lex patted the empty space next to her on the sofa. "Come now. Only for a little while. You wouldn't deny your baby sister – you're *one and only* baby sister – some much-needed attention, would you?"

Michael continued to frown down at her. Lex was the last woman in the world who needed more attention.

"Come," Lex repeated, holding out her palm, "Give me your hand."

Michael ignored her request. He knew if you gave Lex your hand, she'd try to take your heart and soul right along with it.

Nevertheless, he decided to indulge her a little.

Removing his cloak, Michael threw it around her shoulders before eyeing the couch with distaste. It was a ridiculous-looking, see-through chaise. It appeared soft and squishy, but it wasn't the slightest bit elastic. Since it was made with Lucien's energy, the item was as sturdy as a steel bench.

Lex drowned herself in the warmth of her brother's coat. And when Michael seated himself adjacent to her, she didn't hesitate to latch onto his arm like an eagle locking in a prey with its talons.

Much like her Father-King, when Lex grabbed hold of someone she loved, she did so with the intention of never letting go.

Chapter 22:
Fighting with fate, am I?

"And you should've seen the Duchess of Cassowary's gift to Father this year: a remarkably large gold-dipped pearl ring. Or so she tried to have us believe. Naturally, I had it appraised and investigated. The so-called *pearl* beneath the gold turned out to be one of her gallstones. When I confronted her about it, she confessed it was her life's wish to have '*some part of her pressed against the King's heavenly body.*' Shameless! Absolutely shameless, Mikey! I swear, this woman would happily slice both her wrists on Father's cheekbones if it meant she got to touch him…"

Lex ranted on as Michael impassively stared ahead at the sprawling dunes of the Neutral Desert.

They were still seated on the Golden settee. Lex kept bringing up trivial nonsense that Michael couldn't care less about.

Lex knew Michael wasn't really listening, but she didn't mind. She was content to snuggle up next to her big brother and have a nice confab. Granted, her brother wasn't one for chitchat nor was he a *snuggable* man. Embracing Michael was like trying to have a tickle fight with a gigantic boulder.

"The guy hasn't cracked a smile since the 12th century, Lexie," her brother Gabriel had told her once, "Don't get me wrong. Mike's my favourite person in the world. He's just not built for comfort and cheer … But even so…"

Even so, the fact remained that Michael was still here at her behest. He wouldn't have done that for anyone else (except

Gabriel, of course). She was special. In that sense, Golden Princess-Regent Lex supposed she was just like any other girl in the world: she had an insatiable need to feel special.

"Mind you, not all of Father's gifts were so deviant. Lady Pochard presented him with a custom embroidered portrait of his coronation ceremony back in 1030 AD. It was a rather majestic sight. And she did all the needlework herself, can you believe?" Lex nudged his side with her shoulder. "I've grown quite fond of her over the years. She's graceful, kind, and selfless. Wise beyond her centuries, and I find her utterly charming. So much so that I think she might be a real contender."

That last word got Michael's attention. *Contender.* "For what?"

"For the Phantom Queenship, of course."

Michael slashed his eyes at her. "Lexie—"

"There's no going around it, Mikey. It's time we resurrect Operation-Trophy-Wife for you," she sing-songed. "You'll be surpassing your First Millennia of life soon enough, and at the rate you're going, you're headed for everlasting spinsterhood."

"Lexie—"

"Now, now," she bopped him lightly on his nose. "You can't keep flirting around with matrimony forever."

Michael had never flirted with anyone a single day in his life. If they threw themselves at him, it was their choice to do so, their mistake to make.

Lex patted him on the knee. "It's high time you settled down with someone respectable and gave me a little nephew and/or niece to gush over."

For his part, Michael had no need for a spouse, and no desire for children. "Lexie—"

Leaning in, she whispered softly, "It's what Mother always wanted for you."

Michael turned away from her, his silver eyes streaking back to the dunes. The refusal that was on precipice of Michael's lips withdrew and fell back down his throat at the mention of Lana.

"Fine," he scraped out.

Lex smiled like a lioness that caught sight of its dinner. She knew mentioning Lana would clinch the deal. At the end of the day, the dreaded Phantom King Michael was just like any other boy in the world: he had an unnatural attachment to his mother. Even now, with Lana stuck somewhere between life and death, Michael was determined to make her happy.

"Splendid!" beamed Lex. "I have a slew of nice girls in mind. I shall arrange for you to meet them over the next few weeks."

Michael grunted. *Nice* wasn't exactly his type. *Nice* would never survive in his realm of magic, murder and mayhem. The nastier the better, in his case. But he didn't dare say it out loud to his sister.

"I was thinking you'd come to the Gold Kingdom to meet with any potential partners. We offer a much more romantic backdrop, wouldn't you say? No offence Mikey, but you're not likely to find true love in the Phantom Realm. If anything, I'm pretty sure that's where love goes to die…"

As Lex prattled on, neither Michael nor the three Totems inside him were paying much attention. Much to her benefit, they were entirely unaware of her schemes.

There was a reason Lex wanted Michael married and breeding. It had nothing to do with their Mother's wishes. Nor was it affiliated with Lex's penchant for meddling and matchmaking.

This was all very strategic. This was her plan… or at least, one part of it.

Children of Chosen Kings usually didn't inherit thrones. The Totems chose the King and throughout history only one Prince had picked up where their monarch left off and that was

Michael. He was living proof that while succession was rare, it was still possible.

And tonight, Junior came very close to acquiring the Grey throne.

In Lex's mind, that solidified her theory: the Valentas were special.

They already had three Kings in their family: Lucien, Lana (formerly), and Michael.

Whose to say they couldn't have more Kings? Whose to say they couldn't *create* more Kings in the family?

Lex felt her primary purpose in life was to ensure the continuous safety and success of the Golden and the Phantom realms. But in order to do so, the realms had to remain in their hands, in perpetuity. They couldn't allow an outsider to prance in, inherit everything they had created as a family, and cast them out. They couldn't allow the Totems to choose a non-Valenta as the next Gold King or the next Phantom King.

That's why Michael – whether he liked it or not, whether he wanted to or not – would have to do his bit. He would have to get married and generate children who could potentially inherit a Kingship. Lex would make sure of it.

She didn't care if Michael was an unmovable object. He'd haul her brother down the aisle in an armored tank if she had to. Anything to get him married and multiplying.

And, it's not as though Lex was resting everything on Michael's shoulders. She was making her fair share of contributions to the Valenta's Great Dynastic Plan.

Totems made the final call when it came to selecting Kings, but that didn't mean they couldn't be influenced. She knew her Father's Golden Totem was watching everything through his eyes. *Good.* What most people didn't realize was that Lex's entire career as the Golden Regent was one long audition tape for Kinghood.

Truthfully, Lex didn't want to be a King. She enjoyed all the privileges, freedoms, and loopholes that came with being a Princess far too much to give it up. If it were up to her, she'd be a Princess forever.

Their subjects called Lucien *"the Eternal Monarch"* because thus far, no one had succeeded him. Other Kingdoms, like the Reds and the Blues, were already on their what? 125th King? 88th King? The Gold Kingdom, in its lengthy history, was still under the rule of the same monarch it had since its birth.

Lucien was a constant, steadfast figure in a perpetually changing world. But what would they do if something dire ever happened to him? Or even Michael? The Valentas would become commoners, sweeping the streets they used to own. Lex nearly shuddered at the thought. That was no life for her!

Lex genuinely hoped her Father remained the Gold King forever. But if that wasn't possible, then she wanted the Golden Totem to know that she was the next best person for the job…

Granted, she might've lost a few brownie points tonight. She imagined the Golden Totem wasn't too pleased with her using the King's Gift, thereby breaking one of the key laws of the Neutral desert. But Lex doubted she left a bad impression. Afterall, the Golden Totem had chosen Lucien, a man who always believed the rules never applied to him. In that sense, Lex was no different from her Father-King.

Even if said Totem didn't choose her, it could still choose Gabriel or one of Gabriel's children, or one of Michael's children as the next Gold King. As long their Kingdoms stayed in the family.

As the wind picked up, a phantom sound rung through her ears.

"You're fighting with fate, my love," said the spectred-voice of her Mother.

Lex shook it off, ignoring the warning in the ghost's tone.

As with everything, Lex wasn't one to sit quietly on the fence. She was always on one side of the garden or the other. Warm and loving when she wanted to be; cold and distant when she had to be. A romantic who loved the idea of destiny; a realist who refused to leave everything to fate.

In this case, she wasn't going to resign the Valenta Dynasty to forces outside of her control. She wasn't giving up her family's history, their achievements and their rank to predestination. If she had to, she would make fate bend, kneel and bow to her will. It wouldn't be her first time.

Chapter 23:
Why did the angels ghost us?

"Father's talking to himself again." Through a pair of roof-prism binoculars, Junior watched as Lucien floated directly beneath a circle of sinister-looking clouds.

Slices of lightning rippled across the grey sky. Lucien had manifested a pair of translucent golden wings, providing a heavenly glow against the looming darkness. His Father looked as he always did whenever he was airborne: angelic and avenging, like he couldn't decide whether he wanted to save the world or smite it.

"He's not," said Lex. She paid Lucien no mind as he nonchalantly stirred up a dry thunderstorm.

While their Father was on the wing, Junior and his sister remained on the surface level, sitting side by side on a blanket with the desert looming large all around them. The glitz and glamour of last night's attire was long gone; they were back in neutral-toned linen shirts and trousers, safari jackets, and sturdy boots.

Neither of the Valenta siblings were worried about getting struck by the thunderbolts for they were all made by Lucien, and their Father-King's energy knew better than to hurt his children. There was no need to worry about the rain either. All the droplets were evaporating in the air before they could even reach the ground. And as for the thunder... well, thunder was nothing but sound; it wasn't anything worth fearing.

"He is, though. Look at him. I can see his lips moving. He's clearly talking to himself," Junior dropped his binoculars as he shot a look toward Lex.

"He's not," she repeated blandly.

Lex was stretched out across the blanket as though she were getting a suntan. Junior figured she must be receiving some supernatural sustenance from Lucien's electric show. The Golden Gift she wielded came directly from the Divine energy currently stored in Lucien's body. Energy pulling on energy. In that sense, their Father-King was like the sun to her, and she was out here photosynthesizing.

If they were back home or anywhere else in the world, Lex would've manifested her own wings and taken flight as well. But she was playing by the rules (this time) and refraining from using her powers on Neutral soil.

"He is!" insisted Junior. "I catch him doing it all the time back home."

"He's not," she said thrice-over.

The Prince could see his Father-King's ethereal form reflected on her aviator sunglasses. "Has he gone mad, do you think?"

"He's always been a little mad. All Kings are like that. It's practically a prerequisite for the job. But even so, he's not talking to himself."

It was their last day in the desert, and there was nothing left to do. All their guests had departed. The only people remaining were the Golden Family, along with their Secutors, personal staff, and guards. Lucien had given his employees the day off to enjoy the Neutral Realm. Last Junior heard, they had all gone westward, closer to the borders, to explore the safari zone. They wouldn't be back until tomorrow afternoon when it was time to go home.

Even Alecto had been sent away for medical testing. Junior had wanted to avoid that, but his family had insisted. Alecto was a wild bird, and they needed to ensure he didn't contain any harmful diseases before transporting him over to Golden soil.

So, it was just the three Golden Royals, left to their own devices.

It was a rare day for Lucien and Lex. No political meetings, no diplomatic calls, no social engagements, no spiritual quests. The King and the Regent were free to do as they pleased today. But all they seemed to want to do was a fat lot of nothing.

Lex was resting. *"Doing nothing is the greatest luxury, Little Wing,"* she had told him with a long yawn.

Lucien was flying. *"A King is never bone-idle, my boy. He is always working in service to his people, and to God. I assure you every cell within this immaculate form of mine is doing God's work at this very moment,"* he had said primly before soaring off into the sky.

Junior was bored. He was pouring through a folder, which contained the ancient celestial sketches Lucien had brought with him on his search for Eden. They were the same pictures

Junior had been perusing with disinterest yesterday. Occasionally, he'd stop and lift his eyes heavenward. Every time he did so, he caught Lucien seemingly talking to himself.

Lucien had promised to take his children camel-riding when he was done, but the Prince had no idea how long it would be until his Father's feet touched sand again. If he so wished, the Gold King could stay up there for all the hours of eternity, monologuing to himself.

"Who's he talking to then, Lexie?"

"His Totem," Lex replied truthfully and immediately, inwardly, cursed herself for it. She shouldn't have stayed up last night, chewing the fat with Michael. Now, in her drowsy state of mind, she was letting important information slip out. It was a mistake to mention such Divine entities around her little brother, especially given his recent encounter with the Grey Totem. Sure, Junior had forgotten all about it, but Lex still needed to be careful. She couldn't risk triggering any lost memories in her brother's head.

Lex tried shrugging off her verbal misstep as a means to divert Junior. "Or maybe he's talking to God or some such spiritual superior, I don't know," she said cooly.

Once again, Junior's head shot up to Lucien, eyes narrowed in inspection. His Father-King was an easy man to love, but a difficult one to understand.

The Gold King was constantly surrounded by courtiers, diplomats, loyal subjects, enemies posing as friends, and enemies with whom he was occasionally friendly. He had a slew of devoted admirers and dedicated adversaries to keep him company. And yet, Lucien was possibly the loneliest man in the world. Junior was positive his Father-King had no real friends to talk to. Was that why he was always talking to God? Or was God the one purposely making his Father lonely?

Lucien absolutely, unequivocally loved God – perhaps to the point of bone-crushing loneliness. He looked for God *everywhere* in his life. Lucien was here now in pursuit of Him. That sort of intense devotion to a higher power, along with his commitment to his children and his citizens, left very little room in his heart for anyone else.

Then again… Junior's dark eyes slowly sank back down to the images on his lap. Lucien was a King, and Kings were never truly alone, were they? There was always something else – *some such spiritual superior* – there with them, inside of them, yanking at their blood cells.

"Lexie…" He moved his palm along the sketch of a seraphim, sweeping his fingers along a neat row of bloodshot eyes that made up the core of the angel's body.

"Hmm?"

"…Do you think Totems are angels?"

Slowly, Lex turned to him. She said nothing.

"I mean… I know Father says his Totem came to him shaped like a big-glowing-golden-griffin-thingamajig. But that's not what it really is, is it?" Junior carried on at Lex's silence. "It's like how the Red King says his Totem is a dragon. It's not really a dragon giving him powers. Just like it's not really a griffin inside Father right now. The shape the Totem takes is meant to be symbolic, right? … No one knows what Totems are *really* like, except for Kings, and they're not telling us the whole story. They could be angels, for all we know."

He observed his reflection on her glasses as he awaited her response.

After a while, Lex's silence became far too loud for him to cope with.

"Well, what do you think?"

"I wouldn't know," she said in a vacant tone.

Junior frowned. "But you were there when Mike saw his three Totems."

Lex's long, swan-like neck craned eastward, presenting him with a view of her perfect profile. She didn't like summoning *that* particular memory. Junior had only been an infant at the time; far too young to recall the pain of it all. But for the rest of the Valenta siblings, it had been the worst day of their lives – for Michael had seen his Totems mere seconds after Lana had *died*. The 2nd Phantom King succeeding his predecessor. The son inheriting his Mother-King's throne. The first Royal inheritor in the history of Chosen Kings. The first and only one, thus far.

"I witnessed Michael talk to an empty sky," said Lex. "I didn't actually see the Totems themselves."

"But—"

Lex snapped her head back to him. Beneath the shades, her eyes were cutting and sharp. "Only people who've been chosen can tell you the truth about Totems. And that's never happened to me," she said evenly. "You should ask Father or Michael."

"Mike only speaks five syllables a day, and he'd never spare any of them on me," scoffed Junior. "And Father will do what he always does whenever anyone asks him a simple question."

"Which is?" Lex asked, as if she didn't know.

"He'll start monologuing until they forget what they originally asked."

Lex hummed for lack of a better response. She couldn't deny the accuracy of that assumption. Lucien's verbal tirades were as inevitable as death and taxes; though they were not always as peaceable as death and were often far more painful than taxes.

"Besides, he'll just scuttle out the same scripted response. The one all the Kings like to say," Junior cleared his throat, deepened his voice, and said mockingly, "*It's highly classified information, among Kings only.*"

It was a popular response that many Kings, their Father included, gave to the general public. *We can't reveal such sensitive information, as it's to be kept among Kings only*, they'd tell everyone gravely as though they were part of some secret society.

"Father never gives any straight answers," said Junior grumpily.

"We're lucky he lets us ask the questions," said Lex. "He never granted Mikey and Gabby such a privilege when they were growing up."

"How come?"

"Father was a different man with them. Not like how he is now, with us."

"Junior's got it easy," Gabriel had once told Lex. "Every time that boy acts out, Father dismisses it as a hormone imbalance," he grumbled, his tone laced with a twinge of jealousy. "Michael and I weren't even allowed to have hormones."

Lex shifted away from Junior again, signalling her desire to end the conversation.

Junior cast her a strange look. Lex was acting oddly today. He noticed it this morning when she hadn't yelled at him for using her jade face-roller to clean his tongue. She hadn't even bothered pasting on her usual camera-ready smile before stepping outside to face the world. Her exhaustion was too obvious.

With all her daily responsibilities, the Prince assumed his Sister-Princess-Regent felt far more tired than she let on. But today was the first time she actually *looked* tired. Hence, the need to eclipse half her face with those large dark spectacles.

He couldn't even begin to understand what was going on in her head. Lex was as labyrinthine and secretive as Lucien, if not more. Even her secrets had secrets.

Junior could tell something was troubling her, but it was obvious she didn't want to talk about it or about anything else for that matter. Her silence was a request for privacy and space.

If he was a good little brother, he'd respect her wishes and give her a little bit of peace.

But he wasn't.

Poking a finger at her side, he prodded, "So, what do you think about the Totems?"

"Junior," she groaned, "I already told you. I don't know—"

"I'm not asking you what you know. I'm asking you what you *think*."

With a long, drawn-out sigh, Lex shot up to a seated position and faced her brother. "Do I think Totems are angels?" She repeated his original inquiry. "I don't know, and I don't have much of an opinion on the matter, *but* ... anything's possible, I suppose."

"You said angels used to talk to people, right? Maybe they still do, only now, they're called Totems, and they only talk to Kings."

"*I don't know, I wasn't around when angels allegedly conversed with mortals,*" had been her exact words.

"Allegedly," she stressed the word. "I said they *allegedly* talked to people. No one knows for sure."

"The Bible says they did."

"You've read the Bible?"

"Father ordered me to."

One perfectly plucked brow shot out of the rim of her glasses. "And you actually did as you were told?"

"I didn't need to read it, OK? Father read most of it to me in lieu of bedtime stories."

Lex hugged her knees, bringing them up to her chest. She gazed up at their Father-King. "It's in every monotheistic scripture – the Torah, the Bible, and the Quran," she said softly. "They all suggest the same thing: angels interacted directly with mankind. Occasionally, they even appeared to people in human form… Now, if we were to *assume* that's true, then somewhere along the centuries and the millennia, they must have stopped."

"But why?"

"I don't know. It appears they withdrew from all communication without any explanation whatsoever."

"So what? They ghosted us?"

Lex flitted her face back to him. Due to her glasses, he was still unable to read her expression, but he detected a bit of amusement in her tone as she said, "Can't blame them, really. Humanity isn't easy to love."

"We're not that bad," he said in defense of mankind.

"Oh, I'm not so sure, Little Wing." There was a slight twitch at the corner of her lips. "We create our own trouble and fall into the snares of our own making. Perhaps they thought it best to leave us to our self-inflicted fates."

"Still… we have our moments… We've got music and art and sports and money," Junior listed off all the fantastic concepts humanity had created, all the wonderful things this world had to offer, "We've got friends…and family… and we help each other out on occasion." Out of nowhere, for reasons unknown to him, another thought came to his mind, "And sometimes, we help people we don't even know for no reason whatsoever. So… you know, we're not that bad. Not all the time."

Lex's smile was wistful. She wondered if Junior would ever gain enough self-awareness to realize that he, like their Father before him, was an eternal optimist. If he did, it would be much later in life. Right now, at the tender age of 12, Junior was a subconscious optimist, trying (and failing) to play the part of a nonchalant pessimist. He wanted people to think he was as cool and detached as Michael, when in actuality, he was as bright and sanguine as Lucien. But he was still too young to fully embrace who he was at heart. He was still too green to appreciate everything that would one day make him golden.

"You may have a point," she acknowledged, "Even in scripture, angels – much like Totems – only appeared to certain people at specific times. Perhaps nothing's changed in that regard," with a nod towards the King in the sky, "And they're only revealing themselves to a chosen few."

Junior's gaze plunged to the picture atop his lap. The seraph gaping back at him with its blood-soaked eyeballs looked more beastly than ethereal. More demonic than angelic. He didn't want to admit it, but he supposed there was another possibility: the Totems were angels posing as demons, and they had everyone fooled.

He flipped the page, coming across another angelic entity. It was the same angel Junior had been colouring in yesterday: a low-grade principality wielding a flaming sword as it protected the sanctity of paradise from the sins of men.

The memory of Terry and Meryl in the forest, all possessed and petrifying, coursed through him. Whatever demons had gotten into them weren't so awful, he reasoned. They weren't out to harm anyone. They were only protecting the tree from people who wanted to use and abuse its powers.

Squinting up at his Father once more, he admired the shiny golden wings Lucien had manifested. They looked magnificently crystalline.

If Totems are demons, maybe they're the good kind, Junior thought to himself.

The Prince wasn't as ignorant as people assumed. He knew Lucien had done a lot of damage with his powers, but there was no denying that his Father-King had also created many beautiful things with them as well. You couldn't breed such beauty from pure wickedness. There was no way the supernatural entity inside Lucien was eternally evil.

Maybe Totems are just like us. Trapped in a place between good and evil. Stuck smack dab in an empty patch of space between free will and fate.

Junior sighed. Lucien had said the desert was where great men found answers to life's questions. But since coming here, all he had gathered were more and more questions.

"Why are you contemplating such things, Little Wing?" Lex observed him gingerly. Junior's sudden burst of spiritual keenness had thrown her off guard. To think, yesterday, this was the same boy who didn't want to talk about anything but topless women.

"I dunno," muttered Junior.

He truly didn't understand why he was asking such things. He was fascinated by the supernatural, but he was never interested in all *that spiritual stuff.* Like his Father-King and Sister-Princess-Regent, Junior wanted the ability to move mountains, but he had never bothered with who or what would be giving him that ability. Not until now ...because now, something had changed.

"Father's gonna give me the Golden Gift when I turn 18, right? He promised he would," he said. "I guess I wanted to know where those powers come from."

"They come from him."

"Don't give me that. You know what I mean. I know the Golden Gift comes from the Divine energy inside his body, but where did that energy originally come from? It wasn't always there, trapped between his blood and bones, was it? Someone installed it in there, didn't they? But who?"

With a sigh, Junior fell back onto the blanket. Thoughts of a future birthday began to rake through his mind.

18 felt like a lifetime away, but it wasn't. It was only a few short years into the fading future. When it happened, everything would change. By that age, his valensmen-biology would've kicked in, hitting the pause button on the aging process. He'd go on looking like a teenager for ages. He wouldn't see a single facial wrinkle or any signs of senescence until he hit his Seventh or Eighth Century of life.

And, more importantly, 18 was when Junior would receive access to the Golden energy. Soon enough, he'd be able to manifest his own wings and take to the skies alongside Lucien and Lex. That was the plan, at least.

"As someone who has those powers, all I can tell you is that it's best not to look into it too much and accept it for what it is," said Lex.

"Which is?"

Lex leaned in like she was about to tell a big secret. "A blessing," she said plainly. "A gift."

Releasing an exasperated yawn, she resumed her tanning pose.

"Lexie, I was thinking—"

"I know." Lex cut him off crisply in a way that implied they had reached the end of the conversation, whether he liked it or not. "The desert will do that to you. There's nothing to do here but think."

Lex knew the dangers of the desert didn't rest solely on dust storms and dehydration. What made the desert truly terrifying was that you could hear your own thoughts echoing in the emptiness.

"But none of this really matters," she whispered gravely, "So, do us all a favour and forget all about it."

Chapter 24:
You don't want to leave, do you?

It was their final hour in the desert, and Junior couldn't shake the gut feeling that he was forgetting to take something with him. Lucien's staff had assured him nothing was amiss. His belongings were properly packed, and even Alecto was all caged up and ready to go home with them. But Junior was certain he was leaving something behind. Problem was, he couldn't remember what he was deserting in the desert.

He felt strangely forlorn about leaving this place. It was like a love song that made you feel as though you were missing someone who never really existed. It was all so very odd.

Looking out into the sandy hills and the dramatic sunset, the Prince concluded everything about the desert was odd. It was boiling hot throughout the day, and bitterly cold by nightfall. It was a place for solitude and stillness, but it was never silent. The dunes were always roaring, booming or squeaking. People came here looking for answers but ended up leaving with more questions.

Their Golden campsite was gone. There was no longer a gleaming dome to magically shield them from the elements. The staff tents had disappeared as well. Lucien had vanished them all with a casual sweep of his hand. He then proceeded to do the same for the plush-looking seating area he had created for Lex.

"The King maketh, and the King taketh away," Lex had said with a faint smile as she watched the shiny, semitransparent sofa evanesce like a spectre.

Behind him, Lucien's staff members were bustling about, packing everything into SUVs. Jeremiah was chatting with Lex's Secutor beside one of the cars. Now knowing the full extent of Jeremiah's job as a Secutor, Junior could barely make eye contact with him without feeling a deep sense of awkwardness, regret, and shame.

Lex was already back at work, lightly pacing around with a receiver to her ear as she took a diplomatic call from some foreign emperor two galaxies over.

"I know that look," came the voice of his Father-King as he crept up on Junior.

Junior tossed his head back and lifted his eyes to meet Lucien's. "What look?"

"You don't want to leave, do you?" Lucien placed a warm, firm hand on his son's shoulder. "I told you kids, the Neutral Realm is a life-altering place where—"

"I know, I know," said Junior, hoping to stop his Father from free-diving into a tangent, "It's where great men with too much time on their hands came to find God... because God lives out here in the desert. I know."

"God lives *everywhere*, my son," Lucien corrected with a smirk.

If He lives everywhere, then why are you always searching for Him? Junior wanted to point out, but he didn't. Instead, he decided to humour the man. A tiny ghost of a grin began to play on the Prince's lips.

"I know, my Father," Junior threw back at him, mirroring the man's tone.

They smiled at one another before returning to the view. Staring out into a vibrant sky of pink, orange and gold, they enjoyed the small window of time where the sun hung in the balance between daylight and darkness. It reminded Junior of his Mother – far beyond his reach, trapped in a place between life and death. He wondered if his Father was thinking of her too, but he didn't dare ask. He didn't want to ruin the little moment they were having.

As they witnessed the daily disappearance of the sun's upper limb below the horizon, Lucien asked, "Did you enjoy our vacation?"

"Yeah," Junior found himself answering with honesty, "I really did."

His entire experience had teetered back-and-forth between slightly tedious and strangely adventurous. Overall, it hadn't been unpleasant by any means.

"What about you, Father? Did you enjoy your birthday? Be honest."

"I'm always honest."

Junior held back a sigh. He knew Lucien preferred to be an honest man. That didn't mean he always was one.

"And yes," continued Lucien. "I had a splendid time."

"But you didn't find what you were looking for. You didn't find Eden."

"The journey is half the reward." Lucien gave him a bright smile that could've rivalled the sun. "Besides, I still got to enjoy a lovely celebration in my honour."

"But your party was so bor—" Junior stopped himself in the nick of time from saying *boring*. "Bo-bo-bodacious and a little much. I thought you wanted to get away from all the *creature comforts*."

"Yes, well… one needs to have a touch of extravagance when entertaining guests," shrugged Lucien. "You ought to know that by now."

Money was never an issue for the Gold King. He gave generously to his loyal subjects. For every event he threw, the guests always walked away with over-the-top gift bags and free bars of gold. In return, however, the gifts Lucien received were nothing to brag about. The Prince heard one woman tried to give his Father her gallstones as a birthday gift this year. He shuddered at the thought.

"Do you even like those people, Father? I know, you always say a King loves his subjects as his own children. But I mean… if you weren't a King, and they weren't your courtiers, would you like them?"

Junior had never been too fond of the members of Lucien's royal court, the Osprey. As an absolute monarch, Lucien had bestowed various titles and privileges upon his courtiers. Junior couldn't understand why, especially when they didn't seem the least bit deserving.

Members of the Osprey operated in a state of perpetual passive-aggression. They were generally dismissive of people who earned a living or decided to do something with their lives beyond owning property. In Junior's opinion, they were a bunch of phonies, always covering up their pretentiousness with a thick layer of propriety.

Lucien stared down at his son as though he were trekking the boy's trail of thoughts. The Gold King's voice rang like a bell, loud and clear and yet infinitely soft as he said, "We need take time to appreciate the people who love us. Even those who love us for all the wrong reasons."

Junior sighed and shook his head. He didn't know why he bothered asking Lucien anything. This was a man who wouldn't give you a straight answer if you asked him if water was wet.

With Lucien's attention reverted to the disappearing sun, Junior took a moment to observe his Father's profile.

Lucien looked like a young man. By valensmen standards, Lucien was still a young man. He'd only been breathing in air and taking up space for a little over 2,000 years. That was nothing for a valensmen. Nothing but a few grains of sand in an hourglass. Even so, Junior knew Lucien's extensive history. He knew everything his Father had accomplished in such time. He'd read up on it. He'd heard about it from everyone and anyone.

Thus far, Junior had only ever encountered a mildly bad-tempered forest. But Lucien, in his lifetime, had wandered the wilderness, survived the jungle, and created his own paradise on Earth. There was probably a universe of meaning behind every word Lucien uttered, but Junior wasn't ready to understand any of it.

"Come along, son," Lucien said, his eyes still fixed ahead, his right palm stretched out for his son to take. "It's time to go home."

Junior glanced down at his Father's hand. His eyes shot over to all the sand and sage stretched out for miles and miles in front of them.

Godshoots forest was nowhere in sight, but the Prince longed to see it again. He found himself wanting to experience everything again. Camel-riding with Lucien and Lex. Exploring hidden caves with them. Stumbling across mummified cats. Dancing with masked women (even if they weren't bare-breasted). Getting buzzed on Divine juice. Bunking off into the unknown with his friends. Feeling the infinite power and warmth emanating from the Tree – the Tree – the Tree—

Junior grimaced as he tried to conjure up the memory. What was it called again? The Tree of – Queens. Yes, that was it. He didn't understand why he was having so much trouble remembering it now.

Alongside those moments, he also enjoyed meeting the b– meeting the – meeting—

Junior frowned at his sudden spurts of senility.

Meeting ... the vulture. Yes, that was it. *Meeting Alecto,* he assured himself, relief flooding his face. *Anyhow...*

This vacation was ending the same way all great holidays ended: with a desperate desire to stretch it out for another day, another week, another month...

"We can always come back," Lucien told him.

The Prince blinked up at his Father-King. He wondered if Lucien had the power to read minds. Either that, or Junior needed to perfect his poker face.

"Your entire body betrays you, Prince J.R.," the new Grey King would tell him one day, many years from now, "Your thoughts. Your feelings. You wear it all over you like it's a damn uniform."

"Yeah, I'd like that," Junior said, pure honesty pouring out of him. "Let's come back again."

Grabbing Lucien's hand, Junior turned to leave.

"What's wrong?" He asked when Lucien stayed put, refusing to budge. "I thought we were leaving."

"We are." Lucien pulled his son back to his side. "But let's give it another minute. Enjoy the view. It simply won't be the same the next time."

"I'm sure all this sand will still be here, Father."

"I should think not. Dunes are everchanging landforms, molded by wind and waves of storm. The ones we're seeing now are unique. We shall never encounter them again."

"Uh huh." Junior gave him a wry grin. "But it'll still be the same old sand."

Lucien chuckled. "I suppose the desert never really changes, and yet no man leaves here quite the same, and if he returns, he'll step through this *same old sand* as a new man."

His Father's words washed over him again. Junior didn't understand. But someday he would.

Someday, many years from now, with his memories restored and his features matured, he would return to this desert as J.R. Valenta.

J.R. wouldn't come back to the desert with his family, but he wouldn't be alone either. A forgotten friend and an elusive enemy would be here, waiting for him. No longer the same boys, they'd meet again as two entirely different men.

Author's note:
Where do we go from here?

Boys to Enemies is a companion piece to *The King's Energy* series. From here on, you can either go forward or backward.

Go forward into the fading future:

Check out the continuation of J.R.'s (Junior's) story in the book *Golden Phantoms*.

Go further back in time:

Explore the origins of the Tree of Queens and get to know Gold Queen Lana and the Anatolia family (sorcerers for hire) in the book *Secret Society of Kings, Witches and Spirits*.

About the author

FARHANA is the author of *Secret Society of Kings*, *Witches and Spirits*, *Boys to Enemies*, and *Golden Phantoms*. She has more than ten years of work experience in copywriting, editing, and content marketing.

Connect with the author:

TikTok: @farhanabooks
Instagram: @farhanabooks
Tumblr: farhanabooks.tumblr.com
Linktree: https://linktr.ee/farhanabooks